Acclaim for Kath

"Kathleen Fuller's *The Teacher's Bride* is a heartwarming story of unexpected romance woven with fun and engaging characters who come to life on every page. Once you open the book, you won't put it down until you've reached the end."

—Amy Clipston, bestselling author of *A Seat by the Hearth*

"Kathy Fuller's characters leap off the page with subtle power as she uses both wit and wisdom to entertain! Refreshingly honest and charming, Kathy's writing reflects a master's touch when it comes to intricate plotting and a satisfying and inspirational ending full of good cheer!"

—Kelly Long, national bestselling author, on *The Teacher's Bride*

"Kathleen Fuller is a master storyteller and fans will absolutely fall in love with Ruby and Christian in *The Teacher's Bride*."

—Ruth Reid, bestselling author of *A Miracle of Hope*

"*The Teacher's Bride* features characters who know what it's like to be different, to not fit in. What they don't know is that's what makes them so loveable. Kathleen Fuller has written a sweet, oftentimes humorous, romance that reminds readers that the perfect match might be right in front of their noses. She handles the difficult topic of depression with a deft touch. Readers of Amish fiction won't want to miss this delightful story."

—Kelly Irvin, bestselling author of the Every Amish Season series

"Kathleen Fuller is a talented and a gifted author, and she doesn't disappoint in *The Teacher's Bride*. The story will captivate you from the first page to the last with Ruby, Christian, and engaging characters. You'll laugh, gasp, and wonder what will happen next. You won't want to miss reading this heartwarming Amish story of mishaps, faith, love, forgiveness, and friendship."

—Molly Jebber, speaker and award-winning author of *Grace's Forgiveness* and the Amish Keepsake Pocket Quilt series

"Enthusiasts of Fuller's sweet Amish romances will savor this new anthology."

—*Library Journal* on *An Amish Family*

"These four sweet stories are full of hope and promise along with misunderstandings and reconciliation. True love does prevail, but not without prayer, introspection, and humility. A must-read for fans of Amish romance."

—*RT Book Reviews*, 4 stars, on *An Amish Family*

"The incredibly engaging Amish Letters series continues with a third story of perseverance and devotion, making it difficult to put down . . . Fuller skillfully knits together the lives within a changing, faithful community that has suffered its share of challenges."

—*RT Book Reviews*, 4 1/2 stars, on *Words from the Heart*

"Fuller's inspirational tale portrays complex characters facing real-world problems and finding love where they least expected or wanted it to be."

—*Booklist*, starred review, on *A Reluctant Bride*

"Fuller has an amazing capacity for creating damaged characters and giving insights into their brokenness. One of the better voices in the Amish fiction genre."

—*CBA Retailers + Resources* on *A Reluctant Bride*

"This promising series debut from Fuller is edgier than most Amish novels, dealing with difficult and dark issues and featuring well-drawn characters who are tougher than the usual gentle souls found in this genre. Recommended for Amish fiction fans who might like a different flavor."

—*Library Journal* on *A Reluctant Bride*

"Sadie and Aden's love is both sweet and hard-won, and Aden's patience is touching as he wrestles not only with Sadie's dilemma, but his own abusive past. Birch Creek is weighed down by the Troyer family's dark secrets, and readers will be interested to see how secondary characters' lives unfold as the series continues."

—*RT Book Reviews*, 4 stars, on *A Reluctant Bride*

"Kathleen Fuller's *A Reluctant Bride* tells the story of two Amish families whose lives have collided through tragedy. Sadie Schrock's stoic resolve will touch and inspire Fuller's fans, as will the story's concluding triumph of redemption."

—Suzanne Woods Fisher, bestselling author of *Anna's Crossing*

"Kathleen Fuller's *A Reluctant Bride* is a beautiful story of faith, hope, and second chances. Her characters and descriptions are captivating, bringing the story to life with the turn of every page."

—Amy Clipston, bestselling author of *A Simple Prayer* and the Kauffman Amish Bakery series

"The latest offering in the Middlefield Family series is a sweet love story, with perfectly crafted characters. Fuller's Amish novels are written with the utmost respect for their way of living. Readers are given a glimpse of what it is like to live the simple life."

—*RT Book Reviews*, 4 stars, on *Letters to Katie*

"Fuller's second Amish series entry is a sweet romance with a strong sense of place that will attract readers of Wanda Brunstetter and Cindy Woodsmall."

—*Library Journal* on *Faithful to Laura*

"Well-drawn characters and a homespun feel will make this Amish romance a sure bet for fans of Beverly Lewis and Jerry S. Eicher."

—*Library Journal* on *Treasuring Emma*

"*Treasuring Emma* is a heartwarming story filled with real-life situations and well-developed characters. I rooted for Emma and Adam until the very last page. Fans of Amish fiction and those seeking an endearing romance will enjoy this love story. Highly recommended."

—Beth Wiseman, bestselling author of *Her Brother's Keeper* and the Daughters of the Promise series

"*Treasuring Emma* is a charming, emotionally layered story of the value of friendship in love and discovering the truth of the heart. A true treasure of a read!"

—Kelly Long, author of the Patch of Heaven series

A
Love
Made
New

Other Books by Kathleen Fuller

A
Love
Made
New

AN AMISH OF BIRCH CREEK NOVEL

KATHLEEN FULLER

ZONDERVAN

A Love Made New

© 2016 by Kathleen Fuller

This title is also available as an e-book. Visit www.zondervan.com.

Requests for information should be addressed to:
Zondervan, *Grand Rapids, Michigan 49546*

ISBN: 978-0-310-35367-6 (repack)

Library of Congress Cataloging-in-Publication Data
Names: Fuller, Kathleen, author.
Title: A love made new / Kathleen Fuller, Kathleen Fuller.
Description: Nashville, Tennessee: Thomas Nelson, 2016. | Series: An Amish of
Birch Creek novel
Identifiers: LCCN 2016013640 | ISBN 9780718033200 (softcover)
Subjects: LCSH: Amish--Fiction. | Mate selection--Fiction. | Self-realization in
women--Fiction. | Man-woman relationships--Fiction. | GSAFD: Christian
fiction. | Love stories.
Classification: LCC PS3606.U553 L69 2016 | DDC 813/.6--dc23 LC record
available at https://lccn.loc.gov/2016013640

Scripture quotations are taken from the Holy Bible, New International Version®,
NIV®. Copyright © 1973, 1978, 1984, 2011 by Biblica, Inc.® Used by permission of
Zondervan. All rights reserved worldwide. www.zondervan.com. The "NIV" and
"New International Version" are trademarks registered in the United States Patent
and Trademark Office by Biblica, Inc.®

Any Internet addresses (websites, blogs, etc.) and telephone numbers in this book
are offered as a resource. They are not intended in any way to be or imply an
endorsement by Zondervan, nor does Zondervan vouch for the content of these sites
and numbers for the life of this book.

Publisher's Note: This novel is a work of fiction. Names, characters, places, and
incidents are either products of the author's imagination or used fictitiously.
All characters are fictional, and any similarity to people living or dead is purely
coincidental.

Printed in the United States of America

19 20 21 22 23 / LSC / 5 4 3 2 1

To James, the love of my life . . . always and forever.

And now these three remain: faith, hope, and love. But the greatest of these is love.

1 Corinthians 13:13

Glossary

ab im kopp: crazy, crazy in the head
ach: oh
aenti: aunt
appeditlich: delicious
bruder: brother
daag/daags: day/days
daed: father
danki: thank you
dawdi haus: smaller home, attached to or near the main house
Dietsch: Amish language
dochder: daughter
dumm: dumb
dummkopf: idiot
Englisch: non-Amish
familye: family
frau: woman, Mrs.
geh: go
gut: good

gute nacht: good night
haus: house
kaffee: coffee
kapp: white hat worn by Amish women
kinn/kinner: child/children
maedel: girl/young woman
mamm: mom
mann: Amish man
mei: my
mudder/mutter: mother
nee: no
nix: nothing
onkel: uncle
schee: pretty/handsome
schwesters: sisters
seltsam: weird
sohn: son
vatter: father
ya: yes
yer: your
yerself: yourself

Prologue

I'm getting married.

Abigail Schrock could hardly stop herself from whispering the words out loud as she made her way to Joel Zook's house. She even skipped a few steps, which was immature for a twenty-two-year-old, but she couldn't help it. After dealing with months of pain and tragedy, grieving the loss of her mother and father, and helping her younger sister, Joanna, heal from the accident that took their parents' lives, Abigail's heart was wide open to receive happiness.

She had been a bit disappointed Joel hadn't contacted her while she was in Middlefield with Joanna for the past six weeks. Now that she was back in Birch Creek, however, and Joanna was preparing for her own wedding, Abigail knew her time had come. When Joel approached her after church this morning and invited her over, weeks of worry and insecurity disappeared. Joel was going to propose.

She felt that truth deep in her soul as she arrived at his house, ran up the steps, and knocked on the door. Maybe she should just go inside. After all, Joel's parents would be her in-laws soon. Might as well start treating them like family.

She waited, tapping her foot when the door didn't open immediately. Until church this morning, she and Joel hadn't seen each other since the middle of August, at her parents' funeral almost two months ago. But she understood why. He had been busy, working extra hard at his job at Barton Plastics, probably saving every cent for their future together. Impatient, she knocked on the door again, a little annoyed that he hadn't thrown open the door and grabbed her into his arms like she had imagined he would.

Finally she heard footsteps on the other side of the door. It opened, and her heart leaped. Joel. Lean, tall, and so handsome she could stare at him all day. She'd known him her whole life, and he had finally shown interest in her seven months ago after she asked him on a date. Unconventional, for sure, but she couldn't wait forever until he came around. He'd needed a little nudge and she had been happy to give it to him.

"Hi, Abigail."

The screen door still separated them. All right, so he was going to be a little standoffish. That made sense, considering his parents were probably a few feet away in the living room, spending the Sabbath relaxing or napping. Whatever, she wasn't here to think about his parents. She grinned. "Hello, Joel."

He opened the screen door and stepped onto the porch. Then he closed both doors behind him before he faced her.

Now he would hold her. She'd ached for him ever since she had snuck out of the house to meet him near the Yoders' cornfield the night before the accident. They had gone into the field, hidden from sight, the silvery moonlight illuminating Joel's face enough that she could see in his eyes that he cared for her. Then he proceeded to show her how much.

He coughed, bringing her out of her thoughts. Which was a good idea, because she wanted to focus on the present, on the proposal she knew was coming.

"Abigail, it's over."

She blinked, unsure that she heard him correctly. "What?"

"I'm breaking up with you."

She staggered back. This couldn't be right. He wouldn't leave her, not now. Not when she needed him the most, when she was still reeling from the deaths of her mother and father. Not when she had spent weeks caring for her injured sister.

"It's for the best, Abigail."

The sentence hit her like a blast to the chest, churning up familiar, brittle feelings. *There's nothing special about you.*

For most of her life, she had felt that way. Insignificant. Ordinary. She was the middle sister, sandwiched between her older, smarter sister, Sadie, and her younger, sweeter sister, Joanna. Dating Joel, one of the most eligible and most sought-after men in Birch Creek, had made her feel special. *He* had made her feel special. Now he was dumping her.

He looked down at her, remorse in his slate blue eyes.

She should probably give him credit for showing a little regret, but she couldn't bring herself to give him anything. Her hands went to her chest. Her *ample* chest. The sleeves of her dress tightened around her arms as she tried to catch her breath. She'd gained weight since her parents' and Joanna's accident, at least twenty pounds, if not more. At five four, every pound was noticeable. "I thought you were asking me to spend the afternoon with you," she said, still shocked. *I thought you were going to ask me to marry you.* "Now you're saying our relationship is over?"

Joel nodded and stepped away, putting more space between them.

"But it can't be." She wanted to see the warmth in his eyes that had been there before she left. Instead he seemed more distant than he'd been before they started dating. She couldn't accept this. She refused to. "I love you," she blurted out of desperation.

His face pinched as he looked away. "I never said I loved you."

Another slam in the chest. No, he'd never spoken the words. But he had showed her, hadn't he? They had shown each other, as the cornstalks rustled around them. "I gave you everything, Joel." Well, almost everything. That night he had wanted more. She had wanted more. But she had told him no. She wanted to wait until after a wedding. He'd been disappointed, but he had agreed that waiting until after marriage would be the right thing to do and what God would want them to do. She had assumed they were talking about *their* marriage.

He kept his gaze down.

Coward. Or maybe not. Maybe it wasn't that he was afraid to look at her, but that he didn't *want* to look at her. She wasn't the thin woman he'd dated before the accident. He'd seen that at church this morning. But was he so shallow he would break up with her over a few pounds? Okay, more than a few . . . but still. This didn't make any sense. Unless . . . she gulped, fearing she knew the answer to her question before she asked it. "Is there someone else?"

Silence.

Despite everything, she went to him, still desperate and detesting herself for it. She put her hands on his chest and looked up at him, her pride shattering into pieces. "Please, Joel. I can't lose you too. Not now."

When he finally looked at her, his eyes weren't filled with love or longing or attraction or even remote affection. He took her hands and put them at her sides. "I'm sorry, Abigail. I'm really sorry. But Rebecca and I—"

"Rebecca Chupp?" Cute, petite Rebecca, with hair the color of apple cider, perfect teeth, and hips half the size of Abigail's.

"*Ya*, Rebecca." He sighed. "Things between us just . . . happened."

"What does that mean?"

"It means . . . we're over." He turned from her and went inside, the screen door bouncing shut behind him. Then he closed the front door, shutting her out of his life for good.

Every nerve ending in her body went numb. "Joel," she whispered, hoping he'd somehow hear her, come outside, hold her tight, and tell her this was a bad joke. Or that he'd lost his mind for a moment, but realized he couldn't live without her. That she *was* something special. She waited . . . and waited. Stared at the door and prayed it would open again. It didn't.

Somehow she managed to turn and walk down the porch steps, leaving tattered pieces of her heart in her wake. How could she have been so wrong about her and Joel? Wasn't it her turn for happiness? Sadie had married Aden Troyer soon after the buggy accident, and Joanna was marrying Andrew Beiler in a week. Beauty and love had risen from the ashes of her sisters' grief.

Why hadn't it for her?

She glanced over her shoulder at the empty front porch, then hugged her chest, more aware of the roundness of her body than ever before as she walked toward her house. The aching pressure of rejection made her struggle for air. What had she done wrong? What was wrong with her? Had he turned to Rebecca because she had refused to have sex with him? Had Rebecca given him what she wouldn't? Or was he simply not attracted to her anymore?

"Abigail?"

Hope rose within her. Joel. He'd come back for her after all. She whirled around, but that hope disintegrated when she saw the man who had spoken her name. His voice was deep like Joel's but carried a different timbre. In her desperation she'd confused Asa Bontrager with Joel, even though the men looked and acted nothing alike. She started to panic. Had Asa seen her and Joel? Worse yet, had he heard Joel break up with her?

Stuffing down her panic, she uncrossed her arms and lifted her chin, forcing herself to smile. As she had since her return from Middlefield, she made sure to keep her inner pain to herself. She refused to let anyone see her breaking inside, not when Joanna was so fragile and Sadie was trying to piece together the family's grocery and tool business. "Asa. I didn't realize you were there."

He strode toward her, coming close enough that she could smell the peppery scent of the wintergreen gum he was chewing. "I was out for a walk." Thick black brows straightened over pale gray eyes. "Are you okay?"

She regarded him for a moment. Joel was handsome, but when it came to looks, Asa was in a class of his own. She was two years older than he was and had paid little attention to him in the past, not only due to his age but because guys like Asa didn't give second glances to girls like her. Every girl in Birch Creek had a crush on him at one time or another before he'd moved to Indiana at age fifteen. Those boyish good looks had changed to manly handsomeness, but Asa wasn't the one she wanted. Joel was.

"I'm fine," she said, maintaining a light tone. It was becoming easier to outwardly fake her true emotions. She'd had plenty of practice lately. "I was just . . . visiting Joel." He'd find out soon enough what happened. News traveled fast in Birch Creek. But Asa wasn't going to hear about it from her. "I'm headed home."

"Would you like some company?"

Why would he want to walk with her? Not that it mattered. She wanted—no, she needed—to be alone. *"Nee."* She couldn't keep her arms from crossing again, and she didn't have the strength to fake another smile.

He dropped his gaze and kicked at a chunk of gravel on the side of the road. "Okay. Just thought I'd ask."

His kind tone reached inside her, bringing her close to tears. So much for hiding her feelings. Without saying good-bye, she turned and hurried away.

But after a few moments she discovered he was still behind her. He'd hung back a decent distance, but that didn't matter. All she could think about was how she looked from behind. She hadn't altered this particular dress and it was tight in all the wrong places. Heat crept up her cheeks.

After several minutes she couldn't stand it anymore. She spun around. "Quit following me!" She cringed. Where was her carefully crafted composure now?

Asa held up his hands. "I'm not," he said. "Okay, technically I am, but we're going in the same direction. You didn't want me to walk with you, so . . ." He shrugged. "Not sure what else I'm supposed to do, except walk on the other side of the street. I can do that, if you want me to." He looked at her, his gray gaze intense. "I don't want to upset you."

She blew out a long breath. "I'm not upset."

He tilted his head but gave a noncommittal shrug. "Whatever you say."

She sighed. She was being ridiculous. Of course he wasn't staring at her or even following her. "You don't have to walk on the other side of the street."

But he didn't answer her. Instead he kept his eyes locked on hers, pinning her in place.

Then she saw something in the intensity of his gaze that made her forget all about Joel Zook.

She shook her head, hard. Not only was she upset, she was also seeing things. "I . . . I've got to *geh*." She spun around and rushed off. He didn't call after her. By the time she reached her house she was in a full run. Out of breath, out of shape, she was losing the battle with her tears. The reality of her breakup with Joel hit her again. *How could I have been so stupid to think he would want to marry me?*

For the next few minutes she stayed hunched over, her face in her hands, forcing the tears to subside. When they did she stood, wiped her cheeks, and tried to figure out how to tell her sisters that Joel had dumped her. Somehow she'd have to be happy for Joanna's upcoming wedding at the same time. She wouldn't spoil her sister's happiness. But how could she do that when Joel had discarded her like week-old trash?

When Abigail ran off, Asa had to battle the urge to chase after her. He grimaced and shoved his hands into his pockets as he watched her disappear down the road. Their conversation could have gone better. He glanced heavenward, something he'd been doing a lot of lately. *What's happening here, Lord?*

He listened for a response. He heard crickets chirping, birds tweeting, a cow lowing. But nothing that sounded like heavenly communication.

He blew out a breath. God might not be speaking to him now, but that didn't mean he wouldn't be. Lately he'd been talking to Asa loud and clear. But right now Asa could use some divine guidance about his sudden and inexplicable feelings for Abigail Schrock. She was Joel Zook's girl. But that didn't seem to make a difference to his heart.

He started walking again. He hadn't been lying when he said he was going in the same direction she was. He'd decided to take a walk instead of spending another afternoon alone in his wreck of a house. That's when he saw Abigail leaving Joel Zook's. Saw the pain on her pretty face. And knew he couldn't ignore her, even though he was sure she wanted to be alone.

It wasn't long before he passed by her house. He was surprised to see her standing on the front porch, figuring she would have already gone inside. He squinted. Was she crying? What happened between her and Joel wasn't any of his business, but if Joel had hurt her . . . His protective side kicked in. Instead of acting on it he went to the opposite side of the street. If she noticed him now, she probably would think he was stalking her. Not the impression he wanted to make. From the moment he'd seen her at church this morning, he couldn't stop thinking about her. And despite himself, he couldn't help slowing down, determined to keep his eye on her until she went inside.

He was struck by how strange his forbidden attraction to Abigail was. Then again, his life had been nothing but strange since he'd moved back to Birch Creek.

But why Abigail?

He halted his steps. She was the complete opposite of the

only woman he'd ever dated—and until a few weeks ago, had been engaged to. Susanna was quiet, almost to the point of shy. Abigail definitely wasn't shy. She was quick to grin and friendly to everyone, with the exception of him a few moments ago. Even then he could tell she was struggling to keep whatever was bothering her bottled up tight under a pretty smile and non-chalant expression.

Looks-wise, Abigail also couldn't be more different from Susanna. His ex-fiancée was tiny, blonde, and fair. Abigail had olive-toned skin, light brown hair, and almond-shaped eyes one shade darker. She was short, but curvaceous. He'd noticed that the moment he'd laid eyes on her that first Sunday she'd returned from Middlefield. That was also the first time he'd seen her since he'd come back to Birch Creek. She had changed from the thin, boyish girl he'd remembered as a young teen into a stunning woman with plenty of curves in all the right places.

He looked at her again. She was in pain and he wanted to comfort her. Yet not only did he not have the right, he knew she wouldn't want him to.

After a few more minutes she went inside. Asa ran a hand over his face, then he quickened his pace and went home, still thinking about her. What he felt for Abigail was more intense than anything he'd experienced with Susanna. Considering he'd nearly married Susanna, that was saying something.

Half an hour later he was standing in his empty living room, staring at the single rocking chair sitting by the woodstove. He'd picked it up at a secondhand store, but he had no other furniture. Most of his money had gone to buying, cleaning up, and restoring the house his parents used to own. It had been forced into foreclosure and then trashed by the former owners. Or by squatters. He had no idea who had caused the damage. He just knew this wasn't the house he now considered home. And it didn't matter how nice he fixed it up, he could never imagine it being home, no matter what God had asked him to do.

Home. Shipshewana had been his real home . . . until God told him to give it all up, then had uprooted everything in his life and taken it away. He told people the move back was for good. Still, there had always been hope in the back of his mind that God would let him return to Indiana, regain the job he'd lost for no reason, and somehow convince Susanna to forgive him for leaving her. Before, he had been content. Not overly happy, but life had been . . . decent.

He yearned for that complacency right now. He didn't like what he was feeling—guilt with a dose of self-loathing thrown in. He was attracted—deeply attracted—to a taken woman. God wouldn't condone this. Asa had spent the last couple of months trying to follow God's will, to be obedient. And he had been until now. Because for the past half hour his mind had been filled with disobedient thoughts.

He plunked down in the rocking chair and stared at the empty woodstove. Then he closed his eyes, and as he'd done more of lately than ever before, he started to pray. For direction. For forgiveness. For his heart to change. And for Abigail to find peace.

CHAPTER 1

Three months later

Abigail's mouth ached from holding her smile. As she watched Joanna marry Andrew Beiler, she struggled to be happy for her. Deep down she was. After everything her sister had gone through—being the only survivor in the buggy crash that killed their parents, spending over a month in rehabilitation for a broken pelvis, and having a permanent scar on her face from when she was thrown out of the buggy—she deserved to marry the man she'd loved since she was a young girl. Andrew and Joanna were perfect for each other. They'd had some problems along the way to get to this point, but as she saw her sister gaze into her new husband's eyes, she knew their relationship was stronger than ever. Andrew's love had never wavered.

She glanced around the living room, widening her grin as much as she could at the crowd of friends and family who were in attendance. She probably looked deranged. But as Joanna's maid of honor, she didn't want to wreck her sister's day by revealing her turbulent emotions.

With each minute that passed Abigail struggled to hold on to her composure. She glanced past Joanna and saw Asa, who was standing on the other side of Andrew. Her eyes met his and he gave her a small smile. It didn't help. He was Andrew's best man, but she'd had limited contact with him since the day Joel had broken up with her. Which was fine with her. She didn't want to see him anyway. He'd witnessed the aftermath of the most humiliating experience of her life.

After what seemed like hours, Bishop Yoder finally pronounced Joanna and Andrew husband and wife. Abigail couldn't watch as her sister and new brother-in-law exchanged a quick kiss. She looked at the crowd again, which was a mistake. Out of the corner of her eye she saw Joel and Rebecca. Bitterness churned in her stomach. Rebecca had visited Abigail to apologize a week after Joel broke up with her. "It happened so fast," she'd said, worrying the strap on her purse. "I know it wasn't right . . . but we couldn't help it. We fell in love."

Love. Even from across the room and surrounded by a crowd of people, Abigail could see the way Joel looked at Rebecca. He'd never looked at her with such all-consuming affection. Joanna had asked Abigail if it was all right if Joel was invited to the wedding. Abigail didn't protest. It wasn't as if she had a choice—everyone else in their small district had been invited. To exclude Joel and Rebecca would show everyone that Abigail hadn't forgiven them. And according to her faith she had to.

But some days, like today, she wasn't in a forgiving mood.

She felt Joanna touch her arm. The ceremony was over. Abigail pasted her smile back in place and hugged her sister. "Congratulations! I'm so happy for you." And she meant it. She released Joanna and looked at Andrew, her smile feeling less forced. Despite her own pain, she was truly excited for them both.

Andrew grinned as he reached for Joanna's hand. Abigail glanced at their fingers clasped together, and happiness gave way to envy. More people crowded around to congratulate the newly married couple. The Schrock house was large, but to Abigail it became suffocating. She needed a break from all the wedded bliss.

She slipped out of the living room, but not before seeing Sadie and Aden gazing tenderly at each other. Another rock-solid marriage. Another reminder of what she didn't have.

She went outside and stood on the back patio, thankful for the cold January air. Snow tipped the ends of the evergreen trees in her backyard and a thin layer covered the ground. She hugged her arms around her shoulders, already shaking from the freezing air, but she couldn't bring herself to go back inside and get a coat.

"That was a lovely wedding." Irene Beiler, Andrew's older sister, came up beside her.

Abigail turned and tried to muster another smile. She only managed half of one. "*Ya.* It was very nice."

"I'm glad they finally tied the knot. I was a little worried because . . . well, you know."

Abigail nodded. Joanna and Andrew were supposed to marry last October, shortly after she'd returned from Middlefield, but her sister had called off the wedding at the last minute. At the time Abigail had been furious. How could Joanna throw away the love of a good man who wanted to marry her? Later she understood why Joanna had terminated the wedding, and it had been the right decision. "I don't think anything would have prevented them from getting married today."

"True. They had some things to work out, and I'm glad they did. I've never seen *mei bruder* so happy." Irene hugged her arms. "It's freezing out here. Are you coming back inside?"

"In a little bit. It's too crowded in the *haus* right now."

"I'll take the crowd over the cold. See you later."

Once Irene was gone, Abigail's smile slid from her face. She stared straight ahead, the cold air not only dulling her body but also her emotions. She should be used to that dull ache. It had been her constant companion for the past three months. But she'd take the numbness over sharp pain any day. She moved off the patio and walked through the yard, snow covering the toes of her shoes. After walking for a few minutes, her feet grew numb.

But she continued to trudge in the snow. Her lips were stiff, she couldn't feel her nose, and it felt like she had cinder bricks tied to her ankles. And still she walked, toward the copse of trees to the left of the property where the family dog, Homer, liked to play. Homer was leaving with Joanna and Andrew after the wedding. Abigail would miss the adorable mutt, but he and Joanna were attached to each other. Homer had been a fitting wedding gift from Sadie to their younger sister.

"Abigail."

This time she recognized the voice behind her. Asa. She closed her eyes, composed herself, and tried to make her lips curve into a smile. It was getting harder and harder to do, and not because of the cold. She turned and faced him. "Hi," she said, as if standing in the frigid weather in nothing but a dress on her sister's wedding day was the most normal thing in the world.

But Asa wasn't smiling back. "Why are you out here without a coat?" He was wearing his Sunday clothes—black pants, white shirt, and black vest. He'd left his black hat inside and his dark, wavy hair collected the snowflakes that had started to fall. He had the thickest hair she'd ever seen, and it was the most unusual blue-black color. His lashes were also full and thick. They surrounded his eyes, pale gray irises rimmed in darker gray. His square jaw always seemed to have a shadow of dark stubble. He wasn't as tall as Joel, who was nearly a foot taller than she was. But she still had to look up to him.

She yanked her gaze from him and shivered. What was she doing, staring at him like . . . like he was the most beautiful man she'd ever seen? Probably because he was. That was a fact.

Without a word he took off his coat and put it around her shoulders, then blew out a frosty puff of breath. He smelled good, like he'd been chewing cinnamon gum. Or eating a cinnamon roll. What she wouldn't do for a cinnamon roll right now. Great, now she was thinking about food. Then again, when wasn't she thinking about food? Since her breakup with Joel, she'd tried several diets, only to fail every time. At first she'd told her sisters she was trying to lose weight. But after her failure, she kept the rest of her attempts to herself.

Her smile disappeared. She couldn't even keep that steady. She was a mess.

"Keep it as long as you need to," he said, the sleeves of his white shirt billowing in the bitter wind.

She couldn't let him freeze out here. She started to pull off his coat, but he held up his hand.

"I mean it, Abigail. If you're going to stay outside, you have to have a coat. I don't want you to get sick."

She stilled at his words. He sounded like he cared. Like he *really* cared. Her heart sparked back to life and she started to snuggle into the welcome warmth of his coat, breathing in the scent from the fabric. Even his coat smelled good, and she caught hints of wood smoke and cinnamon. Then she stopped moving. Her heart froze over again and she took off the coat.

"Abigail—"

"It doesn't fit." She handed him the garment.

He looked at the coat, then back at her. "You barely put it on."

Something brittle snapped inside her. "Fine. You want me to prove it?" She stuck her arms through the coat, the fabric straining at the seams. The front of the coat gaped open. Asa was lean. She was anything but.

His eyes—those gorgeous eyes—filled with pity. "It's better than *nix*."

She yanked off the coat and heard a couple of the stitches pop. That was the last straw. She threw it at him before turning and fleeing into the woods.

At this point, Asa wondered if he'd do anything right when it came to Abigail. When he found out she and Joel had broken up, he was thrilled. He felt guilty, but happy. Now he didn't have to feel awful about his interest in her. But he had noticed she wasn't herself. Her smile had a bitter hint to it and the joy had left her eyes. So he held back, kept his distance because he knew what it was like to mourn a breakup. Yet moments ago when he saw her standing in the yard without a coat on, he couldn't stay away. *I guess I should have.*

He stared at the grove of trees. She couldn't stay out in the cold much longer. He'd seen her red nose, saw her body shaking as she had struggled into his coat. He closed his eyes. He hadn't meant to embarrass her. And now he had no idea what to do.

Go after her.

Asa looked up toward the gray sky, shocked. Snowflakes fell into his eyes, but he didn't blink. This was the first time he'd clearly heard God's voice in months. But he hesitated. He wasn't cut out for this knight-in-shining-armor routine.

The question popped into his head before he could prevent

it. *Are you sure, Lord?* Then alarm pulsed through him. Who was he to question God?

Go after her.

He put his coat back on and trudged into the woods. He'd learned the hard way what happened when he ignored God. That's how he'd lost his life in Shipshewana before ending up in Birch Creek.

Although it was midday, the light was dim in the woods because of the snow and gray sky. He was about to call Abigail's name when he saw her silhouette outlined a few feet away. A jolt of attraction went through him. He was surprised she'd been embarrassed that his coat didn't fit her. There was nothing to be embarrassed about. He was thin, thinner than when he'd lived in Indiana. He'd not only lost everything, he'd lost weight too, although he was slowly gaining some back. He liked how her curves contrasted with his leanness. He'd seen shame in her eyes where it shouldn't have been. Anger too. *What should I say to her, Lord?* When God didn't answer, he realized he was on his own.

Asa tried to be quiet as he came up behind Abigail. With his second step he snapped a twig with his boot.

She spun around, visibly shaking. "Please *geh*, Asa. I want to be alone."

He moved toward her. "I don't think that's a *gut* idea."

"I didn't ask *yer* opinion."

Her words were sharp, but she sounded more resigned than angry. She surprised him by not backing away. Now that he could see her face, he noticed the defeat in her eyes. "Abigail," he said, softening his voice. "You can't stay out here much longer. You'll freeze." When she didn't respond he added, "What about *yer schwesters*? They'll be looking for you. Do you want Joanna to leave her wedding to find you?"

Her delicate brows lifted. "I hadn't thought about that. You're right. I have to *geh* back. I don't want them to worry."

For once she was listening to him. He planned to accompany her back to the house, but she brushed past him so quickly he had barely turned around before he saw her toe catch on the thin trunk of a dead birch tree lying on the ground. Instinct drove him to grab her around the waist to keep her from falling.

Wow. She was soft. Very soft. She also smelled good, a sweet combination of vanilla and peppermint. His arm tightened around her. Her plump cheeks were flushed with cold. His fingers gathered a bit of her dress as he squeezed her side, her face inches from his. He was close enough to kiss her. He *wanted* to kiss her.

She wriggled in his grasp. "What are you doing?"

He couldn't think. He couldn't speak. He almost couldn't breathe. Holding her like this . . . there were no words for how he felt.

"Asa?"

Her urgent tone took him out of his daze. He released her. "Uh, sorry." But he wasn't, not really. He locked his eyes with hers. Maybe it was wishful thinking on his part. Wishing and hoping that the reason she was still there, that she was standing in the cold gazing at him, was that she felt it, too, the tug of an invisible cord tying them together.

Then she backed away, stepping over the dead tree. Her eyes still wide with what he could now see was confusion, she turned and left.

Asa didn't follow. Instead he looked up at the treetops. "Okay, Lord. I have *nee* idea what I'm doing." Abigail had to think he was *ab im kopp*. After everything that had happened in the past few months, he probably was.

He started back toward the Schrocks' house, determined to avoid Abigail. He was out of line holding her the way he had. Although she wasn't with Joel, she hadn't shown an inkling of interest in Asa, either. He didn't want to scare her away.

But it was hard when he was so scared himself. His feelings frightened him. The intensity, the unexpectedness, and the way he felt and heard God pushing him toward her. He wished he knew why. He wished he could step back and look at the situation logically, the way he usually did. Yet when it came to Abigail, logic was *not* what came to mind.

When he reached the house, he went inside the mudroom and removed his coat and wet boots. He could hear the murmur of the wedding guests as they ate and visited, sounding like they were having a good time. As he passed through the kitchen, he saw Sadie, Irene, Rhoda Troyer, and Andrew's mother, Naomi, cutting a variety of pies.

He walked into the living room, intent on visiting with the rest of the wedding guests so he could put Abigail out of his mind. But he'd taken only two steps forward when he saw her, separate from everyone else, and his heart started hammering in his chest. And although he knew he shouldn't, he couldn't keep himself from going to her again, even though she had left him only moments before. She was alone . . . and he needed to let her know she didn't have to be.

CHAPTER 2

W hen Irene went back inside the Schrocks' house after talking to Abigail, people were milling about in the living
room, the low hum of conversation punctuated with a loud laugh
or two. It was crowded in there, so she decided to go back into the
kitchen to offer help. But she delayed when she saw her mother
alone near the stairs in the living room. That wasn't like *Mamm*.
She was always social at gatherings and weddings. Irene went to
her, frowning a bit at her mother's downcast eyes. *"Mamm?"* She
touched her mother's shoulder. "Is something wrong?"

Mamm turned to Irene, her eyes shiny behind her wire-framed
glasses. Then she shook her head. "Don't worry. Everything is
fine." She looked over at Joanna and Andrew, who were visiting
with a few of their friends. "It's *mei sohn*'s wedding day, and he's
married a wonderful woman. I'm happy for both of them."

"But?"

"But . . . I wish *yer vatter* was here."

Irene nodded. She wished *Daed* was here too. Familiar resentment burrowed in her heart. A force of habit she'd developed
over more than a decade. She calmed the feeling by reminding

herself that what she had believed since she was thirteen years old wasn't true. Her father hadn't abandoned her, Andrew, and *Mamm* for another woman. Not that the real reason he left was much better. But he hadn't betrayed their family. He had never forsaken his love for *Mamm*—and according to her mother, he had never stopped loving his children. Yet it would take more than the truth and a few reassurances from *Mamm* to make her fully believe it. "Have you heard from him lately?" she asked, trying to sound nonchalant.

Mamm shook her head. "Not since I told him about the wedding. The *second* wedding," she said, a small smile coming over her face. "I'm so relieved this one went through."

"Me too."

"It was *gut* that Andrew and Joanna waited until they were ready."

Irene agreed. She nodded her head in her brother's direction. "They seem at ease with each other, don't they?"

"As they should." *Mamm* glanced at Irene. "I know. It wasn't always that way. But seeing them so happy . . . I now know they've healed."

"*Ya.* I think they have too." She scanned the room. The entire Amish community of Birch Creek had gathered to celebrate. Except for one person—their former bishop, Emmanuel Troyer. As soon as she thought of his name, she spied his son, Solomon.

Against her will, her heart did a small flip.

She turned away, irritated. At one time she would have been glad for his attention, for a cheeky smile that made her believe he was thinking only of her, or for a playful wink of his green eyes. Irene didn't want her heart to go out to him. She once had hopes for a relationship with Sol, back before he was put in the bann and his father left the community. But he hadn't showed any interest in her since that time, and now she knew his flirting had been just a game to him. He couldn't be trusted.

Then again, could any man?

She glanced at her brother again. He was a good man. There were many good men in Birch Creek, including Sol's brother, Aden. He had changed since becoming part of the Schrock family.

Supposedly, Sol had changed too. She rubbed the back of her hand, remembering Andrew and Joanna's first wedding last fall. Joanna had left Andrew before exchanging vows, devastating him. Feeling helpless to do anything, Irene had gone outside. Sol had been there. He had checked to make sure she was okay. A small act of kindness, but it had meant so much.

Irene couldn't refrain from looking at him again. He was sitting next to his friend Jalon Chupp, who had his own bad reputation to contend with. But he hadn't gone to the same extremes Sol had. He hadn't been put in the bann, and he hadn't been a thief.

Sol lifted his head and his eyes met hers. She wanted to look away, but something kept her gaze fixed to his. He seemed sad, like he was on the outside looking in, even though he was sitting in a room filled with people. As soon as she had the thought, he broke eye contact.

"I should help Sadie and the rest of the women in the kitchen," *Mamm* said. "Are you coming?"

Irene glanced at Sol again. She hoped one day he would find happiness. True happiness. She had a feeling that was something he hadn't experienced much of in his life. "*Ya,*" she said, pulling her gaze away from him. "I'm coming."

Abigail stood in the corner of the living room, trying to get warm. If she had any sense, she would move over by the woodstove and let the heat from the fire seep through her bones. But there was a small gathering of people huddled there, visiting and enjoying themselves. She didn't want to be a killjoy and she didn't feel like talking to anyone.

But there was more to her reluctance to join the wedding guests than being considerate and wanting her space. Not only was she shaking on the outside, but she was shivering on the inside. Asa Bontrager had touched her. Granted, he was keeping her from falling, but he could have let go of her right away. Her cheeks burned at the memory of him squeezing her side. Had he noticed how fleshy she was? How fat she had gotten? Of course he had—she couldn't hide her weight gain from anyone.

Truth was, she'd struggled with her weight all her life. It had been easier when she was younger. She had never been stick-skinny, but she had been on the thin side. When she turned sixteen, something had happened to her body and her metabolism. She had to work extra hard at her chores and eat less food than her sisters. Sometimes she went on secret crash diets to stay slim, making sure no one noticed that she pushed food around on the plate so it appeared she had eaten more than she actually had, or she would volunteer to wash dishes so no one would know she hadn't finished her meal. It was why she had been so aware of Joanna not eating after the accident. Her sister had become dangerously thin, while Abigail had gained weight. Now Joanna was at a healthy weight, and Abigail continued to gain.

She still wasn't sure if her weight had any bearing on Joel breaking up with her. She had never asked. But Rebecca was thin, even thinner than Abigail was when she and Joel started dating. At one point she was so tired of stressing about it that she forced herself not to dwell on her chubby figure. But Asa brought that to the fore when he grabbed her.

And yet, Asa touching her and making her aware of her weight wasn't what bothered her the most. It was the way he looked at her *while* he was touching her. Like he wanted to kiss her. Which couldn't be possible. She was upset and he was being a nice guy. He'd always been nice, even when they were kids. No, the smoky look she saw in his eyes had nothing to do with him wanting to kiss her and everything to do with the fact that she was tired, cranky, envious of her sisters, and possibly losing her mind.

She looked up and groaned inwardly. Asa was coming toward her. Why wouldn't the man leave her alone?

"Getting warmed up?" he asked when he reached her.

He was irritating. And endearing, which was driving her to distraction. The more he showed her kindness and concern, the bigger the hope that he wasn't just taking pity on her as she feared. At the same time, she didn't need this complication in her life. But how could she let him know without being rude? "I'm feeling better," she said, deciding to be straightforward. She'd never been interested in playing mental or emotional games with people, and she wasn't about to start now. "You don't need to check on me anymore."

"You sure?" One thick black eyebrow lifted, his voice filled with doubt. "You're still shivering."

"I'll warm up soon." She smiled as brightly as she could to prove it to him.

His eyebrow lowered and an intensity filled his eyes. "I'm not leaving until I know you're okay."

Her smile slipped from her face. "Why do you care?" she whispered, needing an answer for his sudden and strange interest in her. When he paused, dread filled her. *I knew it. He does feel sorry for me. The jilted sister. The fat sister. The lonely sister—*

"Because I do." He moved closer. "Because to me you're worth caring about."

That made her freeze in place. Once again the smoky warmth she'd seen in his eyes when he held her in the woods returned, along with a tickle in her belly. And in that moment she knew she could easily kiss Asa and not think twice about it.

"Asa!"

He gave her one last lingering look before turning around to see Christopher Beachy standing behind him. Asa, Andrew, and Christopher, along with a couple of other boys, used to pal around together when they were young.

"Been looking all over for you," Christopher said, his mouth forming a grin above his light brown beard. He glanced past Asa's shoulder and nodded. "Hi, Abigail. Mind if we borrow him for a minute?"

Asa glanced at her, frowning with confusion. "I don't think—"

"That's fine, Christopher." Abigail put her smile back on, relieved. "We were finished talking anyway."

Asa gave her a look that definitely said he was *not* finished before Christopher dragged him off to a group of young men who were standing by Andrew. Abigail turned and headed for the kitchen, but she couldn't resist looking over her shoulder.

Asa was watching her. Then he grinned . . . and she nearly melted.

She turned from him and bumped into Karen Yoder, one of Joanna's friends. "I'm sorry," she said, barely looking at her as she rushed by. Instead of going to the kitchen she went into the bathroom, which was thankfully empty. She leaned against the door and closed her eyes. Whatever she thought was going on with Asa wasn't real. She was still reeling from Joel's betrayal, still grieving her parents, still wishing for things that could never be. That was the only reason she felt so drawn to Asa, the one man in Birch Creek who had shown her little more than polite kindness. But kindness was all it was, nothing else. She had to remember that.

CHAPTER 3

The morning after Andrew and Joanna's wedding, Sol went back to work. Since he'd lost his carpentry job before he was put in the bann, he now worked from home. After years of making large pieces of furniture, he was constructing birdhouses to sell in Sadie's store. The money wasn't nearly as good as having a steady job, but the birdhouses were selling, especially to *Englisch* customers. Then again, they didn't know the person behind the craftsmanship. If they did, maybe the birdhouses wouldn't sell as well.

He scooped up the last of the sausage gravy on his plate with a piece of biscuit and glanced at his mother. She'd continued to make his favorite dishes after his father left, but she didn't eat much herself. Sol was worried about her. She'd lost weight and had become even more withdrawn than he was. She'd never been much for socializing, which made sense considering the secrets their family had kept for so long. But she didn't need to lock herself up inside, either. "*Mamm?*" he asked. "You okay?"

She looked up from the slice of uneaten toast on her plate,

her eyes unfocused. Then she blinked. "Did you need more gravy, *sohn*?"

Sol shook his head and popped the gravy-soaked biscuit into his mouth. When he finished chewing he said, "I'm *gut*. Can I get you anything?"

"*Nee*. But that's nice of you, Sol."

He took a swig of his coffee and waited for her to say something else, but she looked down at her toast and remained silent. It was like this at every meal—little conversation but plenty of silence. He stood, then picked up his plate and coffee cup. "I'll wash these, *Mamm*."

She shot up from her chair, surprising him. "I'll do it." She took the dishes from him.

"I don't mind." Sol had never seen his *daed* wash a dish. Or sweep the floor or dust the furniture or cook a meal. He drew strict lines between men and women's work and had made those lines clear to both Sol and Aden so they didn't cross them. Because whenever they crossed a line . . .

Sol pushed down the pain those memories always caused. *I'm not mei father . . . I refuse to be like him.* But deep down he knew he had more in common with Emmanuel Troyer than he wanted to admit, especially when it came to their tempers.

But God had changed him. Sol knew it in his mind, felt it in his heart. The angry fire that burned inside him for so long had been tempered. But he was terrified of going back to his past, of slipping into the man he'd once been. And if he had to live a life exactly the opposite of his father's not to, he'd do it—even if it meant washing every dish in Birch Creek. He put his hand on her arm and repeated, "I'll do it."

She looked up at him, and he saw a sheen of tears in her eyes. He grimaced. The last thing he wanted to do was make her cry.

He wanted to help her. She had been as much a victim of his father's controlling ways as he and Aden had. He couldn't tell her that. She wouldn't believe it. So it was up to Sol to show her that not only was he a changed man, but he forgave her for the past. "Finish *yer* breakfast," he said, gentling his voice in a way he'd never heard his father do. "Let me clean up this mess."

Mamm paused, nodded, and went back to the table. As Sol started to clean the kitchen, he sighed inwardly. He wanted *Mamm* to be happy. He wanted to be happy. But neither of them could be with the shadows of the past hovering over them.

After he finished washing and drying the dishes, he turned to her. She still hadn't touched her toast, and she was sitting with her hands in her lap, staring straight ahead. He wished she could see that they and Aden were all better off with *Daed* out of their lives. But instead she was waiting, patiently and with great faith, for *Daed*'s return. Sol didn't care if he ever saw the man again.

He moved toward the mudroom to get his hat from the pegboard near the back door, but turned back to look at his mother in the kitchen. "I'll be in the woodshop if you need me."

She nodded, but didn't look at him. Sol shook his head, grabbed his coat in the mudroom, and walked outside. The day before the wedding he'd gone to the sawmill and picked up some choice lumber for several new birdhouses. He'd started to unload the wood from the back of his wagon near the barn when he heard a buggy turn into his driveway. He tilted his hat back and peered at the driver. He hadn't expected to see Jalon here so early.

He watched his friend park the buggy and tether his horse to the post. His black mare flicked her tail as Jalon walked toward Sol.

"Hey, Sol."

Sol leaned the wood plank against the side of the wagon. "Jalon. Surprised to see you here already."

"I have to be at work early today, so I thought I'd take care of that order I mentioned yesterday."

Sol nodded. He and Jalon had drifted apart over the years, but it had been good to sit and visit with him yesterday. When he mentioned to Jalon that he was taking custom orders for birdhouses, his friend had expressed interest in ordering one. Sol hadn't realized his interest was so urgent. "Is the birdhouse for anyone special?"

"Possibly." Jalon glanced away.

Sol realized he had no idea Jalon was seeing anyone. Then again, why would he? He'd kept himself separate from the community as much as he could since his public confession. The shame of admitting what he'd done still consumed him, bringing him to his knees sometimes. But there was another reason they had drifted apart. Sol wasn't the only one in the community who had succumbed to the draw of alcohol. "Anyone I know?" he asked, diverting the path his thoughts threatened to travel.

"*Nee*. She's not from here."

When Jalon didn't add any more information, Sol didn't press. "Do you have a particular design in mind?"

Jalon pulled a folded piece of paper from his pocket. "I saw this in a book at the library and made a copy." He handed it to Sol. "You think you could make that?"

Sol studied the birdhouse. It wasn't too fancy, but it wasn't plain either. He frowned at the black-and-white photo, noticing the different shades of gray on the birdhouse. "This looks like it might be painted."

"It is."

"I just stain the birdhouses. I've never painted one before."

"Oh." Jalon rubbed his chin. "You think you could slap a coat of paint on it?"

"Maybe. Or you could."

Jalon shook his head. "*Nee.* I'm *nee gut* with a paintbrush. I'd ruin it."

"Sounds like you want this birdhouse to be done just right." He glanced at the paper again.

"I guess it will be okay if it's stained," Jalon said.

But Sol shook his head. "I want you to be happy with it." He'd have to find someone who could help him, which filled him with dread. That would mean facing people in his community and asking them. He imagined most of them, if not all, would probably say no. The citizens of Birch Creek said they'd forgiven him, but he knew they hadn't forgotten what he'd done. He'd stolen their money—well, both he and his father had stolen it, but Sol had shouldered the blame. Everyone knew he was an alcoholic too. He was also many other things that no one knew about. Yet he'd seen the stares, felt the eyes of those in the congregation who still judged him. No, it wouldn't be easy putting hat in hand and asking for someone to help him with his business.

"I'll figure something out," Sol said, then took a pencil out of his tool belt. "Let me know what colors you want."

"Pink."

Sol's brow lifted and Jalon quit talking. His friend's cheeks turned bright red.

"Also, blue," Jalon continued after clearing his throat. "Like a sky blue or a bird's-egg blue. And bright yellow."

Sol wrote down the colors. This was definitely a gift for a woman. "When do you need it?"

"Not for a couple of months."

"If I can find someone to paint it for me quickly, I'll have it to you sooner than that."

"All right. But you don't have to hurry."

Sol put his pencil and the paper back in his tool belt. Something strange was going on. Jalon had always been a straightforward guy in the past. When they were drinking, they weren't only straightforward, they were cocky, Jalon only a little less so. He also wasn't a mean drunk like Sol had been. Maybe that's what had Jalon so hesitant. He didn't trust Sol, and Sol didn't blame him. "Jalon, I promise I'll get it done on time. I haven't missed a delivery date yet, not since . . ." He drew in a deep breath. "Not since *Daed* left."

Jalon met him in the eye. "I know you'll keep *yer* word."

That sounded more like Jalon. "*Gut.* I just didn't want you to think I wouldn't. I haven't been all that responsible in the past."

Jalon shoved his hands back into his pockets. "And I'm the last one to cast stones. We're two of kind, you know. Might be why we were such *gut* friends."

Were. Sol didn't miss Jalon's meaning. This was a business transaction, not a renewal of friendship. Sol was surprised how much that hurt. He took a step back. "*Danki* for the order," he said, as if Jalon were a stranger. "You can pay for the birdhouse when you pick it up." He started to turn away.

"I miss hanging out with you."

When Sol turned around, Jalon added with a half-grimace, "Sorry. That sounded corny. And kinda girly too."

But Sol didn't care. He put his hand on Jalon's shoulder. "I've missed you too. I'm sorry I ruined our friendship."

"We both had a hand in that." Jalon frowned. "I started brewing beer when I was fourteen. Not exactly a model citizen myself." He rubbed his forehead. "I keep thinking about that day in church. When you admitted *yer* drinking. I should have joined you up there. I should have confessed."

"Confessed? I thought you quit drinking when you joined the church a couple of years ago."

Jalon paused. "That was the plan. Didn't work out that way. But when you had the guts to tell everyone you're an alcoholic . . . I haven't had a drink since."

"Me either."

"It's . . . it's been hard, Sol. Not gonna lie about that."

"*Ya.*" Sol knew the struggle, the draw of drink. It would be something he would fight for the rest of his life. "Work helps."

"It does. But it doesn't fix it. It doesn't take the craving away." Jalon glanced at the sky. "I pray every day for the strength to resist it."

Sol nodded. "Maybe . . . maybe we should pray for each other."

Jalon cleared his throat again. "Maybe we should." He took his hands out of his pockets. "Anyway—thanks for making the birdhouse. Let me know how much I owe you."

"Will do."

"I better get over to Ben Lapp's. We're doing some construction work near Akron and the taxi driver picks us up from his *haus.*" He looked at Sol. "I'll talk to you soon." He turned and walked away.

As Jalon got in his buggy, Sol called out, "Don't be a stranger." *Now who's being corny?*

Jalon paused mid-climb and grinned. "I won't."

As Jalon left, Sol grabbed the board and smiled. A genuine smile, which he wasn't used to. Oh, he'd been a grinning fool in the past, smiling to cover up the pain of his secrets, or to try to charm a girl into giving him what he wanted. The last woman he'd tried it with was Irene Beiler. His smile faded and he cringed. Out of all the girls he'd shown an interest in, she was the one he could have gotten serious about. But he could never risk being serious. And Irene deserved someone better than an alcoholic with more baggage than a charter bus. He thanked the Lord that nothing had happened with her other than harmless flirting. And now it was better for him to keep his distance . . . even if he couldn't keep his eyes off her every time he saw her.

He pushed Irene from his mind. He thought about Jalon again. It was good to have his friend back. It was also good to know not everyone in the community felt the need to keep their distance. He went inside his small shop, which he'd built after his father left. It wasn't much bigger than a shack, but it was all he needed. He set the board down on a table. Who could he ask to paint the birdhouse? He imagined he'd need to hire someone. Jalon wouldn't be the only customer who would want a painted house.

After he unloaded all the wood, he hitched his horse to his buggy and headed to his brother's. Maybe Sadie or Aden knew someone who could paint. He tapped the reins against the horse's flanks. A few months ago he wouldn't have asked his brother for anything. Now he was one of the few people Sol could go to. *How the tables have turned.*

CHAPTER 4

Irene had offered to help clean up after the wedding at the Schrocks', and she was about to head out the door when she saw her mother descend the stairs, carrying her purse. "I didn't realize you were coming with me," Irene said, wrapping a navy blue scarf around her neck. "I almost left without you."

"I'm not going to the Schrocks'," *Mamm* said.

Irene saw the shadowed yet determined look in her mother's eyes and knew exactly where she was going—the post office. Not the one in Langdon, which was the closest one to Birch Creek, but the one where *Mamm* had a post office box no one but she, *Mamm*, Andrew, and Joanna knew about. She gave her mother a small nod as she buttoned up her coat.

Mamm smoothed her hair, even though it was already tucked neatly underneath her white prayer *kapp*. "The taxi will be here soon. I'll be gone all day." She paused at the front door. "Do you need anything while I'm out?"

"Just for you to be careful."

Mamm paused and smiled. "I will. I'll see you later."

After her mother walked out the front door, Irene went to

37

the mudroom off the kitchen to get her boots. She glanced at the door to the new addition of the house, where Andrew and Joanna had decided to stay last night instead of engaging in the usual tradition of visiting friends after the wedding. Andrew and Asa had worked together to build the addition several months before, which included a small kitchen and bathroom, right after Andrew and Joanna had been officially engaged. Then the wedding had been canceled, and Andrew had admitted that he'd been thinking about tearing the addition down. When he and Joanna reconciled, Andrew and Asa expanded the space a little more. It wasn't exactly a *dawdi haus*, but it did provide privacy for her brother and his new wife until they had their own family. When that happened, then her mother—and probably Irene too—would move into the addition and let Andrew and Joanna have the main house.

Irene sighed as she shoved on one black snow boot. She had mixed feelings about a future that entailed her living in the addition with her mother. Since her father's future with their family was unknown, *Mamm* had resigned herself to living apart from her husband. Irene didn't like the idea of her mother being alone. Yet that's what would happen until, or if ever, her father returned.

But while Irene wasn't thinking about marriage, or even dating, she wasn't settled on the prospect of being a spinster. Actually, she was very unsettled about the idea. Not that there was anything she could do about it. No viable prospects lived in Birch Creek.

No. There had been one . . .

She shoved on her other boot. Whether she ever married was in God's control, and she wouldn't wring her hands over it. She left the house and went to the barn to hitch up the buggy she shared with her mother. As she headed to the Schrocks', tiny flakes of snow drifted in the air, and by the time she reached her destination, another thin layer of snow blanketed the ground. So far January hadn't been too snowy, and Irene could still see patches of green grass peeking out of the snow here and there, but it was bitterly cold and she was eager to get inside the warm house. She pulled into the driveway, passed the grocery and tool store on her left, and tethered her horse to the hitching post by the barn. She took a blanket out of the buggy and covered her horse with it, then shivered as she went to the main house.

Aden welcomed her inside. "Sadie mentioned you were coming over this morning."

"*Ya.* I told her I would help clean up."

"There's not too much to do," he said as they walked into the toasty-warm kitchen. She took in the covered containers and plates on the table and counters. "Everyone was very generous," Aden added.

"I can see that." She wasn't surprised. When it came to gatherings in Birch Creek, there was always more than enough food. Andrew and Joanna had taken some of it home, but the rest of the wedding guests insisted on leaving the leftovers with the Schrocks. The new bishop, Freemont Yoder, had taken only one container of pepper cabbage salad, even though his large family could have used the extra food. Although he wasn't supposed to be, Freemont could be a prideful man when it came to taking care of his family. But no one was perfect, and so far he had been a good and fair bishop. After what had happened with Aden's father, she wasn't going to complain.

"Sadie's in the store." Aden leaned his hip against the counter.

"I'm surprised you opened today."

He shook his head. "We didn't. Sadie needed some time to catch up on the books, though. With the excitement and

KATHLEEN FULLER

preparation for the wedding, she's been spending less time in the office, so she was eager to get back to work." He gestured to the table of food. "Help *yerself* if you're hungry."

"I ate before I came over." She took in the huge spread again. "Maybe I shouldn't have, though."

Aden grinned, and Irene regarded him for a moment. He'd always been a nice *mann*, but a loner while they were in school. Before his marriage to Sadie, Aden had been withdrawn, but now he was friendly, outgoing, confident, and clearly in love with his wife. Irene was amazed at the transformation—and how loving and being loved could drastically change a person for the better. At least it had in Aden's case.

"Abigail should be down soon." Aden drummed his fingers against the back of one of the kitchen chairs.

"*Geh* ahead and get on with *yer daag*," Irene said, shooing him out of the kitchen. "I'll get started in here."

Looking relieved to be set free from any potential kitchen duty, he said, "I think I'll see how Sadie's doing with the books."

Irene hid a smile as he left the kitchen. *I'm sure that's not all he's going to do.* With the store closed, he and Sadie would be alone. She sighed again. *Be content, whatever the circumstances.* And she should be, now that she'd given over her nonexistent love life to God. Yet she didn't feel content, not always, and especially around couples.

She was relieved when Abigail entered the kitchen carrying a stack of small oval rag rugs. She'd done enough ruminating on the subject, and she was eager to do something, anything, to get her mind on something else.

Abigail greeted Irene with a smile, her round cheeks lifting and making the corners of her brown eyes crinkle. "*Gut* morning," she said.

"Morning, Abigail." Irene returned her friend's smile and then caught something flicker in her eyes. The middle Schrock sister was known for her spunk and warmth. And today her smile was friendly enough. Yet there was something a little off about it, as her smiles had been since her breakup with Joel Zook. She wouldn't blame Abigail if she wasn't as cheerful as she seemed. Yet she did seem to take everything in stride, continuing to be pleasant, to crack a joke here and there, and to handle her parents' deaths with grace. Still, Irene suspected that not all was what it appeared to be where Abigail was concerned, although she hoped it was just her imagination. Abigail deserved the happiness her sisters had.

"*Danki* for coming over." Abigail nodded at the pretty rugs hanging over her forearm. "It won't take me long to run these out to the store. Sadie's been expecting them. She also mentioned she had some more orders for me."

"That reminds me," Irene said, "*Mamm* wants to put in an order too."

Abigail nodded, her smile slipping a bit.

"Is that okay?" Irene asked.

"*Ya*, but it might be a little while before I can get it to her. I'm falling a little behind with so many orders."

"That's a *gut* thing, *ya*?"

"It is." She paused. "I have to admit, I'm getting overwhelmed. This was supposed to be a hobby for me, not a business. But Sadie's so excited about the success of the rug sales . . ." She shrugged. "I'm doing the best I can."

Irene leaned against the counter. "Do you need some help? I don't know how to weave a rug, but I'm a fast learner. I can also help cut fabric and sew . . . whatever you need done."

Abigail's brow lifted. "That's a great idea. But I couldn't pay you very much."

"I don't need much pay. It will be fun. Maybe you can teach me how to weave once you get caught up on the orders."

"I will. It's not hard."

"I tell you what," Irene said, going to Abigail. "Why don't you work on the rugs today and I'll take care of all the clean up?"

Abigail shook her head. "*Nee.* I couldn't let you do that."

"*Ya*, you can. And I don't mind. Like Aden said, there's not much to do. Just a bit of picking up and straightening."

"I don't want to keep you from *yer daag*."

"Trust me, I don't have anything pressing to do at home. *Mamm*'s gone and"—she couldn't restrain herself from rolling her eyes—"I'm sure Andrew and Joanna wouldn't complain about having a little more privacy."

A swift shadow passed over Abigail's eyes. Then it disappeared. "I'm sure they wouldn't. I'm glad they're happy. Joanna deserves it. So does Andrew."

"Since that's settled, let me get started on cleaning."

"I appreciate it, Irene. And *yer* offer to help with the rugs."

"Maybe I can start after I finish with the *haus*. I'm sure it won't take me all *daag*."

"I'll be back in a bit, then." Abigail went through the mudroom, opened the back door, and left.

Irene looked at all the food on the table. She could combine a few things into one large container. Cookies, mostly. After she finished that task, she stacked the empty containers and plates next to the sink. When she glanced at the kitchen floor, she squinted. Crumbs were scattered everywhere amid traces of dirt tracked in from outside. She'd tackle this mess before washing the dishes.

After sweeping the floor, she found the mop and a bucket in the mudroom. She went to the sink and put the bucket in it, turned on the tap so the water ran slowly into the bucket, then looked underneath the sink for vinegar. Vinegar mixed with warm water always worked magic on a wood floor. She searched the cabinet but didn't see any. When she heard the back door open and close, she said, "Abigail, do you know where the vinegar is?"

"*Nee.*"

Irene stilled at the deep voice behind her. Solomon Troyer.

CHAPTER 5

Irene slowly stood and turned to look at Sol. He was standing in the doorway to the mudroom, as if hesitant to fully enter the kitchen. His dark blue coat covered his broad torso. She tried to pull her gaze away from him, but she couldn't. He'd always been more muscular than Aden. Snowflakes blanketed his shoulders and were visible on the band of his straw hat. When she met his green gaze, she felt a familiar, and unwanted, stirring.

Even before he'd started flirting with her last year, she'd always been physically attracted to Sol. It was hard not to be. But there had also been an underlying darkness about him too, which had confused her at the time. Now she knew the source of it. She'd been lucky not to fall in love with him then. He would have broken her heart the same way her father had broken her mother's.

Yet she continued to look at him, oddly powerless not to.

"*Yer* bucket is overflowing," he said.

She spun around to see that not only was the bucket full, but the sink almost was too. "Oh *nee*." She turned off the tap, but not before water sloshed onto the floor. More water spilled when she picked up the bucket. "I'm supposed to help clean up, not make a bigger mess." She put the full bucket on the counter so the sink could drain, then looked for a dish towel. Finding one lying on the counter nearby, she picked it up, knelt down, and started wiping up the excess water.

To her surprise Sol crouched beside her with another dish towel, helping her dry up the spilled water.

"I've got this," she said. "You don't have to help."

But he didn't say anything, just continued to clean up with her. Once the floor was nearly dry, he stood first. She rose right after him and her shoulder crashed into the bottom edge of the bucket, tipping it toward her. She gasped as warm water flowed over her and dripped onto the floor.

Sol's eyes widened. Then his lips twitched, almost forming a smile.

Irene blew out a breath and snatched the bucket off the floor. "It's official," she said. "I'm pathetic. Who else would make two messes while trying to clean up one?"

"You're not pathetic. Here."

She thought he was going to hand her the dry dishcloth he was now holding. Instead he used it to pat the water from her shoulder. After a moment he slowed his movements, his eyes scanning her from shoulder to toe. A startled look entered his eyes, and he almost shoved the cloth at her as he jumped back. "Sorry."

She barely heard his apology. His nearness, coupled with the still-dark emerald hue of his eyes, almost made her speechless. "I-it's okay," she said. Why did she sound breathless?

He moved farther from her. "I . . ." He gulped. "Do you know where Aden is?"

She saw his features go blank, and whatever had been in his eyes disappeared. If there had been anything there at all. That was enough to bring her partially to her senses. "He's in the store with Sadie."

Sol nodded, then hurried out of the house without saying another word.

Irene turned around and leaned over the sink. Her dress was wet, and despite the heat in the kitchen she felt cold. She couldn't say the same for her cheeks.

No, Sol wasn't the same man she'd been attracted to last year. He was different, in a way that made her interest in him months ago pale against what she was feeling now . . . and she had no idea why.

Sol shook his head as he walked from Aden and Sadie's house to Schrock Grocery and Tools. What had he been thinking, touching Irene Beiler like that? In the past he wouldn't have missed the chance to flirt with her. He would have used the opportunity to get close to her, closer than he had been in the kitchen. To sneak a kiss. Possibly something a little bit more.

That was before his life changed. Before God saved him from himself.

But today something in her eyes had shot straight through his soul, enough that it scared him. She should be repulsed by him. Instead, she seemed the complete opposite. He'd seen the longing in her eyes. Recognized it, because he felt the same thing.

But Irene was a good woman. She was sweet and kind and had a heart bigger than Birch Creek. She was the kind of woman who deserved a man of integrity, one with an unblemished past and no baggage.

A man the opposite of Sol.

A brisk wind seemed to go through him as he opened the door to the store. He saw Abigail behind the counter, staring in confusion at several pieces of paper spread in front of her. She looked up as he walked inside. "Hi, Sol."

He nodded his greeting and gestured to the papers. "Looks like you're studying for a test."

"I might as well be." She leaned forward and put her chin on her hand. "I don't get this."

"What?"

"Paperwork. Specifically accounting paperwork." She scowled. "Apparently I haven't been recording the sales of *mei* rugs, *yer* birdhouses, or Joanna's baked goods correctly." Then she straightened. "That doesn't mean you haven't been getting *yer* money and the correct amount," she added quickly.

"Oh, I know. I've been paid right and fair."

"But Sadie has a system." She frowned again. "I'm not a fan of systems. She knows that."

Sol didn't want to get in the middle of Sadie and Abigail's business. "I'll leave you to it, then. Irene"—he nearly fumbled over her name—"said Aden is here."

"Back in the office." Abigail gathered up the papers into a crooked pile. "I'm done with this today. I'm going back to the *haus.*"

Sol nodded and headed for the back of the store. The office door was partway open. He was about to knock when he saw Aden and Sadie in a passionate embrace through the crack.

He leaned against the wall and closed his eyes. That was the last thing he needed to see. He was glad for his brother, who had always loved Sadie, even when she despised both him and Sol. But seeing Aden kissing his wife just drove another nail into the coffin of hope he had for a happy future. He couldn't imagine getting married. He didn't know how to be a husband, and he especially didn't know how to be a father. All he knew was violence. Control through fear. Coping by drinking . . . something that had never completely gone away.

"Someone out there?" he heard Aden say.

Sol took a breath as he pushed open the door. He fought to appear nonchalant. "Hey, Aden. Sadie."

Sadie nodded at him, her cheeks flushed, and sat down at the desk. He swallowed, remembering the last time he'd been in this office with her. *Daed* had a horrific plan for Sol to marry her so his father could get his hands on the lucrative natural gas rights on the Schrocks' property. And Sol had gone along with it, not because he loved her, but because he had seen it as his escape from a life he hated. But Aden had thwarted the plan, angering both his father and Sol, even though his actions had been out of love.

And while Sadie forgave Sol for the past, there was still a distance between them Sol was sure would always be there.

He turned to Aden as Sadie focused on a stack of papers on the desk. "I wanted to talk to you about the birdhouses."

"You're going to keep making them, *ya*?" Sadie asked, looking up. "They're selling very well."

One thing he'd learned about Sadie since her marriage to Aden was that she was very serious about the family business. The grocery and tool store had flourished under her management. "*Ya*, I'll still make them. I like creating them, better than the carpentry work I was doing before."

"*Gut*," Aden said. "I'm glad you've found something you enjoy."

Sol knew his brother's words were genuine, and he marveled at how easily Aden had forgiven him for the abuse Sol had put him through most of their lives. For Sol, forgiving himself wasn't easy. Right now it seemed impossible. "I thought about making a few different kinds of houses instead of the same plain ones. Also, maybe painting some of them. I'll need to find someone who can paint, though. I'm terrible at it."

"Sadie's a *gut* artist," Aden said.

Sadie shot Aden a quelling look. "I don't have time to paint birdhouses."

Her tone wasn't rude, but it held double meaning. She didn't have the time, but she also wasn't going to go out of her way to help Sol, either. He didn't resent her for it, not when it was his fault she felt that way.

Aden's brow furrowed as he nodded apologetically to his wife. "Sorry, I shouldn't have mentioned it."

Sadie's expression softened. "It's okay." She turned to Sol. "Once the honey comes in from the hives, I anticipate we'll have even more business."

Sol nodded. "I understand. Do you know anyone who might be interested in painting them?"

"I'll ask around," Aden said with a nod.

"*Danki.* I'll pay them, of course."

"I'll let you know if I find anyone."

Sol was relieved Aden had taken the initiative on this. "Guess I better get back to work," Sol said, pushing his hat lower on his head. "Sadie."

She lifted her chin and gave him a tiny nod. "Sol."

He went back outside and to his buggy. The snow was coming down harder now and he needed to get home before it became too slushy on the roads. As he drove down the Schrocks' driveway, he glanced at the house. From here he could see Irene and Abigail through the kitchen window. He couldn't take his eyes off Irene, remembering the softness of her features when she chuckled over spilling the water. Then he remembered himself and stared straight ahead. He didn't need to think about Irene or any other woman. *You get what you deserve.* After the sins he'd committed, he deserved nothing.

CHAPTER 6

As Abigail waited on customers in the store one day in late February, she thought about how January and now most of February had come and gone. Each day had folded into another with almost icy boredom. She knew she should be thankful for a respite after what had seemed like an endless barrage of grief and pain.

Her rug business was going well, though—almost too well. She was having trouble keeping up with the orders even with Irene's help. And Sadie was still nagging her to do a better job of keeping track of her business records. But Abigail had never had a head for business, and as winter stretched on, her growing apathy didn't help.

Not only had her listlessness not improved, but resentment had reared up a week before Valentine's Day when she opened a shipment of Valentine's Day cards. "We're selling these now?" she'd asked Sadie.

Sadie nodded, picking up one of the cards. "Just a few. I ordered them a bit late, but Joanna has made some special chocolates for the holiday too. Nothing too fancy." She looked at Abigail before setting the card back in the box. "I can put these out," she said, reaching for the box.

Abigail had caught the flash of pity in her sister's eyes. Which was ridiculous. It had been months since she and Joel broke up. Asa had left her alone, too, except for occasionally nodding and smiling at her in church. That cemented in her mind that his earlier attention had been because he was considerate. There was no deeper meaning than that.

"I can set them out," she said, wishing she felt as cheerful as she sounded. Then she smiled. And she kept that smile on her face as she rang up the first customer who eagerly chose a card along with some candy for his sweetheart.

Now with March drawing closer, Abigail spent more time in her room weaving and less time in the store. Business had trailed off a bit, and she used the time to work. It was easier not to think about how alone she felt when she was working.

On Saturday afternoon she sat on the edge of her bed, unable to bring herself to work on another rug. Instead she stared at the wooden loom frame across the room. She'd had it for several months, but she couldn't summon the interest in trying it out. She pulled her gaze away, got up from the bed, and headed downstairs to the kitchen. She was bored and lonely—and that usually propelled her to find something to eat.

She glanced out the kitchen window. Snow was falling in heavy layers on the ground, much like it had most of the winter, with only a couple of thaws that never completely melted all the snow. Sadie and Aden were manning the store. Abigail glanced at the pantry, then at her body. She hadn't gained any more weight, but she hadn't lost any either. Eating a snack when she'd had lunch a couple of hours ago was a bad idea.

Forcing herself not to look at the pantry, she sat down at the table and ran her finger over the polished wood. Loneliness once again crept over her. She was distancing herself from her sisters, even from her friends. But that wasn't what caused this deep ache in her heart. She missed her parents. She wished *Mamm* was here. That she could talk to her about the emptiness she couldn't escape.

Then again, she knew what *Mamm* would say. *There's a lesson to be learned from this, Abigail. And once you've learned it, you will be stronger than before.*

What was there to learn from having her heart smashed into pieces? From seeing the man she had loved in love with someone else? Seeing her sisters happy and living life and feeling guilty for resenting their happiness? Most of all, feeling paralyzed to do anything about it?

Abigail shot up from the chair and opened the pantry door, giving in to the craving with mindless fervor. She pushed aside the flour and sugar containers and reached all the way back for her hidden stash. When she found the pile of candy bars, she didn't even bother to go back to the table—she grabbed the first one and ripped it open. Chocolate and sugar melted in her mouth, temporarily soothing her hurt and frustration. That's how the cycle had been lately—momentary relief followed by guilt and self-loathing. Knowing that didn't keep her from cramming the rest of the candy in her mouth as she shut the pantry door—at the same time the back door opened.

A frigid blast of air slammed into her. She flinched, her mouth full of chocolate. She stilled mid-chew when she saw Asa standing in the doorway to the mudroom.

∞

The last thing Asa expected to see when he walked into the Schrocks' house was Abigail gaping at him with wide eyes, a chocolate bar poking out of her mouth—and looking adorable. He stifled a sigh at how fast his resolve disappeared and shut the door to keep out the frigid cold. On the way over he had promised himself he wouldn't be affected by her. Since Andrew's wedding, he'd forced himself to leave her alone. God had been silent on the matter and Asa figured he must have misinterpreted his feelings for Abigail, especially since nothing bad had happened when he didn't seek her out. Unlike when he'd been disobedient in Indiana, his life hadn't fallen apart.

Keeping his distance had also given him perspective. There wasn't a deep, connecting attraction between them. He had merely sympathized with her—she had experienced a lot of disappointment lately and he knew what that was like. Of course, none of that changed the fact that he still thought she was cute.

He continued to look at her, his heart hammering in his chest. He was such a liar. He felt deeply for Abigail, and that was never more acute until this moment when he was in close proximity to her after keeping so much distance between them.

He was also filled with dread. He hadn't wanted to see her, not under these circumstances. He thought she'd be at the store, and he'd stopped there first. When Sadie said Abigail was home and to not bother knocking when he went inside, he hadn't known Abigail would be in the kitchen. He thought he'd have a few more minutes to prepare himself, to think of what to say to her. Because that morning when he'd overheard Joel talking to a mutual friend at work about what he planned to do tomorrow at church, Asa knew he had to talk to her.

Her wide eyes narrowed, but she kept her gaze on him. It took him a second, but he recognized the emotion in her eyes and it surprised him. Defiance. She went back to chewing her candy bar, slowly and with a lift of her chin. When she finished that one, she unwrapped a second one, broke off a piece, and put it into her mouth.

There wasn't anything intimate in the way she was eating or how she was looking at him. But there was some sort of challenge going on that he didn't understand, as if she was daring him to say something about her eating two chocolate bars in succession. He didn't care if she ate a whole box. What he did care about was her reaction to Joel's news.

He took off his hat. "Hi, Abigail," he said, unable to think of a better way to start the conversation.

She finished chewing, still staring at him. Then she paused before tossing the rest of the candy bar in the trash. She crossed her arms over her chest. "Hi."

He noticed she had a smudge of chocolate on the corner of her lip. His arm lifted and he realized he was about to walk over and wipe it off her mouth with his thumb. He forced his hand to his side. He was back to losing all common sense when he was around her—something he'd never had to deal with before.

"Do you need something, Asa?"

He gripped the rim of his hat. Maybe he shouldn't say anything. The situation wasn't his business. But then he imagined Abigail's face in church tomorrow when she heard about Joel and Rebecca, and he couldn't walk away even though he wanted to. "I need to talk to you." He glanced at the chairs around the table. "We should probably sit down."

He saw a spark of worry in her eyes. "Why?"

He pulled out a chair for her. "I'll tell you once you sit down."

"Asa, just tell me what's wrong."

"I'll tell you when you sit down." He parked himself in a second chair and looked up at her.

"Now you've got me worried." She sat down next to him, and he wondered if she noticed she was so close he could touch her hand if he wanted to. *And I want to.* He bent the brim of his hat until he thought he'd crease it permanently. Which was hard to do with a stiff Amish hat. He pulled in a breath. "Abigail . . . I heard something at work today."

Her face paled. "What?" Then she frowned. "Is it about Joel?"

Now he really wished he hadn't come here. He kept a grip on his hat as he said, "Joel and Rebecca are announcing their engagement tomorrow."

The rest of the color drained from Abigail's face. She didn't move. The small smear of chocolate now shined like a brown beacon from the corner of her lip. He waited for her to say something. Even a cough would be good right now. Anything but the catatonic reaction she was having now. Then she spoke. "I . . ." The garbled word sounded like it was forced from her lips.

His heart swelled with compassion. Now he was glad he'd ignored his cowardly instincts and told her ahead of time. "I'm sorry."

She looked down at her lap. "*Danki* . . . for . . . telling . . . me."

This wasn't good. He leaned forward and looked in her eyes. "Abigail? Are you okay?"

She didn't respond.

Take her hand.

His whole body jerked and he nearly dropped his hat. This was the first time he'd heard God's voice in months. Before he returned to Birch Creek, he'd never heard God speak in actual words. Now it was as though his brain was tuned in to a divine frequency. *I don't think I should—*

Take her hand.

An unseen force seemed to propel him to put his hat on the table. Or maybe it was his own volition—he was starting to get the two confused lately. He glanced at Abigail's lap. Her hands lay there, limply, right beneath the gentle swell of her abdomen. He leaned forward and covered his hand over her plump fingers.

She still didn't move.

At least she wasn't pushing him away. He curled his hand around hers. "I really am sorry. I thought you should know so you wouldn't be surprised in church tomorrow."

Abigail nodded.

Her lack of reaction gave him time to look at their hands entwined together. She had the softest hands, especially the tops of her fingers. He moved his thumb across the inside of her palm.

That seemed to bring her back from whatever void she'd gone to. She pulled her hand from his and jumped up from the chair. "I'm sorry, Asa," she said, her lips curling into a strained half-smile. "I've been rude. Do you want anything to drink? To eat? I can make *kaffee*, we've got, uh, candy bars . . ."

He rose from the chair and went to her. "*Nee*. And you haven't been rude."

"*Ya*, I have." She put the heel of her hand on her forehead, not looking at him, and her pretend smile disappeared. "I don't know what's wrong with me lately. I know how to be hospitable."

"Abigail, it's okay."

"*Nee*, it's not." She finally looked at him. "But trust me, I'm over Joel. I'm happy for him and Rebecca. I really am. I should have expected it, anyway. It's not like they've been secret about their relationship."

His heart went out to her. The words had poured out of her like water rushing over a cliff.

"I should probably check to see if Sadie needs help at the store." She moved past Asa without looking at him. "I . . . I hope you don't mind seeing *yerself* out." Then she opened the door and disappeared into the blowing snow.

As soon as she stepped out the back door, Abigail froze as the windy cold whipped around her. Joel was engaged. Or at least he would be, officially, when it was announced in church tomorrow. She didn't understand her reaction to the news. She was over Joel. When she thought of him now, it wasn't with love, but with regret. Yet here she was, unable to sort out how she felt. Asa probably thought she was *ab im kopp.*

The door behind her opened. She flinched and closed her eyes. Asa. He always seemed to be around at her most embarrassing moments. She nearly died inside when he caught her stuffing her face with candy. Then she grew angry at the thought of him judging her. Never mind that he never did actually judge her. But she knew what he had to be thinking. *As fat as she is, she shouldn't be eating that candy.* She even imagined the words in his deep voice. So she did the only thing she could think of to keep her humiliation at bay—she continued to eat. He wouldn't see her hidden shame, at least not reflected on her face.

"Abigail." He came up behind her and she felt his coat across her shoulders. Typical Asa. He was kind enough to warn her about Joel and Rebecca. Why wouldn't he be just as kind dealing with her reaction to the news?

"Come inside," he said, his hands on her shoulders, as if he was making sure she wouldn't whip off his coat and throw it back at him again. His coat didn't fit her any better than it had weeks ago. Yet she seemed to be enveloped with warmth.

She turned toward him and looked up into his eyes. Snowflakes speckled his blue-black hair. He was wearing a short-sleeved shirt. She knew he had to be freezing. Yet neither of them moved as their gazes locked. Then he brushed his thumb over the corner of her mouth.

"Chocolate," he whispered, drawing his thumb away.

That one word was the equivalent of an ice bucket sloshing over her. She had chocolate on her mouth from her candy binge. She stepped away from him and went back inside. A moment later she heard the door shut behind her.

She leaned against the counter, trying to slow her heartbeat, her lips still tingling from where he had touched her. Then her stomach rebelled and she put her hand over it. She shouldn't have eaten that much chocolate at once. She shouldn't have gone outside in the cold. She shouldn't be so affected by Joel's engagement news.

She shouldn't want Asa Bontrager to touch her again.

She heard him come up behind her and she took in a deep breath. It was time for her to be practical. To not let her emotions and impulses take over like they normally did. To not read anything into Asa's kindness. Fortifying herself, she removed his coat, turned, and smiled. "*Danki*," she said, handing it to him. "That was *dumm* of me, to forget *mei* coat." Her voice sounded like a cross between a bullfrog and one of Homer's squeaky dog toys, so she cleared her throat. "I appreciate you letting me know about Joel."

He took the coat and peered down at her with a concerned gaze that reached clear to her cold toes. "Are you sure you're all right?"

"Of course!" She laughed to show him she was fine. It came out like a strained garble, but it was the best she could do. Then she managed part of a real smile. "Honestly, Asa, I'll be okay. I've been through worse." She hadn't meant to say that last part.

"I know." His voice and gaze were steady. "That's why I'm worried about you."

"Don't be." She moved past him and pushed the kitchen chairs back under the table. Then she smiled at him again. "Everything is okay."

"Are you sure?"

"Positive." Her smile widened, and it even reached a little bit of her heart. "I appreciate *yer* thoughtfulness," she said.

Something flickered in his eyes before he took his hat. He put it on his head. "If you need to talk, let me know."

"I will."

"I mean it." The intensity in his eyes nearly undid her. "I'm here for you, Abigail." He put on his coat, gave her one last look, and left.

Somehow, deep in her heart, she knew he meant it.

CHAPTER 7

Naomi finished polishing the coffee table in Rhoda Troyer's living room. Tomorrow would be the first time Rhoda had hosted church since her husband, Emmanuel, left. Rhoda could have refused to host and no one would have questioned her about it. Naomi was surprised she had agreed; this had to be hard for her. That was why she was here helping her friend get ready for tomorrow's service and fellowship.

Sol was out positioning the benches for morning worship in the barn with a couple of other men. Naomi also wondered what he thought about hosting the service, but she wouldn't ask. She knew what it was like to want to keep feelings close to the heart.

"What's next?" she asked Rhoda as she stood, feeling a bit of a pinch in her back from bending over. Getting older wasn't for the faint of heart. Although she was only in her early forties, her body felt older than that. Raising two children, being separated from her husband, not knowing where he was and only gaining contact with him through letters . . . it had all taken its toll on her over the last twelve years. She still missed Bartholomew, just as much as she had since the day he left. His smile. His sense of adventure. His gentle touch. She glanced at Rhoda, who was dusting off a lampshade, and felt compassion. Emmanuel had only been gone a few months, but Naomi remembered that those first months of being without Bartholomew had been the hardest.

"I think we're almost finished." Rhoda smiled, but her eyes remained sad. Naomi once again thought having church service so soon was a bad idea. Emmanuel had been their bishop for over twenty years, since before Naomi moved to Birch Creek. Since he'd left, Rhoda had attended every church service and was attentive to Bishop Yoder's sermons. But hosting church? Naomi thought that could wait until next year.

"I appreciate *yer* help," Rhoda added. "It's nice to have company."

So maybe that was it. They had a common bond, even though it was for different reasons. Naomi and Rhoda had grown closer since Emmanuel left. Naomi had been the first woman to visit Rhoda and try to encourage her shortly after Emmanuel's departure. But Naomi had also been wrapped up in her own family drama, with Andrew and Joanna having relationship problems. Shortly after, Andrew had confronted her with the lie she and Bartholomew had concocted about his departure. Although their intentions had been to keep their children safe, they had deceived them. Bartholomew wasn't the man they thought he was. He hadn't left the family because he wanted to. His illegal actions from his youth had caught up to him. They were all paying the consequences, and she didn't know how much longer they would be paying them.

She went to Rhoda, leaving her own troubles behind so she

could comfort her friend. "Since we're finished cleaning, how about we have a cup of *kaffee* before I *geh* home?"

Rhoda smiled again, and this time a little of the emotion reached her eyes. "I'd like that."

Naomi followed her into the spotless kitchen. Rhoda prepared the coffee while Naomi sat down. From her chair at the table she could see snow falling outside the kitchen window. She'd have to leave soon before it got too thick. But there was still time to visit with Rhoda.

Rhoda set a mug of coffee in front of Naomi, then sat down. She didn't say anything, just stared at the steam rising from her own mug.

"Do you need any help preparing the food?" Naomi asked, then blew the steam from the hot beverage.

"*Nee.* I went to the grocery store yesterday and stocked up. Besides, you know everyone brings food, whether or not they decide to stay for a visit."

This was true. The citizens of Birch Creek were generous. The community had pulled together even more after Emmanuel left. "I thought I might make some deviled eggs for tomorrow." Those had been one of Bartholomew's favorite snacks.

Rhoda's eyes widened and she shook her head. "Emmanuel wouldn't like that."

Naomi frowned, the mug still near her mouth.

"He never approved of the name of those eggs."

"Deviled?" Naomi's brow lifted. It was a cooking term, and she honestly never thought about the word *devil* being a part of the word.

"*Ya.*"

"So you never made them?"

"I never will make them," she said in all seriousness. "I would appreciate it if you would bring something else. When Emmanuel comes back and finds out we served deviled eggs in his home, he will be upset."

"When is he coming back?"

Rhoda glanced at her mug. "In God's time."

Naomi set down her mug. How many times had she told herself the same thing about Bartholomew? That he would return at God's behest, and not a moment sooner? Still, it was a bitter pill to swallow, not knowing when he would return, waking up every morning wondering if this was the day she would see her husband again, only to go to bed that night alone once again. "I'm sorry," she said, her heart going out to her friend who was no doubt suffering the same way.

"*Nee* need to be sorry." Rhoda took a drink from her coffee as if they were talking about the weather instead of her absent husband. Determination replaced the sadness in her eyes. "*Mei* Emmanuel will return."

Naomi wasn't sure what to say. She looked at Rhoda with concern. Her brown hair had gotten grayer the past few months, and more lines creased her forehead. There was always a strain tugging at her mouth and melancholy in her eyes. For Rhoda's sake she hoped Emmanuel would return soon. But other than his family, he had little reason to come back to Birch Creek. He was in the bann for several reasons—hiding funds from the community, leaving his wife, abandoning his bishop duties. If—when—he returned, he would have to confess. He would be forgiven, of course. But in the back of her mind she wondered if Emmanuel Troyer would ever face what he had done. They had been fortunate the community hadn't split when he left.

"Have you heard from him?" Naomi asked. Normally she

wouldn't pry like this, but Rhoda's confident stance made her wonder if Emmanuel had been in contact with her.

Rhoda lifted her chin, but Naomi saw her bottom lip tremble slightly. "*Nee*. I have not."

Naomi pressed her lips together and picked up her mug. While she didn't have Bartholomew's physical presence, he was still very much a part of her life. She didn't know what she'd do if they hadn't remained in contact through letters over the years, even though he wasn't supposed to make contact with her or his family. He had agreed to forge a new life, to leave his old one behind. But he hadn't. Not really. Like her, he had faith that one day he would see his family again. And it hadn't been long after he left and she and the children moved to Birch Creek that she received his first letter, with instructions on how they could communicate in the future. She at least had something tangible to hang her hope on. But Rhoda . . . she'd received only silence from her husband. Yet she still held on to hope.

The kitchen door opened and Sol came in. There was a mudroom off the Troyers' kitchen, so he had already taken off his coat, hat, and boots. "Hi, Naomi," he said, then blew on his hands, which were red from the cold.

"Hello, Solomon."

"Snow's getting heavy." Sol went to a cabinet and removed a mug, then hesitated before pouring coffee. "You might want to head for home soon. I can bring *yer* buggy around for you if you want."

"*Danki*." She had parked her horse and buggy near the Troyers' barn. "I appreciate it." She turned to his mother. "But Rhoda, are you sure you don't need help with anything else?"

She nodded. "*Ya. Danki* for coming over."

Sol set his empty mug on the countertop and left the kitchen. "I'll be right back."

A couple of minutes later, Naomi went to the mudroom and slipped on her boots, then her navy blue coat and scarf and black bonnet. She tied the bonnet around her neck and pinned her cape over her coat.

"Here." Rhoda came into the mudroom. She handed Naomi a thermos. "Hot coffee. For the drive home."

Naomi smiled, touched by the thoughtful gesture. "I'll see you tomorrow, then."

Through the small window of the mudroom Naomi saw Sol bring around her horse and buggy. Outside, she thanked him again, climbed into the buggy, and left, praying for Rhoda, Sol—and, of course, Bartholomew—as she made her way home.

Bartholomew Beiler opened the door to his apartment, shut and locked it behind him, and tossed his keys on a small table. He pulled off his work boots and left them by the door, then went to the recliner and plopped down. Fatigue washed through him. He had put in another twelve-hour workday on the assembly line at Taylor and Sons, which he'd been doing since he started at the glass factory almost five years ago. He was tired, but he didn't mind the work. The longer he stayed there, the less time he had to spend alone. He was willing to work Saturdays, so they were happy to give him plenty of overtime. He was happy to get it.

He leaned back against the chair and ran his hand over his face. Twelve years of this, being separated from his family, living alone, living in this world but not remotely a part of it. His only friendships were superficial, the ones he had at work, and he had to keep it that way. Sure, the guys invited him out for drinks sometimes after a hard shift. A few of them had felt sorry for him over the years and tried to get him to come to their houses for Thanksgiving or Christmas. But Bartholomew—or Jack Collins, as everyone else knew him—always had an excuse.

It was his fault he lived like this, friendless and separated from his family. He'd made the decision to rebel against his strict Amish parents in the worst possible way—by dealing drugs. Then he'd met Naomi.

He sighed at the thought of his wife. His beautiful, strong, courageous wife. She had changed him, made him want to be a better man. And for a time, he was. But because of his mistakes she had to finish raising Irene and Andrew alone. She was both their mother and their father. She was also his rock, the first person he thought of every morning when he woke up and the last he thought of every night before he went to sleep.

He bolted from the chair, frustrated. Naomi had changed his life, but the past had caught up to him. He was arrested, then turned state's evidence. His information had led to the arrest of several people high up in a complex drug ring in Florida. But not everyone had been caught, and for their own protection his wife and children had to move to Birch Creek, a small Amish community that was barely a blip on the map. He was sent even farther away with a new identity to start a new life. But he couldn't . . . not when all he wanted was his wife and children by his side.

He went to the kitchen and flung open the fridge door. The refrigerator was nearly empty except for a six-pack of pop and a bottle of mustard. He had a couple pizzas in the freezer. Another gourmet dinner tonight. He grabbed one of the cans, shut the door, and was about to pop the top when he heard a knock on the door.

Ice chilled his veins. Although he knew he was under protection by the U.S. Marshals Service, Bartholomew remained constantly on guard. Slowly he set down the can and crept to the door. He peered through the peephole, then blew out a relieved breath. After unlocking the two chain locks and the dead bolt, he opened the door. "Hey, Mike."

A tall man built like a football linebacker strolled through the door. His salt-and-pepper hair was cut short against his head, the bristles brushing the top of the doorjamb as he walked inside. "Jack," he said with a nod, taking a quick visual survey of the small living room. There wasn't much to look at—a short couch and matching recliner, a flat-screen TV perched on a cheap stand, and an old coffee table. Still, Mike's eagle-sharp eyes continued to peruse the room.

"Want something to drink?" Bartholomew asked, closing the door.

"Sure."

"Coke okay?"

"Since I'm on duty, absolutely."

Bartholomew got Mike a pop and handed it to him. He didn't keep any liquor in the place. Ever since he married Naomi and joined the Amish church, he hadn't touched a drop of drink and his drug tests at work had been cleaner than clean.

Mike sat down on the couch and opened his drink. Bartholomew sat down in the recliner and turned to him. "What made you decide to stop by?"

"You know the drill. Gotta check on you every once in a while. Make sure everything is in line." He tipped his beverage toward Bartholomew. "Not like you would ever step out of bounds, Jack."

Bartholomew didn't respond. He didn't know how much of his past Mike knew, and they never discussed it.

"Have any plans for the weekend?" Mike asked.

"Nope." Bartholomew took a long drink.

"You never do." Mike put his drink on the coffee table, leaned back against the couch, and sighed. "We've been doing this a long time. You're supposed to live a new life, Jack. Not hide away for more than a decade."

"I go to work. That is my life."

"It's not much of one."

"It is for me." *At least for right now.* "Any word on . . ." He couldn't even bring himself to ask the question. Each time he did, he was disappointed.

Mike shook his head, grabbed the pop, and took another long swig. Silence filled the room as he stared at the top of the can.

Bartholomew waited to see if the man had anything else to say. He never liked small talk, and unless Mike was here to tell him he was free to go home to his family, Bartholomew was ready for him to leave. He stood, feigning a yawn, hoping Mike would get the hint. "Got to get up early in the morning," he said, taking a step toward the door.

With a curt nod Mike put the pop can on the coffee table and stood. He rubbed his hand across the top of his head. "Maybe soon I can tell you what you want to hear."

Bartholomew refused to get his hopes up. Mike always said that before he left. Tonight was no different. "Night, Mike."

"See you later, Jack."

Bartholomew closed the door behind him, bolted it, and leaned against it. Fatigue sank into him. He wasn't lying when he said he had to get up early, even on a Sunday. That was one habit he still had from when he was Amish. Early to bed, early to rise. It made the days go faster.

He went to his bedroom and sat on the edge of the bed. Then

he leaned forward, running both hands over his hair, which was almost as short as Mike's. One day he would go home, and when he did, he'd grow a proper Amish haircut. He couldn't wait.

Home. He closed his eyes. "When, Lord?" he whispered. "When can I see *mei familye* again?"

God wasn't talking, and Bartholomew opened his eyes. He turned on the lamp on his nightstand and opened the drawer. There they were. Every letter Naomi had written. He looked through them every night. He had them memorized, too, except for the last one she'd sent. She wrote to him more often than he did to her. He didn't want to risk Mike or any of the other guys assigned to watch him finding out he was writing to his wife.

He picked up her latest letter and opened it.

Dear Bartholomew,

Next week Andrew and Joanna will be married. How I wish you were here to be by *mei* side. You would be so happy with *yer sohn*. He has grown into a fine *mann*, and will be a wonderful husband to his wife.

A lump formed in Bartholomew's throat. He knew Naomi's words weren't said to instill guilt, but they did anyway. He should be there. He shouldn't be in a one-bedroom apartment working a factory job he hated, spending every night alone, missing all his children's milestones. Yet these were the consequences to be paid. And he would pay them without complaint.

There was more to the letter, sweet words of love that Bartholomew savored. Naomi's writings were always a balm to him. After he finished reading, he carefully folded the letter, put it back in the envelope, and placed it in the drawer. Then he saw Andrew's letter and picked it up.

He'd been surprised his son had written to him last year. Obviously Naomi had told him, and probably Irene too, the real reason he left the family. To keep his wife and children safe, he had insisted Naomi tell everyone that he left the family for an *Englisch* woman. But now it seemed Andrew knew the truth. His son had penned few words, but they were important.

When you're free, come find me.

Bartholomew folded the letter and closed his eyes. One day he would be back with his family, for good, and on his own terms. An image of Naomi came to his mind. Six years ago, but he remembered it like it was yesterday. The last time he saw her. The federal government had insisted on moving him around the first few years, and he was living closer to Birch Creek. He took advantage of that and sneaked away to visit her.

He surprised her by doing something a bit childish—climbing up a tree and trying to sneak into her bedroom through the window. But she'd been in the room, seen him, and opened the window to let him in. Before he climbed inside he grabbed her face and kissed her. "Sorry," he'd said, pulling back. But he wasn't really sorry. The lingering kiss had brought him alive again, after feeling dead inside for so long. "I couldn't help myself."

She let him into her house and back into her heart. When she laid her cheek against his chest . . . even now as he thought about that time, his heart raced.

"I can't believe you're here," she'd said, looking up at him with love he didn't deserve. She was still so beautiful, and he couldn't resist unbinding her hair, running his fingers through the soft strands. She'd questioned him. "You're not supposed to be here."

"You couldn't expect me to stay away forever."

He opened his eyes. No, he couldn't stay away from his family forever. He refused to. And when he returned to them, he would never leave again.

CHAPTER 8

A bigail ground her teeth as everyone congratulated Joel and Rebecca after the service. As the two of them milled around the edges of the Troyers' barn, Rebecca beamed, her pretty cheeks glowing as Joel stood by her side—tall, lean, handsome, and clearly in love with his wife to be.

Abigail wanted to throw up. When Asa told her about Joel's announcement yesterday, she'd convinced him she was fine. She'd almost convinced herself. But right now, nothing was further from the truth.

Andrew, Asa, and Aden were standing on the opposite side of the barn from where Sadie, Joanna, and Irene had formed a circle around Abigail. Now Joanna moved to stand by her side and took her hand.

For the first time in weeks the ice around Abigail's heart began to thaw. Her family was lined up in solidarity behind her. Well, Asa wasn't part of her family but he was Andrew's best friend. His actions told her he was also on her side. What she didn't understand was why. She only knew she was grateful.

"I'm fine," she said, lifting her chin. Make that a double chin, one she noticed in the bathroom mirror this morning before they left for church. She looked at slim Rebecca Chupp and tried to stem the jealousy within her. But she no longer looked at Joel and wished they were still together.

He glanced up and their gazes met. Joel was so tall he could see over everyone in Birch Creek. A bit of the happiness in his eyes dimmed. She frowned. He almost looked apologetic. He hadn't seemed all that apologetic when he broke up with her.

"Are you sure you're all right?" Irene asked.

Abigail broke eye contact with Joel and looked at her friend. Since she and Irene had started working together, they had grown closer. It was nice to have someone to talk to while they made rugs, even if they only talked about superficial things. There seemed to be an understanding between them that certain subjects wouldn't be discussed—Joel, Asa, and, surprisingly, Sol. Abigail had noticed Sol standing off by himself today.

Abigail glanced around at her family and friends again. This time her gaze met Asa's, and it mirrored what she saw in everyone else's—sympathy. Her smile disappeared. The Schrocks had been on the receiving end of enough pity to last a lifetime. There was only one way to reassure him—and everyone else—that she didn't need anyone's sympathy. Straightening her shoulders, she said to the women around her, "Excuse me." Then she walked over to Joel and Rebecca.

The small crowd around the couple parted to let her through, although she hadn't asked them to move. They also ceased talking, except for a few hushed murmurs. What, did they expect her to make a scene? To accuse Joel of loving and leaving her? *I wish I could.* The thought flashed through her unbidden. Okay, maybe she hadn't settled everything in her mind and heart where Joel was concerned, but she wasn't pining after him anymore. She had moved on, and it was time everyone else had too. "Congratulations," she said, making a conscious decision to speak to Rebecca first.

Rebecca smiled. Abigail still wondered what part Rebecca had to play in Joel's betrayal. Had she gone after Joel the moment Abigail left for Middlefield? Had she ever said to him, "Joel, this isn't a *gut* idea. Abigail just lost her parents. She's helping her younger sister recover. Maybe we shouldn't do this"? Or had Joel wooed her?

Did the answers really matter?

"That means a lot coming from you, Abigail." Rebecca's sweet, melodic voice sounded sincere. "*Danki* for wishing us well."

"*Ya*," Joel said. "*Danki.*"

Abigail looked at him. He wasn't smiling. He looked confused. A small part of her was glad. *Let him be off-kilter for once.*

"May God bless *yer* marriage." One more smile, this time aimed at Joel. Then she turned her head up, pretending to ignore the people looking at her. Yet despite her determination to show them all she was fine, imagined voices rang in her head.

Poor Abigail. Both her schwesters married . . . and she's single and alone.

She'll find someone else . . . maybe.

Wow, she's packed on the pounds.

She almost tripped over her feet at that last thought, suddenly aware of the tightness of the top of her dress, the way her sweater didn't quite close over her torso underneath her coat, which strained a bit at the buttons. Then she was reminded of the thickness of her legs. Her stupid double chin. Tears pricked her eyes. *Not now. Don't cry now.* She blinked and kept on walking, ignoring not only the congregation but also her sisters, their husbands, and Irene.

Her steps quickened and she walked around the back of the Troyers' barn, breathing in the cold, sharp air. Her eyes watered. That had been so much harder than she'd thought it would be. She gasped for breath, her legs shaking, as negative thoughts and pain crashed into her.

The sound of boots crunching on snow made her lift her head. Her legs steadied slightly as she saw him draw near. *Asa.*

∞

She's amazing.

He'd gone after her when she disappeared behind the Troyers' barn. She'd surprised him. No, she'd shocked him. He'd watched her every move as she approached Rebecca and Joel, her chin lifted with defiant confidence. She didn't have to congratulate them in front of everyone. Everyone would have understood if she hadn't. But she'd done the bravest thing he'd ever seen. She'd extended grace. And she'd done it with a smile.

But she wasn't smiling now. She looked pale, as if she were a bit in shock. He wanted to go to her, but her body seemed to have closed in on itself a little, as if warding him off. He steeled himself, expecting her to tell him to go away. But she didn't. Instead, her body started to shake.

He didn't need God to propel him to her or to tell him what to do. He went to her, putting himself between her and the cold, intermittent wind. "You're crying."

"It's the wind." She didn't avert her gaze, but she wiped at her left eye with the back of her hand. Then she stared at him, unflinching with her chocolate-colored eyes. They were beautiful, with light brown lashes and a few specks of gold dotting the irises. Despite the sheen in her eyes, he could still see warmth in those depths hiding behind a wall of pain. He wanted to take a sledgehammer and destroy that wall, smashing it to dust.

"I don't understand," she said.

"What?"

"You."

That makes two of us. He wasn't himself around her. Not even close. She jangled his nerves, jumbled his thoughts, and made him question his sanity. "I'm a simple guy."

She held up her hands. "Don't . . ."

"Don't what?"

"Be charming. Or whatever it is you're doing." Her eyes started watering again. "I don't need anyone feeling sorry for me."

"I don't feel sorry for you."

"Then why are you here?"

Ever since he'd arrived in Birch Creek he'd wondered why God had led—and kept leading him—to Abigail Schrock. Now he knew. He understood about loss, could identify with the hurt confusion swirling in her gorgeous eyes. And in his heart, he knew he needed her too. But he had to keep that to himself, at least for now. "Rugs," he blurted, unsure where the word had come from.

Her left eyebrow arched while her right one stayed straight. Her skeptical expression was cute. "Rugs?"

"I need some. I'm almost finished fixing up *mei haus*, at least the downstairs. Now I need to start filling it."

"With rugs."

"With everything. Furniture, rugs . . ." He shrugged. "It's an empty shell right now."

"You can buy the rugs at the store."

"I don't know what kind to get. Maybe you could bring over some samples? Then I can see what will work in *mei haus*." Did he really just say that?

"Seriously? You can't pick out a rug by *yerself*?"

He held out his hands. "Call me clueless." And crazy.

Her eyebrow lifted even higher for a moment. Then she sighed. "Fine. I'll come over and help you make *yer* difficult rug decision."

Then he saw it. The gleam in her eye. Now her lips were twitching. His shoulders relaxed a little. He hadn't known he'd been so tense. "I'd appreciate any help you can give me."

"I'll see you tomorrow evening, then?"

"Sounds *gut*."

She paused for a moment, then crossed her arms. "I should get back to *mei schwesters*. They'll be worried about me, even though they don't need to be."

Her expression told him she didn't think he needed to worry about her either. He stepped to the side to let her pass. "I should be home around five thirty," he called out before she rounded the barn.

Abigail glanced over her shoulder, gave him a nod, then disappeared.

He leaned against the barn and grinned. His ruse might be dumb, but he was going to see her tomorrow. Then his smile slipped. He was going to see her tomorrow. In his house, which was almost empty right now. He pushed off from the barn. *Okay, Lord . . . what's the next step?*

CHAPTER 9

Sol poured Aden a mug of coffee, then one for himself. His brother had decided to stay and visit with *Mamm* for a while after everyone else left for the afternoon. She was pleased by the visit, but Sol could tell she was tired. When she told him and Aden she wanted to lie down for a little while, neither of them argued. Hopefully she would sleep, not toss and turn like he knew she tended to do since *Daed* left.

He took the mugs and sat down at the kitchen table. Pushing one mug toward Aden, he said, "It's strong."

"That's how I like it." Aden picked up the coffee.

"*Nee*, I mean really strong." He glanced away. "The extra kick, it . . . helps."

Aden paused. "I understand." He took a sip and his eyes grew wide. "You weren't joking."

"Told you." Sol drank the tar-colored brew. What he wouldn't do for a real drink right now. But he would be satisfied with coffee. Liquor would never pass his lips again.

Aden set down his coffee mug and pushed it away a few inches. "We've got some things to talk about," Aden said. "And none of them concern *kaffee*."

Sol set down his mug and gripped it in his hands. "If you're worried about *Mamm*, don't be. I'm taking care of her."

Aden nodded. "I know you are. But there are some things you can't help her with."

Slumping, Sol nodded. "I know. I wish I could."

"Have you heard from him?"

"*Nee*." Sol clenched his fists. But *Daed* was never far from his mind. How he had broken him and Aden. How he'd fooled the community, although Sol thought *Daed* truly believed everything he did was God's will. He'd been gone for several months, and not only had he not sent any word about where he was or if he was okay, he also hadn't sent any money. Sol didn't expect a dime from him, but what about *Mamm*? How could he leave his wife and the mother of his children—sons he'd never shown an ounce of love toward—without funds?

Maybe his father trusted Aden to take care of her. And that would be true. Aden always did the right thing, or at least he tried to. Sol was trying to follow his lead, and he'd been keeping a watchful eye on *Mamm* ever since their father left. She still maintained he was coming back. His office was the same. His clothes still hung in the closet. She still fixed a little extra food in case he decided to show up at suppertime. Sol didn't have the heart to tell her his father was probably gone forever. If hanging on to hope helped her get through the day, he wasn't about to squash that hope.

"I doubt we'll ever see him again." Sol took another swig of his coffee. The bitter taste added to the sourness in the pit of his stomach.

"I don't believe that. *Ya*, I know he would abandon *us*." Aden's jaw jerked. "But he'd never leave *Mamm*. Not forever, anyway."

"*Mamm* agrees with you." Sol rubbed his forehead. "She insists he's coming back any *daag* now."

"What's wrong with her holding on to hope?"

"*Nix*, right now. But someday she'll need to face reality." Sol fisted his hand on the table, then moved it to his lap. He unclenched it and looked at Aden. "She'll have to accept that our *daed* was—is—a terrible person." *And that's giving him more credit than he deserves.*

Aden leaned back against his chair. "Maybe he's not anymore."

Sol scoffed. "You don't seriously believe that."

"*You're* different." Aden leaned against the table and folded his hands. "Maybe *Daed* has changed too."

"That's a big if." Sol sighed. "Let's say you're right, that he has changed. Then why hasn't he come back?"

Aden paused. "I don't have the answer to that."

"Because you have *yer* head in the clouds."

"And *yers* is always in the sand."

Sol counted to ten. He'd been doing that for the past few months, working on controlling his temper. He wasn't mad at Aden, he was angry that his brother was right. He'd covered his pain with alcohol, and when that hadn't worked, he took out his fury with his fists instead of dealing with his problems like a man.

This time he was able to speak without snapping or sarcasm before he made it to five. That was an improvement. "I told her I wouldn't leave her alone. That *nee* matter what happens, she'll always have me."

"She'll have me too. I'm not going anywhere."

"But you have a *familye* of *yer* own. Sadie, maybe some *kinner* soon."

"If God wills. But that doesn't mean I won't be there for *Mamm*."

"*Daed* too?"

Aden pressed his lips together. "*Ya*. I have to forgive him. We both do."

Sol looked at the table. He'd refinished it last Christmas as a present for his mother. She'd had the same scuffed table for years since their father had refused to buy a new one or have this one repaired. Sol had also made other improvements to the house—he replaced their small woodstove with a larger one, bought a new hickory rocking chair for *Mamm*, and was planning to sand and refinish the living room floors when the weather turned warmer. His father had lived frugally, yet had hoarded his own money and the community fund over the twenty years he'd been bishop of Birch Creek. His father had been cruel not only to his own family; he'd also let the community suffer. How was Sol supposed to forgive him for that? For everything he had done?

"Suppose *Daed* doesn't return, at least for a long time." Aden cleared his throat, as if saying the words out loud bothered him. "I don't want *Mamm* living alone."

"I'm here, Aden. She won't be alone."

"You're here for now."

Once more Sol could feel his anger rising even though he wasn't surprised Aden was insinuating that he would abandon their mother. His brother might have forgiven him, but it was clear Sol hadn't earned his trust. "I told you I'm not going anywhere and I meant it."

"That's not what I'm saying. I know you'll stand by her, Sol.

But what about when you get married? What will happen to her then?"

"I'm not getting married."

"Not now . . . but someday."

He didn't answer, just stared at the wood grain on the table. He had come to terms with his future. He'd continue with woodworking—something he really loved now that he was focused and sober and had his own business—and take care of his mother. When—more likely if—his father returned, then he'd deal with that. But love, that was off the table. And somehow he would handle the loneliness, the envy he felt when he saw Aden and Sadie together, or any other happy couple. This was his penance.

"Sol?"

Aden's voice cut into his thoughts. He looked at his younger brother. His red beard had grown out and was now a little scraggly around his chin. He had changed too. Since marrying Sadie and standing up to their father, he had transformed from a weak, broken man to a confident one. "Don't worry about *Mamm*," Sol said. "I'll make sure she's always taken care of."

Aden nodded. He glanced at the coffee mug. "You won't be offended if I don't finish that?"

Sol half-smiled. "*Nee.* I'll finish it for you."

Aden pushed away from the table. "I've got to get back home."

Sol followed Aden to the buggy. Before getting in, Aden said, "*Daed*'s not the only person you need to forgive, Sol."

He couldn't imagine who his brother was talking about. Sol had transgressed, not the other way around. "Who?"

"You." Aden climbed into the buggy. "You need to forgive *yerself.*"

Sol waited until his brother had disappeared down the road

before heading back to the house. He stood outside the back door and hung his head. How could he forgive himself for years and years of sins? How could he live his life knowing what he had done? If he had to forgive himself, he didn't know how.

∞

"I don't know why Asa didn't ask me for decorating advice," Irene said Monday afternoon as she handed Abigail two of the half-finished rugs they had worked on last week. "Actually, I don't know why he needs decorating advice at all. He's never been picky about stuff like that before, at least as long as I've known him. Then again, he was gone for several years. Maybe he's picky about that stuff now."

Abigail shrugged, but she hid the fact that she had wondered the same thing, pondering it enough that she had trouble falling asleep. What did Asa want from her? It couldn't be anything romantic. She and Asa definitely weren't a good match.

She turned to Irene. "Did you and Asa ever date?"

Irene laughed. "Goodness, *nee*. He's like *mei bruder*. You're not the first one to ask me, though. And apparently several girls have found it hard to believe someone exists on this planet who isn't interested in Asa Bontrager."

"That makes two of us." At least she was trying to convince herself of that.

"Hmm," Irene said. "I wonder if he might be interested in *you*, though."

Her friend wasn't helping. "I can't see that happening. I'm sure he's being nice."

"He's always been that." Irene tapped her finger on her chin. "But I can see you two together."

Abigail's mouth dropped open. Then she clamped it shut. "I'm not ready for a relationship."

"Not even a date?"

"*Nee*. Not even a date. And that's the last I'm going to say on that subject."

"All right." Irene looked a little contrite. "I'm sorry I touched on a sore spot."

"You didn't." She had, but that wasn't Irene's fault. Putting ridiculous ideas like dating Asa out of her mind, Abigail placed the rugs on her bed. Five were unfinished and one was ready for sale. She and Irene had chosen a variety of colors—browns, grays, blues, sage and dark greens, and russet and rust. All fairly masculine, if one could call a woven rug masculine.

Irene went to the wooden loom frame and touched the light brown wood. "Are you ever going to use this?"

"*Ya*," Abigail said, a bit too quickly. And she would. Every night she looked at the loom and told herself she would use it the next day. But when she looked at it in the morning, she didn't have a single creative thought. Her life was in a rut. She was stuck as she watched her sisters move on with their happy lives. Yesterday after they'd returned home from the Troyers', Sadie and Aden had sat on the couch together. Both of them were reading—Aden a beekeeping manual and Sadie a book on how to run a business—but they were sitting close to each other. Abigail had tried to focus on her magazine. She'd grabbed the nearest one, which, of course, had to be a cooking magazine. Looking at food after what had happened earlier at church made her want to go to the kitchen and binge, even though she was still full from lunch.

She'd compelled herself not to, but occasionally she'd glance up, only to see Aden looking at Sadie or Sadie looking at Aden.

Finally Abigail gave up and went upstairs. It was obvious they wanted to be alone. She had become a third wheel in her own house.

She snatched the rugs off the bed. "We better get going. *Danki* for the ride to Asa's."

"How are you getting back home?"

"Aden said he'd pick me up at *yer haus* after the store closed."

Outside, Abigail followed Irene through the snow, which was coming down in a heavy cloud of white. Spring would officially start in two weeks, but Mother Nature didn't seem to be aware of that. Abigail thought about canceling with Asa altogether. Perhaps she should, using the weather as an excuse. But she wanted to keep her word. Besides, it wouldn't take long to show him the rugs and take his order. She climbed into Irene's buggy and put the rugs on her lap. They were heavy and warmed her immediately.

The snow continued to fall, making the roads both slushy and slick. When they reached Irene's house, Abigail motioned for her to turn into the driveway. "I can walk to Asa's from here."

Irene shook her head. "It won't take me long to drop you off."

"I don't want you to get the wheels stuck in his driveway." Plus, she needed the extra time. For some reason her gut was churning. Which didn't make any sense. This was Asa. She'd show him the rugs, then she'd leave. It had taken them so long to get here in the thickening snow that Aden wouldn't be very far behind.

"Are you sure? Do you want me to send Aden over to pick you up when he gets here?"

Abigail was already getting out of the buggy. "*Ya*, I'm sure. And I can walk back to *yer haus* to meet Aden. I'll see you later."

Irene nodded and Abigail peered through the snow. Asa's house was only a little farther down the street, but set way back on a hill, against a copse of woods similar to the ones by her house. She hugged the rugs against her as she trudged through the snow. Her boots kept her toes warm and dry, but she couldn't say the same for her legs. The wind kicked up, swirling the snow, and making her dress whip against her calves. Oh, this was a bad idea. She hadn't realized that the falling snow was now on the verge of a blizzard. Her nerves forgotten, she tucked her chin and pushed against the whirling wind and pounding snow.

By the time she reached Asa's house, her feet were no longer dry or warm. Her mouth felt frozen, and each inhale was like razor blades in her lungs. Her heart pounded in her chest as she climbed the hill to his house, the rag rugs wet and weighing at least twice as much as they had when she left Irene's buggy. When she got to his front door, she leaned against it, using her hip to knock on it. *He better be home.* She waited a moment, then moved her hip to knock on the door again—only to have it give way. She tumbled into the living room and fell against Asa.

Asa's eyes widened as Abigail propelled toward him, holding rugs and covered in snow. She slammed into him with such force that he couldn't steady himself and he landed on his rear end. Abigail hit the floor in front of him, facedown in the rugs.

He scrambled to his feet and slammed the door against the wind and blowing snow. He'd knocked off work a little early today to clean up the place before she got there, but the weather hadn't been this bad when he left work. He knelt down beside her. "Abigail! Are you all right?"

She lifted her gaze to his. Delicate flakes of snow covered her cheeks, her nose, even her lips. "I'm very ready for spring."

He wanted to laugh, but her dark expression ended his good humor. "Let me help you up."

"I've got it." She moved to her knees and blew a few snow-flakes off her lips. Then she stood up, looking a bit bewildered, quite disheveled, and very, very cute.

He put his hands on his hips. "What did you do, walk over here from Irene's?"

She nodded. "It seemed like a *gut* idea at the time."

She was shaking again. And red-faced. He caught the weariness in her eyes. The walk and subsequent fall must have taken a lot out of her. "Give me *yer* coat and bonnet, and then sit by the fire." He'd made sure the fire in the woodstove was blazing for her arrival. The house had a cold, empty appearance. It didn't need to feel cold too.

He'd been steadily working to repair and clean the house, but some days his heart wasn't in it. Last fall he'd spent a couple of weeks working on Andrew's addition, and that had taken time away from the renovation too.

For once Abigail didn't argue with him. She took off her coat and bonnet and handed them to him. The skirt of her light purple dress was wet. Although she was cold and looked miserable, he couldn't keep his gaze off her. Regaining his senses, he grabbed his rocking chair and moved it close to the stove. "Here. Have a seat."

She plopped down in the chair, her head hanging, every bit of Abigail-spunk gone. "I'll hang these up on the banister," he said. She didn't respond as he went to the staircase and draped her coat and bonnet over it. He had a pegboard in the mudroom off the kitchen, but her clothes would dry faster in the heat of the living room. He turned and saw the pile of rugs on the floor. They were wet too. There wasn't enough room for them on the banister, so he asked, "Can I set these over the kitchen chairs to dry?"

"*Ya*. Sure."

He took the rugs and hung them over the backs of the two secondhand chairs in the kitchen, thankful he'd recently been able to add them and an old table to his sparse furnishings. When he returned he asked, "Do you want some *kaffee*? I can brew a pot real quick."

She shook her head.

He moved to crouch down in front of her and took her cold hand in his. Her fingers were like ice. "Now's not the time to *geh* silent on me, Abigail."

"I'm tired," she whispered. "So . . . tired."

He knew she didn't mean just physically. The weeks after he first came back, when he was trying to find a job and had only a ratty sleeping bag to sleep on, were physically and emotionally painful. Forcing himself to get up each morning, to not let his circumstances drag him down, had been difficult. "You can rest here. As long as you need to."

Her gaze met his, and he was relieved when he saw a small spark ignited in her eyes. "Why are you being so nice to me?" she asked.

"Because I'm a nice guy."

"It's more than that. You always see me at *mei* worst . . . but you somehow manage to make me feel a little bit better."

He sat back on his haunches. "That's the point." Her eyes filled and she looked away, which made him want to take her into his arms right there. He wanted to sit in the rocking chair and cuddle her in his lap. He wanted to feel the softness of her cheek against his shoulder, to rub his hand down her back and tell her everything would be okay. That despite all the pain she'd been through, God was with her. Wasn't that how he had survived the past few months? God had uprooted him, but he'd also been his closest ally.

But he couldn't hold her. Couldn't tell her what was on his heart. Not yet. He didn't need God to tell him it was too soon. "I'll make that *kaffee*."

CHAPTER 10

As Irene drove to the barn to put up her buggy and stable her horse, she noticed an extra buggy parked outside. Was Aden already here to pick up Abigail? But that didn't make sense. In this weather he wouldn't have gotten to her house before she did. Someone must be visiting. They would have to go home soon—the wind and snow were turning brutal.

She went inside, welcoming the cozy warmth of the house. She removed her coat and bonnet and hung them on the peg-board in the mudroom, then slipped off her boots. Her feet hit the concrete floor, coldness sliding through her stockings. She couldn't wait for something warm to drink and something hot to eat. Then she'd relax with a book after supper. She'd been trying to finish this latest mystery for over two weeks, but she was having trouble getting into the story.

She opened the door to the kitchen and walked inside, ready to greet whoever was visiting, only to halt when she saw Sol Troyer. He was sitting at the table, where four birdhouses sat. She stared at them for a moment. Until he'd started creating birdhouses and selling them at the Schrocks' store, she hadn't any idea just how talented he was. No wonder he was doing well selling them at the store.

But what were they—and he—doing here?

He rose from his chair. "*Yer mamm* ordered these a few weeks back. I was in the neighborhood and I thought I'd drop them off."

She glanced at the birdhouses again. "I wonder who they're for?"

Sol frowned. "I hope I didn't ruin a surprise. She didn't say they were a surprise." He pointed his thumb toward the door. "She went to get her purse."

Irene nodded and inspected the birdhouses. None of them was too fancy, but they were each made of different woods and stained to a dull but pretty gleam that would hold up well in any kind of weather. One was a simple replica of a log cabin, complete with square shingles and a front porch. The other three were more rustic with small angled roofs, a hole near the top, and a perch underneath. She liked all four. Sol was a master craftsman.

"They're lovely, Sol." She looked at him. "You do wonderful work."

His cheeks reddened almost to the color of his hair. He shrugged off her compliment.

Mamm walked into the kitchen. "Sorry it took me so long." She looked at Irene and smiled, then at Sol. "I remembered *yer mamm* wants to try that pineapple fluff recipe I brought over Sunday." She held up a card. "I thought I knew where it was, but it took me awhile to find it. I put it in the wrong note file after I finished making it." She turned her gaze back to Irene. "What do you think of the birdhouses?"

"They're beautiful."

"Aren't they? They'll make lovely gifts."

"For who?"

Mamm's smile widened. "You'll have to find out."

Irene didn't think she was being all that sneaky. Her birthday was next month, and everyone knew how much she loved watching birds. Some of her favorite memories were of sitting on her front porch or in the yard and watching the robins, cardinals, blue jays, finches, and other birds fly around, play in puddles, and pick at the grass.

Naomi handed a check to Sol. "*Danki*," she said. "I appreciate you bringing them over."

"Not a problem." He folded the check and put it in his pocket.

"I also appreciate you getting them finished early. I'm sure you've been busy with lots of orders."

"I have." His voice was quiet and low and he wasn't looking at *Mamm*.

Irene saw him frown. "That's not a *gut* thing?"

"Oh, it is." He glanced up. "But one person wants a painted birdhouse. I can stain wood, but not paint, and I'm running out of time. I don't know anyone who can paint for me, and Aden hasn't been able to find anyone for me either."

"Irene's an excellent painter."

Irene shot a look at her mother. She could paint walls, but she wasn't particularly skilled at it and had never tried any other kind of painting.

"You are?" asked Sol, one reddish eyebrow lifting.

"Oh *ya*," *Mamm* said before Irene could answer. "Especially in school. She would bring home the sweetest pictures, very detailed."

"*Mamm*, that was coloring. With crayons."

"Some were with paints." Naomi turned to Sol. "She's being modest, of course."

"Of course." But Sol continued to look at her with questioning eyes, along with something else she couldn't define that caused a shiver between her shoulder blades. Before she could stop herself she said, "I could try painting one." Her eyes widened. What was she doing? She already had a job with Abigail, although that didn't take up all her time. And it wasn't like her family was hurting for money. Andrew's farrier business was doing well, easily supporting her and her mother and Joanna, along with being able to give extra to the community fund. So why was she offering to work with Sol?

Because he needs you.

The words nearly made her stumble backward. *He needs me?* She met his gaze and, for a brief instant, saw beyond the physical attraction to the deep hurt he held inside. *He needs me.* "I'm not an expert, and the last time I painted something it was this kitchen a couple of years ago." She spread her hands out, gesturing to the walls. "That's not the same as birdhouses, but I could give it a try."

He looked around the kitchen. "Looks nice." Again his voice was low, but appreciative. He looked back at her. "Aren't you working with Abigail?"

"*Ya.*"

"I don't want to give you more work."

"Don't you think that's *mei* decision to make?"

His top lip lifted in a half-smile. "I suppose so."

"Sol, why don't you stay for supper and you and Irene can discuss this further?" *Mamm* said.

Irene had forgotten her mother was in the room. So had Sol apparently, from the surprised look on his face. "*Danki*, but I'm sure *Mamm* has supper ready for me at home. I should get going."

"*Nee* one's going anywhere," Andrew said as he strode into

the kitchen. "I just got home. One of *mei Englisch* customers said we're probably getting at least twelve inches of snow before midnight. The way it's coming down right now, I believe him."

"I'm sure I'll be fine," Sol said.

Andrew shook his head. "You'll end up getting *yer* horse stuck if you *geh* now. You're welcome to stay here tonight."

Irene looked at Sol, who flicked a glance in her direction. She saw his Adam's apple move up and down before turning back to Andrew. "*Danki.* I'll take you up on the offer."

That was a relief. The last thing she wanted was for him to get stuck in a storm. Then she remembered Abigail. "Aden," Irene said, turning to her brother. "He's supposed to pick up Abigail here."

"I'll call and tell him not to come." Andrew started to leave the kitchen, but Irene touched his arm.

"She's at Asa's."

Andrew paused. "What's she doing over there?"

"Showing him some rugs."

"Rugs?"

"*Ya.*" She explained about the rugs to Andrew, his frown growing as she spoke. When she finished talking he said, "It's not *gut* for her to be walking out in this weather, even if she is only coming from Asa's."

"Should I *geh* get her?" Irene asked.

Andrew shook his head. "I'm sure Asa wouldn't let her *geh* out in weather like this."

Irene wasn't sure Abigail being alone with Asa was such a good idea. When she mentioned the possibility of Asa being interested in Abigail, she had been serious. He was acting odd and had been ever since he arrived in Birch Creek. He was different than she remembered, a little less sure of himself, more introverted than he used to be. But she'd noticed how he couldn't keep his eyes off Abigail, especially when Abigail wasn't looking.

"I'll call Aden," Andrew said, "and I'll be happy to call *yer mamm* as well, Sol. To let her know you're staying here tonight. I'm sure she'll check *yer* phone shanty for messages when she starts to worry about you." Then he disappeared into the mud-room. Since Andrew owned his own business, he was allowed to have a cell phone, but he didn't keep it in the house. They also had a phone shanty at the end of the driveway, but in this weather she didn't blame him for using his cell.

She glanced at Sol. He was staring at the seat of a kitchen chair, his strong hands gripping its back. A gust of wind kicked up, rattling the windows.

"Then that's settled," *Mamm* said. "We've got plenty of chicken stew and Joanna's biscuits for supper. And Joanna made a scrumptious peach cobbler last night too. I took a little taste when she wasn't looking." She went to Sol and looked up at him. "You're welcome to stay as long as you need to."

Sol nodded again, and Irene's heart did a tiny twirl. Uh-oh. She needed to settle her feelings where Sol was concerned. Especially now that she would be working alongside him. *He needs you.* She couldn't get those words out of her head. He wasn't the same man who had flirted with her in his parents' basement last fall. His confident swagger was gone, replaced with a shyness that didn't fit him either. He was a man in turmoil; she could plainly see that. But what could she do to help him? Right now, she could paint birdhouses. She'd let the Lord lead her to do the rest.

Andrew came back into the kitchen, this time with Joanna behind him. Very close behind him, Irene noted. She thought living with her brother and his wife would be awkward. But it wasn't. Joanna was so sweet and gracious that she was a pleasure to live with. And Andrew was happier than she'd ever seen him since their *daed* left.

She glanced at Sol again. Did he think about his father often? Was he hoping for him to return? The bishop had left in disgrace. But that didn't mean Sol didn't still love him or want him to come back. Irene's own father was paying the consequences for his mistakes. And, like Sol, she didn't know when her father would be coming back, if at all, and it left a hole in her life.

"I'll help you with supper," Joanna said, moving past Irene and giving a glancing smile to Sol. He released the back of the chair, seeming to relax a bit. At that moment Joanna's dog, Homer, came barreling into the kitchen. He skidded to a standstill in front of her and sat on his haunches, looking up at her with adoration. Or hunger. Irene wasn't sure which.

"Homer, behave." Joanna pointed to the corner of the kitchen. "*Geh.*"

Homer looked at her a little longer, then trotted to the corner and settled himself on the large pillow bed Andrew had bought for the dog. He wasn't any trouble, and along with Joanna he had become a welcome addition to the family.

"Andrew said Abigail is at Asa's." Joanna looked out the kitchen window. "Wow, it's turning brutal out there."

Irene nodded. What were Abigail and Asa doing? Hopefully staying warm and dry. Things might be awkward between them, especially since Asa had been acting so out of character. But at least they weren't out in the blizzard. Irene couldn't imagine either one of them doing something that stupid.

Falling on her face in front of Asa had crushed the dam Abigail had set up around her emotions. She added that to her failures. He'd also seen her tears, although she'd tried to fight them. She thought she'd had everything under control. But she didn't. *God, what is wrong with me?* She hadn't wanted to admit she was tired. Or weak. But there was no use hiding it anymore. Not that she hid anything very well from Asa. He always seemed to be around at her worst moments.

She stared at the cast-iron woodstove, then glanced around the room. It had been years since she'd been in this house, and only then when the Bontragers held church services. He was right; the place did look empty. But it looked new too. The walls were painted stark white. He had the stove and the rocking chair she sat in, which was a little tight on her hips but still comfortable. There was no other furniture, though. No couches, end tables, or even a bookshelf. Nothing decorated on the walls, like a clock or a calendar. No curtains on the windows, which were covered with blowing snow.

She looked at her feet and realized she still wore her boots. For a moment she worried about his wood floor, but then she saw it was scratched and needed refinishing. She'd heard he was fixing up the house after it had been wrecked by the former owners or squatters. Still, she didn't need to make wet spots on his floor. She started to pull off one boot when she heard him from behind her. She froze when she felt his warm hand on her shoulder.

He came around and knelt in front of her. "*Kaffee*'s brewing," he said, then took her boot and slipped it off her foot. He put it in front of the woodstove and turned to her.

A shiver ran through her, even though she was warm from the stove. "Asa, I can take off *mei* boots."

"I know." He lifted her other booted foot. "But I want to do this for you."

She watched as he put her other boot in front of the stove. She curled her stocking feet underneath the chair.

"Do you need a blanket?" he asked.

"I'm fine, Asa." And she was, surprisingly. Although having Asa take off her boots was unnerving, it was also nice to be cared for like this. Once again, he was making her feel special.

"It's really coming down outside." He moved from his knees to casually sit in front of her, leaning his arm over one bent leg.

Looking down at him like this was awkward. But there was nowhere else for him to sit. Suddenly she felt guilty. "I'll leave the rugs with you," she said, getting up from the chair. "You can give them back to Irene when you've decided which one you want."

"You don't have to *geh*—"

"Aden will be at Irene's soon to pick me up. I don't want him to have to wait on me."

"Oh." He stood. "Well then, I'll drive you over there."

"There's *nee* need to get *yer* horse out in this." She took her boots and started to put one on, but she moved too quickly and lost her balance.

His hand went to her waist. "Steady," he said.

Once again she was aware of her body as he touched her. And once again she was mortified. She regained her balance and moved away from him, giving him no choice but to drop his hand. "This is getting ridiculous," she said, voicing her thoughts out loud.

"What do you mean?"

"You. Me. This." She waved the boot in her hand. "I'm always falling or tripping or upset or freezing . . . and you're always there." She paused, lowering the boot. "You're always there."

He swallowed, and she could see his Adam's apple working in the center of his neck. "I'm trying to be." He moved closer to her. "I want to be *yer* friend."

And if she needed any more confirmation that there was nothing romantic between them, he'd just given it to her. She took a deep breath. She should be glad about this. She didn't need to be romantically involved with anyone right now. It was too soon after Joel, and even though he could move on from what they had so quickly, she couldn't. That was also clear to her. She smiled. "*Danki*. I can use a *gut* friend."

"Me too." But as he spoke, his gaze didn't leave hers, and his gray irises turned that stormy dark color that made her feel things she shouldn't be feeling for a friend. Clearly she didn't have any idea how to read a man either. She'd been so wrong about Joel.

"We should get you to Irene's," he said, still gazing at her with enough warmth that she was actually starting to get a little hot.

She shook her head. "Like I said, I'm walking over there."

"Then I'm walking with you."

Abigail shoved on the boot. "*Nee*, you're not. *Nee* sense in both of us freezing."

He held up his hand. "Wait for me. It will only take a minute for me to grab *mei* boots and coat."

But when he left, she shoved on the other boot, then grabbed her coat and bonnet off the banister and put them on as she opened the door. It wouldn't take her long to get to Irene's, and it really was foolish for both of them to be out in this horrible weather. She buttoned up her coat, tied her bonnet, donned her gloves, and then plunged into the wintry night.

∞

It took Asa less than a minute to grab his coat and boots and put them on, only to come back and discover Abigail was gone. What a stubborn woman. Did she really think he was going to let her walk in this storm by herself? He opened the door and headed into the blowing snow, squinting his eyes and wishing he'd brought his hat. How could he have forgotten his hat? And his gloves. Another gust of wind kicked up, ruffling his hair and chilling the tops of his ears. Then again, his hat probably would have blown off his head in this wind.

He searched around in the darkness. Where was she? He'd started to worry when he finally made out the shadowy figure a few feet in front of him, struggling against the driving wind. He blew out a frosty breath and trudged toward Abigail. She wasn't the only one ready for spring.

When he reached her, he put his arm underneath her elbow. She jumped and gave him a frightened look. The storm howled around them. "I've got you!" he yelled, hoping she could hear him.

She nodded. But before she took another step forward, she wrapped her arm around his and held on tight to his coat.

Together they fought the blizzard, and for a little while Asa worried the weather might win. He couldn't remember the last time they'd had such a bad snowstorm. Even in Indiana they hadn't had a blizzard like this. Relief shot through him when he spied the faint light of the gas lamp in the Beilers' window. "We're almost there," he hollered to Abigail.

She moved closer to him.

If it hadn't been snowing, he might have enjoyed the close contact. But their goal was to keep each other from blowing away. When they made it up the steps to the front porch, Abigail let go of his arm. He faced her, leaning down and rubbing his stiff hands against her coat. "You okay?"

"*Y-ya.*" Then she asked, "A-are you?"

It was the first time she'd inquired about his well-being. He felt warm from the inside out as he nodded, then pounded on Andrew's door. Abigail huddled next to him as he blew on his hands. Finally the door opened.

"Asa? Abigail?" Naomi looked from him to her, her eyes widened. "*Gut* heavens, get inside!"

Asa let Abigail go in first, even though he was the one who had on fewer outer layers. The tops of his ears were numb. So were his fingers. He flexed them, looking at the red skin.

Then two gloved hands were around his own. Abigail's. She rubbed her palms over his in a brisk motion. "Better?"

You have nee *idea.* He nodded, not trusting himself to speak.

Naomi paused for a moment, looking at them, before saying, "*Geh* stand by the woodstove."

Abigail let go of Asa's hands and they both moved close to the stove. Asa's frigid body soaked in the warmth like a frozen sponge. He held his hands toward the heat as Andrew, Irene, and Joanna came into the room.

Andrew's brow shot up. "Why didn't you wait the storm out at *yer haus?*"

Shooting a look at Abigail, Asa shrugged.

"It's not Asa's fault." Abigail met Asa's gaze before looking at Andrew.

Joanna went to her sister. "Are you okay? *Yer* lips are almost blue."

"I didn't realize how bad it w-was outside." Her body shook next to Asa's. She looked up at him. "I'm sorry," she said softly.

"I'll get some quilts," Andrew said.

"I'll take *yer* coats," Irene added.

"I'll make some hot chocolate." Joanna patted Abigail's wet coat.

Asa and Abigail handed their coats and, in Abigail's case, her bonnet and gloves to Irene. Andrew and Joanna disappeared and Asa supposed Naomi had gone to the kitchen from the delicious smells wafting from there. His stomach grumbled. Something hot and delicious would be perfect right now.

Then he realized he was alone with Abigail, the crackle of the wood from the stove the only sound in the room. Abigail faced the fire, rubbing her hands together. Then she looked at Asa. "What about *yer* woodstove?"

"It will burn out on its own. I'm not worried."

She sighed. "I'm sorry. You shouldn't have come after me."

"I didn't mind." And he didn't. He would have done anything to make sure she was safe. Even risk frostbitten ears. He touched the tops, making sure they were still there. He couldn't feel his hair against them.

Naomi appeared, holding two mugs. "Hot tea," she said, handing one to Abigail, the other to Asa.

"Joanna's making hot chocolate," Abigail said.

"You'll want that too." She shook her head. "You two could have been lost out there."

"We knew the way to *yer haus*," Asa said, then sipped the tea.

"That's not what I mean. We haven't had one of these storms in years, but in a blizzard like that, when you can't see anything, it's easy to get off course."

Asa hadn't thought about that. It was true, though. And they hadn't brought a flashlight. They could have frozen to death out there. *Thank you, Lord.* He met Abigail's eyes and knew she was thinking the same thing.

They were wrapped in quilts, sipping on hot chocolate in front of the woodstove when Naomi said supper would be ready soon. "Then we'll figure out where everyone is going to sleep."

"I'll help Andrew with the horses after supper," Asa said. He had bedded down his own horse in the stall before Abigail arrived. The young mare would be warm for the rest of the night. If the storm continued into the morning, he'd have to make his way over there. But he'd cross that bridge when he came to it.

"You don't have to. Sol's with Andrew right now taking care of them."

"Sol's here?" Abigail asked.

"Ya. He's not going anywhere either." Naomi went back into the kitchen.

Asa took another sip of his hot chocolate. He'd had Joanna's hot chocolate before, and it was delicious. He wondered if Abigail had her sister's recipe. An image popped into his mind. He and Abigail, seated around the fire at home, sipping hot chocolate . . .

He froze. That was the first time he'd imagined them together. As a married couple. With the image still firmly in his mind, he cast her a side glance. She was staring at the stove, but not with the frozen, glazed expression she'd had earlier. Then she looked at him. Smiled. And he forgot to breathe.

"I guess we're all having a sleepover," she said, turning back to look at the stove.

"When I was younger Andrew and I would split time between each other's houses." He grinned. "Part of me feels like a kid again tonight."

"Even after almost freezing to death?"

"I wouldn't have let that happen." He looked at her, an idea coming. "Think you might be up for a game of Dutch Blitz tonight?"

She arched a surprised eyebrow, then a competitive gleam appeared in her eyes. Oh, wow. This was a side of her he hadn't seen before.

"It's *mei* favorite card game."

"Mine too." He angled toward her and crossed his arms over his chest. "I'll have you know that I rarely lose."

"And I'll have you know that I *never* lose." Then she smiled, a genuine, relaxed smile that almost had him flat on the floor. He didn't need divine convincing anymore to want to be with Abigail Schrock. Now it would take an act of God for him not to want to be with her.

CHAPTER 11

After eating a delicious supper, Sol munched on Joanna's peach cobbler while he stood at the perimeter of the kitchen watching Joanna, Abigail, Asa, and Andrew play Dutch Blitz. Naomi and Irene were washing dishes, and Homer was under the table at Joanna's feet. Outside the wind howled and shook the windows, but inside it was cozy, warm, and comfortable. Everyone seemed at ease with one another. Something he wasn't used to.

He frowned, putting his fork on his plate, only half finishing his cobbler even though it was the best peach dessert he'd ever tasted. Growing up, his father had forbidden games in the house. He and Aden only played when they were at friends' houses or at school. When Sol was a teenager, he'd lost interest in games and became interested in getting drunk instead.

Abigail took her set of cards and shuffled them expertly. Sol couldn't help but catch Asa watching her. The guy had barely kept his eyes off her. She seemed oblivious, though. Sol's frown deepened. He didn't know Asa very well and had no idea what his intentions were where Abigail was concerned. But Abigail was part of his family now. He didn't want to see her hurt, like she had been by Joel.

He stilled. When had he started to care so much about the Schrock sisters? Yes, they were family by marriage. Then again, if Asa ended up hurting Abigail, what could Sol do about it? He was a pariah. And why? Because of *Daed*. Everything always circled around to his father.

Irene came up to him. "Don't tell me you don't like the cobbler. There's something wrong with *yer* taste buds, if you don't."

"*Nee*, it's *gut*. I'm just not very hungry." And he wasn't. Thinking about his father destroyed his appetite.

"*Mamm*'s chicken stew is delicious. And Joanna makes the best biscuits. So flaky and flavorful." She leaned forward. "I love Joanna, but I doubly love that she's a *gut* cook. Andrew's going to have to watch his waistline."

Sol almost smiled at that. Leave it to Irene to make him feel a little lighthearted. She was so sweet and earnest and, of course, pretty, with sparkling blue eyes and blonde hair that never stayed completely under her *kapp*. Right now a few wisps brushed against her cheek, and he wished he could tuck them behind her ear. At one time he probably would have. But he respected her too much now. He hadn't expected her to offer to help him paint the birdhouses. But now he couldn't help but look forward to spending time with her. She wasn't treating him like an outcast . . . she treated him like a person.

"Here," she said, taking his plate from him. Then she glanced at the table. "You don't want to play?"

"It's a four-person game."

"We have two decks."

He shook his head. "I don't really know how."

Her eyes widened. "You don't know how to play Dutch Blitz?"

His jaw set again. "*Nee*. I don't." Another reminder of how barren his life had been—and still was. He couldn't play or enjoy a simple game. "If you'll excuse me . . ." He turned and left the kitchen to be alone in the living room. He sat down on the couch and started counting again, not to curb his temper, but to stifle the ache in his chest. He didn't want to be alone. He wanted to be a part of the fun in the kitchen. To feel like he wasn't always going to be an outsider. Yet he didn't see how that would change. He was too broken inside. He'd hurt too many people.

But something else held him back. He'd spent a lifetime being disappointed. He couldn't bear that again, especially over Irene. Eventually she would find out his true character, and she would abandon him too. It was only a matter of time.

Irene wanted to chase after Sol and apologize, although she didn't know what she'd said to upset him. She'd seen him, off to the side, enjoying his peach cobbler, which of course was the best cobbler she'd ever had because Joanna had made it. Then she saw a shadow pass over his face and he put down his fork. He looked so lonely, and nothing could have kept her from going to him to try to cheer him up. For a brief moment she had even gotten him to smile.

Then she'd mentioned the game and he was back to brooding again. Which made her want to try to comfort him. But he'd refuse, and she wouldn't go chasing after him. He might need her, but he wasn't making things easy.

She took his plate and dumped the rest of the cobbler in the trash bin. Joanna was too busy with the card game to notice she'd thrown away the treat. Then she took the plate to the sink. Her mother was drying the last cup. Irene washed the dessert dish, rinsed it, then took the towel from her mother to dry it.

"It's nice to see everyone having a *gut* time." Naomi turned and leaned against the counter, her gaze on the card players.

Not everyone. Irene glanced over her shoulder. But at least the rest of them were. Abigail had just called out "Blitz!" That meant she won the hand, and she turned to Asa and gave him a triumphant smile.

"Lucky," he said, grabbing the cards and shuffling.

"Not luck. Skill. And give me those." She took Asa's deck and shuffled them for him.

"Hey. I can shuffle *mei* own cards."

"And we'll be here all night if you do," Abigail shot back.

"Um, I think we'll be here all night anyway."

Abigail grinned and handed Asa his deck. Andrew and Joanna had already shuffled theirs. Abigail gave hers a quick couple of shuffles and the game was on again.

"Why don't you join them?" *Mamm* asked.

Irene wanted to. Dutch Blitz was one of her favorite games. But she didn't want to intrude on the two couples. Her suspicion about Asa was right on—he was interested in Abigail. Abigail didn't seem to notice, but it was obvious the way he leaned close to her while he was playing, brushing her shoulder with his. The game was a lively one, but that didn't keep Asa's eyes from watching Abigail. No wonder he kept losing the game.

Maybe that's why Sol hadn't wanted to join them. It was clear that the two couples didn't need a fifth and sixth wheel.

Irene turned to her mother. "It's awkward with five people. You need an even number."

"What about Sol?" Naomi scanned the kitchen. "Where did he *geh*?"

"He was tired." Irene immediately felt bad for the little lie, but explaining about Sol was too difficult.

"Blitz!" Abigail sat back in her chair, her arms across her chest.

"Again?" Joanna said.

"I give up." Andrew lifted his hands. "You're unbeatable tonight, Abigail."

"I told you she was *gut* at this game," Joanna said.

Asa remained silent. Irene watched him watch Abigail, and she hoped whatever feelings he had for her, he would take things slow. Abigail was still fragile, even though she was tough on the outside. She'd suffered enough pain in the past few months. She didn't need Asa adding more.

"Could you fix up Andrew's room for Sol?" her mother asked. "It hasn't been used since the wedding, and I'm sure it needs a little dusting. The sheets are clean, but you should probably replace the quilt on the bed with a fresh one from *mei* hope chest."

Irene nodded. "Sure. I'll do that now."

"*Gut.* And Irene?"

She turned and looked at her mother. "*Ya?*"

"I'm sorry if I overstepped a little while ago. You know, about painting the birdhouses. I feel like I put you and Sol on the spot, and I shouldn't have. It's just . . ." *Mamm*'s eyes filled with compassion.

Irene put her hand on her mother's arm. "I know, *Mamm.* And it's all right. I don't mind helping him."

Mamm patted her hand. "*Gut.* I think he needs someone to reach out to him. To make him feel like he's part of our community again." She pulled away. "*Geh* on. You better get the bedroom ready since Sol is tired."

Nodding, Irene left and headed for her mother's bedroom

to get the quilt out of the hope chest. She passed through the living room and saw Sol sitting on the couch, his head slightly down. She moved toward him, hating to see his strong shoulders slumped as if in defeat. *Mamm* was right. God was right. Sol did need someone in his corner. She took in a deep breath and said, "I'll have Andrew's old room ready for you in a few minutes."

He turned around and looked up at her. "That's okay. You don't have to *geh* to any trouble. I can sleep on the floor if need be."

"Sol Troyer, you're not going to sleep on the floor." She put her hands on her waist. "We have plenty of room in this *haus*. Besides, I'd give up *mei* bed before I let you sleep on the floor."

He stared at her for a moment, long enough to make her cheeks heat. Okay, maybe she shouldn't have said that out loud. But it was true. Surely he didn't think he deserved to sleep on the floor. "Just give me a few minutes to get the room ready for you."

He nodded, still staring at her. This time her cheeks heated for a different reason, and she had to pull her gaze from his. This was all getting complicated—her attraction to him coupled with the strong prompting to reach out. She hurried out of the living room and up the stairs, grabbed a quilt from the hope chest in her mother's bedroom, and made her way down the hall.

She opened the door to Andrew's old room and turned on the battery-operated lamp on the side table. Up until he'd built the addition, Andrew had the smallest bedroom in the house. He'd never complained, saying he didn't need much room. "I'm a guy," he used to say. "I could live in a closet if I needed to." He probably could, and this room was only a bit larger than a closet. There was a bed, the side table, and a small bureau, plus a window and a tiny closet. The wind rattled the glass pane as she stripped the blue-and-white quilt off the single bed, smoothed out the sheets, and placed the fresh quilt on top.

Then she frowned. Pink. The quilt was pink. Not just one shade of pink, but at least a dozen different ones, all laid out in an intricate pattern of flowers. It had been her grandmother's quilt, passed on to her mother. Irene had taken the first quilt off the stack in the hope chest without paying attention.

Then she chuckled at the thought of strapping Sol Troyer wrapped up in a pink flowered quilt.

Her laughter subdued when she heard footsteps on the stairs. She fluffed the pillow, then looked around for something to quickly dust the furniture. She pulled open the top drawer of the bureau, which of course was empty since Andrew had moved all his clothes to the addition. Then she saw a stray sock in the back corner of the drawer. She snatched it, shut the drawer, and began wiping the dust off the dresser.

"You really don't have to do that."

She turned to see Sol standing in the doorway, his hands in his pockets, his shoulders still slumped but not as much as before. "I don't mind," she said, wiping off a small clump of dust. When was the last time anyone cleaned in here? *Mamm* must have been right that it had been since the wedding. "It will only take a—" Dust flew up her nose and she sneezed.

"*Gesundheit*," Sol said.

But Irene wasn't done. She never sneezed only once. Usually it was five, six, sometimes seven times before she was done. Andrew had counted thirteen one time. That had been miserable and Irene had been out of breath by the time she was finished.

"*Gesun—*"

She sneezed again, held up one finger, and continued to sneeze until she thought her head would explode. Finally, she finished, her eyes watering and her nose running.

"Wow." Sol stepped into the room. "Are you okay?"

She nodded, sniffing. "*Ya.* Sorry about that."

"Are you allergic to dust?"

"*Nee.* I've just always sneezed like that." She glanced away, sniffing again. "It's pretty embarrassing."

"If that's the most embarrassing thing you ever do, then you're lucky." He pulled a handkerchief out of his pocket.

She took the handkerchief and blew her nose. "*Danki.*" She was about to hand it to him but thought better of it. "I'll wash it for you."

"That's okay—"

"I'm not giving this back to you after I blew *mei* nose on it." She glanced around. "I think the room is *gut* enough for one night." Then she spied some dust on the side table and started toward it.

"Here." He took the sock from her hand and gave the table a quick swipe. "Done."

"I'll take the sock, then."

"Only if you promise me you'll quit dusting."

She grinned. "Promise."

He handed her the dusty sock. Then they stood in the room for a few moments, Sol not looking at her and Irene trying to think of something to say to fill the uncomfortable silence between them.

"Sorry about the quilt," she said.

Sol looked at the bed. "What's wrong with it?"

"It's pink. And flowery."

He shrugged. "Irene, I'm not picky."

"I just want you to be comfortable."

"And I will be." He smiled a little. It was barely a lift of his lips, but it transformed his face from brooding to handsome, and her breath caught in her throat.

He shoved his hands back into his pockets. "I, uh, wanted to tell you that you don't have to help me with the birdhouses. In case you've changed *yer* mind."

"From a couple of hours ago? I'm not that fickle, Sol. I said I would help you. Who knows, you may fire me after you see *mei* work."

"*Nee.* I wouldn't." He leveled his gaze on her. "I owe you an apology, and I've been trying to think of the right words."

"Apology?"

"For flirting with you last year. For making you think I was interested in you."

His words made her heart sink. She had known he was playing games with her. But hearing him say it out loud stung for some reason.

"I shouldn't have disrespected you like that." He took a step forward, but his hands were still in his pockets. "You deserve better than that. Better than me."

Her skin tingled at the tone of his voice. "Sol, you were a different *mann* back then."

"*Ya.* But . . ." He looked down at his feet, which were covered in thick white socks. "Anyway, I'm sorry. I promise I won't disrespect you ever again." He met her eyes. "I'm a work in progress."

"Aren't we all?" She tilted her head and smiled. "The important thing is that we keep trying."

"I'll never stop trying to be a better person, Irene."

She clutched the sock and handkerchief in her hand, unsure how to respond to his words, to the intensity of his gaze as he spoke. All she could say was, "*Gute nacht.*"

"*Gute nacht.*"

She went to her bedroom and tossed the sock and Sol's handkerchief in the clothes basket in the corner. She sat down at the edge of her bed. Downstairs she could hear everyone laughing as they continued to play Dutch Blitz. But all she could think about was Sol. He said he would never stop trying to be better . . . and she believed him. Maybe someday she could help him believe in himself.

∞

"Are you sure Andrew doesn't mind giving up his bed?" Abigail snuggled under the covers, the pink-and-white quilt pulled all the way up to her chin.

Joanna smiled as she lay beside her. "*Nee*. He said he and Asa used to bunk together in the living room when they were *kinner*. Besides," she said, elbowing Abigail, "it won't hurt him to sleep on the couch for one night."

"I'm sure it will be the only time he ever sleeps there." She grinned at Joanna. "You two seem so happy together."

"We are." Joanna rolled onto her side and lifted her head up, resting it on her arm. Her long brown braid fell over her shoulder. She was wearing a light pink nightgown that went clear to her toes.

Abigail was still wearing her dress. None of the Beiler women had anything to fit her. But she wasn't going to let that ruin the good time she'd had tonight. What had seemed like a disastrous evening had turned into a fun time. She hadn't been able to relax and enjoy life in ages.

"I'm so glad to see you smile again," Joanna said, as if she could read Abigail's thoughts.

"It's *gut* to smile again."

"So," Joanna said, her eyebrows wiggling, "what's going on with you and Asa? Why were you at his *haus* tonight?"

Abigail rubbed the edge of the quilt between her fingers. "He wanted to look at some rug samples and asked me to bring them over. That's all."

"Right."

Abigail blew out a breath, her good mood diminishing. "Joanna, I'm serious. Asa is only a friend." At least she was trying to convince herself of that. Her feelings about him were more confused than ever. "I don't want to get into another relationship."

Joanna nodded, the teasing glint in her eye gone. "I understand. But Asa is a *gut mann*. He's dependable and loyal, and he and Andrew are as close as *bruders*. It's nice to have him as a friend, *ya*?"

"*Ya*." And it was. Joanna was right. Asa had many wonderful qualities. There was no ego about him, and he never made her feel like she was less when he was around. But he made her feel other things, and that bothered her. Like when he looked at her with smoky intensity, as if they were connected somehow. Or the tingles she experienced tonight when he brushed against her shoulder with his, or when their hands had touched as they had reached for cards. Granted, that was part of the game. It was fast-paced and you had to get rid of your cards as quickly as you could. She'd bumped into Andrew and Joanna several times too.

Neither of them had affected her like Asa had, though.

Joanna touched Abigail's arm through the quilt. "I'm sorry. I didn't mean to push. I just want to see you happy."

"I know." And she did. Since their parents' deaths, the three sisters had grown closer. They all wanted one another's happiness. Sadie and Joanna had theirs, and it wasn't only in the form of marrying the men they loved. Sadie had come into her own as the manager of the store. And Joanna had come back stronger than ever from a physically and emotionally devastating accident. They weren't the same women they'd been before that day Cameron Crawford hit their parents' buggy while speeding down the back roads of Birch Creek. "Have you heard from Cameron recently?" Abigail asked.

"Andrew gets a letter from him once a week. They've become friends."

"Are you okay with that?"

"Of course. I'm glad they're writing to each other. Cameron is still thinking about being a pastor. He's been leading Bible study in prison. He says sometimes only one person shows up; other times it's ten or more. He doesn't care whether he meets with one or a dozen. He's just glad to hold the study. He's determined to be a better man for Lacy."

Abigail thought about Cameron's daughter, who was less than a year old. Her mother had died in childbirth, and the grief over her death was partly to blame for Cameron causing the accident. Lacy was now in the care of one of Cameron's friends. Abigail didn't know all the details, but like Joanna, she had forgiven him.

Joanna yawned. "It's been a long *daag*. I'm going to turn out the light, okay?"

"Sure."

A moment later the room was plunged into darkness. Joanna shifted in the bed beside Abigail while Abigail lay on her back, her hands folded across her middle. She continued to think about Cameron, her parents, even Aden and Sol's father. For years her life in Birch Creek had been peaceful. Easy, even. Not anymore. She stifled a sigh, not wanting to disturb Joanna. So much death and loss. And yet everyone continued to live their lives. Forging ahead.

That's what Abigail had to do. She couldn't mope about her life anymore. She had a good start on her business, and if she focused on that more than what she had lost, her business would start to thrive. She would throw herself into her weaving—and that meant using her special loom. Decision made, she closed her eyes, and for the first time in weeks, she prayed with intent.

"It's like we're *kinner* all over again," Andrew said, tossing a quilt at Asa.

Asa easily snatched it out of the air with one hand. Since he was taller than Andrew, he was taking the couch, while Andrew took the loveseat. Asa lay down and threw the quilt over his legs. He didn't really need it. The room was warm enough from the woodstove. Outside the wind continued to howl. Surely it would end soon since the storm had been going on for several hours. He put his hands behind the back of his head and glanced at Andrew. "It's not exactly like it was when we were *kinner*. You didn't have a wife on the other side of the *haus*."

Andrew grinned as he turned off the gas lamp. "*Nee*, I didn't."

The room was immersed in darkness except for the glow from the woodstove. He listened to the crackling wood, his thoughts turning to Abigail. After they arrived at Andrew's, she was different. And when they were playing the card game, he felt like he'd seen a glimpse of the real Abigail, the one that was hidden underneath a layer of rejection, pain, and grief. She'd been so pretty, her full cheeks rosy with laughter, her smile so bright as she trounced everyone several times in Dutch Blitz. She was a good player. But he had to admit he was off his game. He had a hard time sitting next to her, hearing her laughter, seeing the way she fully concentrated on playing. Several times he'd missed playing key cards because she'd unknowingly distracted him. He hadn't minded losing one bit.

He frowned. It hadn't been this way with Susanna. He'd enjoyed being with her. He'd thought they were a good fit. He cared about what happened to her. He had thought he loved her.

Yet what he felt for Abigail ran deep, straight into his bones. Was that God's doing? Was God showing him the person he'd thought he loved hadn't been the right person for him after all?

He rolled on his side. He would ponder this all night if he let himself. He closed his eyes, already hearing Andrew's steady breathing. He was asleep. Asa should be too. But each time he closed his eyes, he saw Abigail's beaming face as she looked at him, meeting his gaze directly without wariness. She looked at him with joy. Joy over winning the game, but still. The glow in her chocolate-colored eyes had surrounded his heart, cocooning it in a pleasant feeling he'd never experienced in his life. Susanna would look at him with adoration, which lifted his ego. But Abigail had touched his heart.

That didn't mean anything had changed between them, other than he had admitted to her that he wanted to be her friend. Now he had to convince her he wanted more without coming off as a weirdo. He wasn't sure how to do that. With Susanna, it had been easy. They had been together because it was expected, especially by both their families. Now he knew he was destined for something more. But how could he show that to Abigail?

He rolled over again, then switched to the opposite end of the couch a few minutes later. The quilt tangled in his legs. He had kept on his pants but borrowed one of Andrew's T-shirts. It hung loose on him because Andrew was so broad-shouldered.

After what seemed like hours, he sat up. This wasn't work-ing. He couldn't lie here all night tossing and turning. Slowly he got up from the couch and crept to the kitchen. Although he didn't know why he bothered being quiet. He knew Andrew could sleep through anything.

He walked into the kitchen. Maybe a snack would help him fall asleep. The wind had quieted down, but flakes still landed on the windows. Since he'd practically lived here as a kid, he didn't bother turning on the light. He was about to open the pantry door when the gas lamp hissed to life. He turned around and saw Abigail in the doorway.

CHAPTER 12

Abigail didn't move at the sight of Asa staring at her. She hadn't been able to sleep, her mind whirring about so many things, mostly Asa. She couldn't keep shifting in the bed or she'd wake Joanna. Food always helped her sleep, and lately she'd been sneaking a midnight snack every night. She'd tried to hold off tonight, but she couldn't. Hopefully Naomi wouldn't mind.

And now Asa was here, again. He'd know she was getting something to eat, again. She should just turn around and go back to bed. But that would be stupid. She could get a snack if she wanted. Even though it would probably be better if she didn't. But she wasn't going to turn around and leave now.

"Hi," he said, not moving from his position in front of the pantry. His voice was soft, sending heat down her spine. She hadn't felt the same jolt with Joel. Not even close.

"I was getting something to eat," he said, looking at her over his shoulder. "Couldn't sleep."

"Me either."

"Do you want something?" He opened the pantry door. "Looks like Joanna's been doing a lot of baking."

That was good to hear. Not only because Abigail was hungry—which she was—but because Joanna hadn't wanted to bake when she first returned from Middlefield.

She hadn't even thought to look for a snack in Joanna's pantry in the addition, where she and her sister were sleeping.

She thought about turning down Asa's offer, though. Was she really hungry, or simply stressed? Or maybe bored? No, she definitely wasn't bored, not around Asa.

He pulled out a container of white chocolate chip cookies and showed them to her. "These look *appeditlich*."

They were. Joanna had often made them when she was still living at home, and they were Abigail's favorites.

"Do you want any?" he asked.

"Just one," she said, going to him. She didn't want to look greedy or piggish.

He held the container to her. "You have more willpower than me." After she took one of the cookies, he grabbed three and closed the container, taking it with him as he sat down at the table. He seemed to be settling in. He glanced up at her, his eyes filled with an unspoken invitation to join him.

Abigail resisted the urge to cram the cookie into her mouth and go back to bed. But that would be rude, and after he'd been so nice to her over the past few months, he didn't deserve that kind of treatment. She joined Asa at the table but moved her chair away from him as she sat down.

Something flickered across his gaze. This wasn't the first time she'd sensed she'd disappointed him. But each time she saw that look, she didn't understand it. Why would moving away from him disappoint him? She set the cookie on the table.

"I'll get us some plates." He shot up from the chair and went to the cupboard. He seemed to know exactly where everything was, and not only did he bring back plates but also two glasses of milk. He set them down. "Probably should have asked if you like milk."

"It's a requirement with cookies."

"I think so too." He sat down and then took a big gulp of milk from his glass. But he didn't eat one of the cookies. Instead he stared at the table.

Abigail picked at her own cookie. This was ridiculous. She never had trouble talking to people. Joel had called her a chatterbox one time, but that was in jest. At least she'd thought it was. Maybe that annoyed him. Maybe that was one of the reasons they broke up. Did Rebecca talk a lot? Abigail couldn't remember. Was she one of those quiet, adoring types? Abigail frowned. She'd never be like that.

"I don't think I've seen so many different facial expressions in less than a minute," Asa said, finally picking up his cookie. She hadn't noticed him looking up.

She smiled sheepishly. "Sorry. Apparently I have an expressive face. Or so I'm told. I can never keep *mei* emotions a secret."

"That's not a bad thing."

"It's not always a *gut* thing, either." She broke off a piece of her cookie and put it into her mouth. This had to be what heaven tasted like. She closed her eyes as she chewed.

"Enjoying the cookie?"

She opened her eyes and blushed. Then she lifted her chin. She wasn't going to be embarrassed about being herself. "*Ya.* They're *mei* favorite, and *nee* one makes them better than Joanna."

"I'll agree with that. I'm partial to chocolate chip, but these are definitely in second place." He held up the cookie and examined it.

"Joanna always puts in extra white chocolate chips," Abigail said. "That's what makes them so *gut*."

He took a bite, looking at her as he chewed. Another jolt hit her. This wasn't good. His black curly hair was wild and sticking out in thick hanks all over his head. For some reason she wanted to smooth it down. Probably because it was messy. Or probably because she wanted to know what it felt like.

She averted her gaze and stuffed almost the entire cookie into her mouth, chasing it with a large gulp of milk. She needed to go to bed. She was clearly tired if she was thinking about touching Asa's hair. But she had to tell him a few things first. "I'm sorry I've been so hard to get along with lately."

"You have?" His full lips quirked up into a half-smile. "Hadn't noticed."

That made her grin. "Then you're dense, because I've been terrible to live with." She sighed and ran her finger down the side of the milk glass. "I haven't been myself, and I feel bad about that. Everything has changed." She looked at him. "I don't like change."

His gray eyes lost their humor. "I don't either. Unless it's *gut* change. Like getting married, having kids . . ." His eyes widened. "Or, uh, getting a promotion at work."

"You got a promotion?"

"*Nee*. I was just using that as an example." He flicked his gaze at her. "Can I tell you a secret?"

"Sure."

He leaned forward. "I don't like *mei* job. Actually, I can't stand it."

"At the plastics factory? Didn't you work at a factory in Shipshewana?"

"*Ya*." He took another drink of milk, finishing off the glass. "I didn't care for that work either."

"What did you do?"

"Put together RVs. I did upholstery. Pretty boring job, but it paid well."

Abigail put her elbows on the table and leaned her chin on her hand. "So what would you do if you had a choice?"

His face turned red, and Abigail realized she'd never seen him blush before. At least not this deeply. It made him more handsome than ever.

"Bookkeeping," he said, staring at the one cookie he had left.

"Really?" That answer was unexpected. She knew he had helped Andrew build the addition on the Beiler house and had done a good job of it too. "I thought you would have said construction."

"Why? Because I'm not smart enough to do math?"

She leaned back at his sudden shift in tone. Gone was the laconic posture, the casualness of his demeanor. She glanced at his hands, which had balled into fists. "*Nee*. I didn't mean that at all. Anyway, you have to do math in construction."

His hands relaxed. "That's true. But that math is easy."

Abigail didn't think so. She was terrible at math. School had been difficult for her. Although she did well, she had to fight for every A she made. She'd been happy to finish school and work in her parents' store. She could operate the cash register, but she was fine with letting Sadie and her parents deal with the accounting. She couldn't think of anything more boring than looking at a bunch of numbers on ledger sheets.

"I shouldn't have said anything." He picked up the container of cookies and started to get up.

Abigail put her hand on the container. Obviously she'd hit a sore spot with him. "Wait," she said. Then she was uncertain what to say next. "I, uh, want another cookie."

He opened the lid and handed her one. There was no look of censure or judgment in his eyes as she took it. Then again, there shouldn't be. Her weight wasn't his business. But what she'd said to irritate him was, and she wanted to know why he'd reacted the way he did. "I'm sorry if I upset you."

He blinked, as if shocked that she would apologize. "You didn't upset me. I'm just used to people assuming I'm not very . . . smart."

She'd never thought that about him. He was far from stupid. "Why would anyone think that?"

He shrugged and put the lid back on the cookie container. "Because I work in a factory, I guess. Or I only have an eighth-grade education."

"So do I. We all do in Birch Creek. That's not a reflection of our intelligence."

"I guess not. But I used to wonder . . ."

"Wonder what?"

"If I would have liked going to high school. Or even college." He sighed. "I like to learn. I always enjoyed school."

"Not me," Abigail said.

"I don't remember you disliking it," he said. "I remember you being happy in school."

"You paid attention to me in school?"

Again, his face turned red. "Not much," he admitted. This time he looked her in the eye and she could see he was telling the truth. He probably had just as few memories about her as she had of him. "But what I do remember was that you were happy."

"I was happy socializing, not doing the schoolwork. Sadie and Joanna were the smart ones."

"You're not *dumm*," he said.

Her eyes narrowed. "I never said I was."

He looked contrite. "Sorry." He brushed some crumbs off the table. "I always seem to say the wrong thing around you."

His voice was so full of self-deprecation that she couldn't resist touching his hand to get his attention. "Not all the time."

His gaze locked with hers, and instead of a jolt this time, she felt something slam into her. Something warm and comforting and pleasant. She pulled her hand away as if it were on fire. "Why accounting?" she asked, desperate to change the subject.

"Numbers fascinate me. The patterns, the rules. I also like the satisfaction when the account balances." He grinned. "I know. I'm *seltsam*."

"A little." She smiled back. "You sound like Sadie. She's been teaching herself bookkeeping. She's really *gut* at it. Unlike me. *Mei* records are a mess."

"From *yer* rug business?"

"*Ya*. I just throw receipts in the box. I pay Irene, but I have *nee* idea what I have left over. I need to open a bank account, but I haven't bothered."

"Where do you keep *yer* money?"

She bit her bottom lip. "Um, in a shoe box under *mei* bed."

"Are you afraid of banks?"

She took in a deep breath. "*Nee*. I'm afraid to admit that I don't understand them. Or interest, or debits and credits. I've been meaning to ask Sadie to show me, but she's so busy with the store, and with Aden." She turned away. "Now I sound *dumm*."

"*Nee*. Uninformed, though. Which isn't a *gut* idea if you're going to have a business."

"I didn't plan to have one. I was just going to make a few rugs to sell in the store. Then people were asking for more."

"The ones you brought to *mei haus* were nice."

"*Danki*, though perhaps you should look at them when

they're dry. When you know which one you want, I'll finish it for you. That's the least I can do for you after walking over here with me in the blizzard."

"That wasn't a big deal." He tapped his chin, drawing her attention to the black whiskers there. They were also above his lip. It gave him a scruffy look she found appealing. She'd remembered Asa being meticulous about his appearance when they were growing up. His clothes were always pressed and he never seemed to get dirty. But since he'd returned, he looked different. Scruffy, like now, and his clothes weren't perfect. Then again, he was a bachelor and living on his own. He probably didn't care about ironing his clothes.

She pulled her gaze from his before he caught her staring at him.

"Tell you what. In exchange for a rug, I'll teach you some bookkeeping basics. We can start by opening a bank account."

"What do you mean, 'we'?"

"I mean I'll *geh* with you. Banks are open on Saturday mornings, and I can take the day off. So the first Saturday we have *gut* weather, I'll come pick you up and we'll *geh* to the bank."

Abigail bit her lip again. She wasn't a child. She didn't need help opening an account. Part of her hadn't been interested in doing anything, so it was laziness and apathy on her part. But she was truthful in that she didn't understand the basics. Yet did she really need his hand-holding? "I think I can do it myself."

"I'm sure you could. But I'd like to *geh* with you."

To the bank. Even though he liked bookkeeping, she couldn't fathom why he would want to accompany her. She couldn't try to puzzle this out anymore—Asa wanting her friendship, but looking at her as if . . . as if he wanted more. And despite her doubt that he did, sure she was seeing things that weren't there, she was tired of being confused. "Asa, I need you to be honest with me."

∞

Asa swallowed, worried she was going to ask the question he dreaded answering. He couldn't be anything but honest with her. Sitting here tonight, admitting his secret that he wanted to be a bookkeeper, sharing cookies and milk and relaxing, had been nice. Very nice. And it had felt right. When she admitted she didn't know anything about bookkeeping, he knew he could help her, which would give him an excuse to spend time with her. Maybe it was a little underhanded, but he was desperate.

"Is there something going on here?" She gestured to him, then to herself. "Between us?"

He pulled in a breath. This would be the time to tell her he wanted more than friendship. She was giving him an opening. But something held him back. More like someone. *God, don't let me make a mistake here.* "Other than friendship, *nix*."

She narrowed her eyes. "I asked for honesty."

"Honest, that's the truth."

Abigail looked at the table and threaded her fingers together. "Then you don't . . ." Her voice grew soft and she wasn't looking at him. "Feel anything?"

Right now he was feeling a lot of things. Any other time he would appreciate straightforwardness. He had a deep-seated feeling that this wasn't the time to lay his heart bare to her. But he couldn't lie to her either. "I think," he said, measuring his words, "maybe something."

Her head popped up and she let out a small chuckle. "Well.

That was definitive." Then she tilted her head. "Do you feel sorry for me?"

He could answer this question easily. "*Nee*. I definitely don't feel sorry for you."

"Because I'd understand if you did." She averted her gaze. "It's been a tough few months for me and *mei familye*."

"I know."

"With *mei* parents dying . . ." She swallowed. "And then Joel dumping me . . ."

His hands curled into fists for the second time during their conversation. "Joel's an idiot."

She half-smiled. "*Nee*, he's not. He just knows what he wants. And it's not me." She looked down at the last quarter of her cookie and frowned. "I can see why."

He barely heard her last words. She was opening up to him and he didn't want to mess anything up. "Like I said, he's an idiot."

Abigail's frown didn't disappear, but she did look at him. "Since I wanted honesty from you, I'll give it in return. Joel broke *mei* heart." Her bottom lip trembled. "Shattered it in a thousand pieces. I'm still putting it back together. I won't *geh* through that again."

"Abigail—"

She held up her hand. "Please, let me finish. If there's one thing you've proven to me over the past few months it's that you're a nice guy. A really nice guy. But so was Joel." She kept her eyes level with his.

What do I do now, Lord? He schooled his features and made sure he could speak without emotion when he said, "I understand."

She let out a breath, as if a heavy burden had been lifted from her shoulders. "That said, I do want to start taking *mei* business seriously. So I'll take you up on *yer* offer to help me with *mei* bank account and show me how to keep the books."

He sat up a bit. "I can do that."

"I feel the need to warn you I'm a slow learner."

"That's all right. I'm a patient man." *In more ways than one.*

She yawned. "I'm heading for bed. *Gute nacht,* Asa." She glanced at the container of cookies. "Thanks for the snack. And that talk. I feel better."

He nodded and watched her as she went back to the addition. Her hair was in a thick braid and he had longed to touch it. She was still wearing her dress, and he couldn't keep his eyes off her as she walked away. He smiled. He'd stretch out his bookkeeping lessons with Abigail as long as he could.

CHAPTER 13

"You sure you don't mind doing this?"

Irene looked at Sol. Although the weather had improved since the blizzard two days ago, it was still cold and snowy outside. She could have put off starting on the birdhouses, but she didn't want Sol to think she didn't want to help him. As it was, he'd been tense since her arrival at his workshop a few minutes ago. He seemed nervous. Very nervous. She smiled, hoping to put him at ease. "Sol, for the last time, I want to help. Besides, I'm sure it will be *fun.*"

He looked at her as if he had no idea what the word meant.

They couldn't have this tension between them. "Sol," she said, making sure to keep her voice soft. "Just tell me what you want me to do."

He looked down at her, and she saw the lines of strain around his mouth decrease. "I've set up a place for you," he said. "It's small, but well ventilated."

She followed him to a room in the back of his shop. It was

chilly in the small space, but not too cold. The workshop was clearly well-insulated.

"I'll just crack this open to let out any fumes," he said. The room was so small that he had to reach over her to lift the window open a few inches. She couldn't help but breathe in the clean scent of his blue shirt, her heart thumping at his nearness.

"Sorry," he said, pulling away from her. "I should have opened it before you arrived."

"That's okay." It definitely was. She looked for signs to see if he was as affected by their nearness as she was, but she didn't see anything. He moved a chair over to a table where he had set up a variety of brushes, small cans of paint, and newspaper. He'd even thoughtfully put an apron next to the supplies.

"I tried to get as many colors as I could find," he said. "But not too many crazy colors."

"*Nee* neon pink, I see."

He smiled. "*Nee.* Definitely not neon."

She looked at the birdhouse on the table. She was glad he gave her a simple one to do for her first attempt. She had decided to go to the library within the next few days to study up on colors and designs and, of course, birdhouses. She did know enough about painting wood, however, to say, "I'll have to prime it first."

He reached around her again and grabbed the can of primer. "Here," he said, handing it to her. But he didn't move quite so far away this time.

"*Danki.*" She looked up at him, breathless. He was so handsome, guarded and vulnerable at the same time.

Then he moved away. "I'll leave you to it," he said.

"Any particular way you want me to paint this?" she said, gesturing behind her.

"Surprise me." Then he grinned. It was a genuine grin, one

she'd never seen before. She'd seen him cocky, sullen, dangerous. But never bright and open like this. She was so surprised at the transformation she couldn't speak.

"I'll be in the workshop if you need anything."

She nodded, still unable to say anything.

He stood in the doorway, as if he seemed eager to leave. "I appreciate you doing this, Irene."

"*Mei* pleasure." And as he nodded and turned away, she definitely meant it.

What am I doing?

Sol leaned over the table, trying to catch his breath. It had been foolish to be so close to her moments ago. He closed his eyes, but all he saw was her pretty face. She was so lovely . . . so perfect.

She was also off-limits.

He opened his eyes and went back to work. He'd hoped she'd change her mind about painting the birdhouses. He probably should have tried to paint them himself. But then they would have looked horrible. So while a part of him was glad she hadn't backed out, another part was on pins and needles knowing she was close by.

He had thought about her almost constantly since the blizzard. How kind she had been to him, to the point of being concerned about him sleeping on a pink quilt. She had also taken his apology with grace. She was special, even more special than he'd initially thought. And that had made him leave the Beiler house before breakfast the next morning. It wasn't that he hadn't wanted to see her again. It was that he wanted to see her too much.

He stood and rubbed the back of his neck. He had work to

do, and thinking about Irene wasn't helping him get it done. He continued with the finishing touches on Jalon's birdhouse and put all his mental attention on his work instead of the lovely woman in the next room.

After working for an hour he decided to take a break. He needed some coffee. He started to open the door of the shop, then realized not asking Irene if she needed anything would be rude. He went to the workroom. The door was open slightly, and he pushed on it, hesitating halfway. He couldn't keep himself from staring at her.

She was a study in concentration, and he could see she was already doing a good job. Three cans of paint were open beside the birdhouse, and she had put on his mother's old apron he'd left for her. He continued to watch, forgetting himself, noticing the way her tongue stuck out a little as she focused on applying a thin, light blue accent line on the edge of the tiny roof. When she finished, she set the paintbrush on the lid of the can and arched her back.

He sucked in a breath, losing his balance and hitting the door, which swung completely open. He stumbled into the room.

"Sol," she said, putting her hand to her mouth, her pretty blue eyes wide and startled. Then she removed it. "You scared me."

His mind flashed back to when he was sixteen. He'd been hiding in the cornfield, waiting for Sadie Schrock to pass by. He'd been drinking, as he always had back then. He'd tried to kiss her, but she escaped. He had seen fear in her eyes then, and again a few years later after she married Aden. In a drunken stupor Sol had tried to assault her, only to have Aden kick him out of the house.

His hands started to shake with shame. "I'm . . . I'm sorry," he said, backing away from Irene. "I . . . I didn't mean to . . ."

She went to him, her face twisted in concern. "It's okay, Sol." She peered up at him. "Don't look so serious. I was just startled."

"I would never hurt you, Irene."

Her body stilled. "Where did that come from?"

He wasn't sure, and he tried to find something to cover himself, to backtrack. He moved away from her and hit his shoulder against the wall. "Never mind," he said, turning to go.

But she put her hand on his arm. "Sol. You don't have to run from me."

He couldn't answer her. He was running because he was a coward. What he wouldn't do for a drink right now. Anything to escape the pain and shame he was feeling.

"You also don't have to be so serious." She smiled, and it reached to the darkness inside him. "Loosen up, for once."

Before he could respond, she picked up the blue paintbrush. He held up his hands. "What are you going to do with that?"

"*Nix*, if you promise you'll relax."

"Irene, I'm—"

She took the paintbrush and drew a streak across his face.

His eyes widened at the same time hers did.

"Sol," she said, moving from him. "I don't know why I did that. I was only teasing you, I didn't think . . ."

He brought his hand to his cheek, feeling the paint there. He looked at her, and she seemed genuinely contrite, and a little confused. There was only one thing to do. He took the brush from her and slid it across her forehead. "Payback," he said, unable to hide his smile. "It's only fair."

"Payback, huh?" She grabbed another brush, and this time she flicked paint at him. "How's that for payback?"

He looked at the front of his shirt, now covered with yellow flecks. The shirt was old and stained, and he didn't care. "That's all you got?" He smeared his brush against her chin, then regretted the impulsive action.

But he shouldn't have, because she took her yellow brush and drew a line down his nose. "How's that?" Then she started to laugh.

He couldn't help but join her, but not before he flicked paint on her apron. She parried by trying to draw an X on the front of his shirt, but the brush was out of paint. He thought the game was over until she dipped her finger in the red paint can and put a dot of paint on the tip of his nose.

"Now you look like Rudolph," she said, giggling.

"Oh yeah?" He reached around her and put his fingers in blue paint. He started to smear them across her face, then held back. She was so close to him he could hear her breathing, smell the scent of paint on her skin. He took one blue finger and traced it across the top of her cheek, his eyes never leaving hers, mesmerized by the darkening blue color and the fringe of dark blonde lashes.

"Sol," she said, sounding breathless.

That brought him out of his stupor, and he stood back. "I . . ."

"If you tell me you're sorry one more time I'm going to dump this can of paint on *yer* head." She picked it up and held it in front of her.

"But you're a mess."

"So? I think you're a bigger mess. At least I don't have a red nose." She looked at the apron. "Besides, what's a little paint? It's water based, so it will come right off."

"*Ya*," he said, still frowning, still waiting for her to be angry. They'd wasted paint and time, something his father wouldn't have tolerated. But his father wasn't here. He wasn't beholden to his earthly father anymore. And for the first time in years, he'd had fun.

"We should wash up," she said.

"There's a sink in the back."

He led her to a small, utilitarian basin and a single tap that dispensed only cold water. He turned it on and she put her hands underneath the flow, only to pull them back. "It's freezing."

"Sorry. You can *geh* in the *haus* and wash. There's warm water there."

She smirked. "I can handle it." But her body shook as she washed the paint off her hands.

"Wait," he said, then grabbed a clean rag from a bin he kept near the sink. He put it under the water, then squeezed out the excess. He held it in his hands, warming it, then handed it to her. "This will be better."

She nodded as she took the rag from him. She dabbed the paint off her face while he washed his hands. Then he splashed the water on his face a few times, turned off the tap, and reached for a dry rag. He wiped his cheeks and forehead as he turned to her. Somehow she'd managed to get all the paint off her face, leaving behind rosy cheeks.

"You missed a spot," she said, pointing to his cheek.

He dabbed at it a few times before she took the rag from him. "Let me." She slowly wiped his cheek, and this time her fingertips trailed against his skin. He closed his eyes at the slight contact, warmth filling him, finding the parts of his heart that had been cold for so long. When he opened his eyes, she was still touching him, still gazing at him in a way that made him want to hold her tight and never let go.

But he couldn't do that. He took the rag from her. "Thanks," he said, his voice and posture stiff. He tossed the rags into a separate bin and turned from her.

"Sol, wait."

He paused, then faced her. "I don't want to hurt you, Irene."

"You couldn't hurt me."

She sounded so confident he almost believed it himself. He hung his head. "I wasn't always like that," he said, whispering, unbelieving that he had confessed it out loud. "I wasn't always safe."

"I know."

He lifted his head, paralyzed with fear. Did she know the totality of his past? What he hadn't confessed that day in church?

"If I was worried about you and me, I wouldn't be here. I trust you." She lifted her chin. "I really do."

"You shouldn't," he said, looking away from her.

"Why not? You haven't given me any reason not to."

The already-small workshop seemed to close in on him. "You don't know me, Irene. Not the real me."

"I know you well enough."

"There are things . . . in *mei* past . . . ."

She moved closer to him, her hand tightening around his. "We all have things in our past."

"Not like this."

She kept her gaze on him, and he nearly melted at the understanding in her eyes. "Everything can be forgiven, Sol. God gives us mercy. We should extend it to everyone else."

He wanted to say something, but his mouth went dry. She could say these words now, but what if she knew what he'd really done? She'd run out that door faster than you could draw a breath.

"We're done for the *daag*," he said, turning and walking away from her.

"Sol—"

But he ignored her plea and walked out of the shop.

CHAPTER 14

Almost two weeks after the blizzard, Saturday morning dawned cold, but it wasn't snowing. It hadn't snowed in a couple of days, and the streets were more passable. Abigail couldn't put Asa and the trip to the bank off any longer. She got up early and went to the store to get the shawl she'd left there yesterday. It was seven thirty and the store wouldn't open until eight.

Although Abigail was able to go home the day after the big snowstorm, the weather had continued to be ruthless. Last Saturday she used that as an excuse to keep her and Asa from going to the bank, which was halfway between Birch Creek and Barton. She'd seen him at the store when he delivered some new shelves, but they didn't talk. She kept herself busy with customers. She wasn't hiding from him exactly, but she didn't want to speak to him either. She was kind of glad the weather wasn't cooperating, because she must have been out of her mind to agree to let Asa help her with her business.

Not that she didn't trust him. But she was embarrassed to show him how much she didn't know. Now that she was serious about it, she also realized she cared what he thought. She thought maybe she should ask Sadie to help her get things straight before she met with Asa. But she never got a chance—Sadie had taken advantage of the terrible weather to put her and Aden to work rearranging the store.

Abigail also kept busy with her weaving projects and started knitting again. A week after the big snowstorm, she'd pulled the box with her collection of yarn out of the closet. She hadn't knitted in a long while, focusing her energy on the rugs. But as she picked up a skein of soft navy blue yarn, she itched to start. She ran her fingers over the yarn, a lump in her throat. She had been planning to use this yarn to make a scarf and cap for Christmas for her father. His were fraying, and she had purchased the expensive yarn, only to put it away in the box after his death.

She took the yarn and her needles downstairs, sat in the chair where her mother usually sat, and started knitting. Outside snow continued to fall as she started on the waffle pattern. She wasn't sure what she was going to make, or for whom. But for some reason she was compelled to knit, to use this yarn, and to sit in her mother's chair. It didn't bring her peace, but it brought her comfort.

Afterward she had sent word to Asa that she was ready to go to the bank if the weather was good on Saturday.

Now she unlocked the door to the store and surveyed the changes. She had to admit, Sadie's idea had been a good one. On the left side of the store were the new shelves Sol had constructed. They held a variety of Amish goods, including Joanna's baked goods, jams Karen Yoder had made, and candles made by Rebecca Chupp. Sadie asked Abigail if it was all right to carry Rebecca's candles. "She approached me last week," Sadie said, looking unsure. "She saw Karen's jams and told me she makes candles. She wanted to sell some to save money . . ."

Sadie didn't have to finish her sentence. To save money for the wedding. Or for their marriage. It didn't matter. Abigail put her hand on Sadie's arm. "You can sell them here." It would be unfair of her not to agree.

Sadie nodded, and the next day Rebecca arrived with a box of scented candles.

Next to the new shelving was another section of wider shelves. These featured Sol's birdhouses. Abigail knew Irene was working on painting the birdhouses and she had done a wonderful job. They were a mix of traditional, rustic, and colorful birdhouses. Aden said the snow and slow business had been a blessing because it allowed Sol to catch up with the orders and to make extra inventory. Abigail thought he must have worked day and night to get so many birdhouses done.

On the other side of the birdhouse display was the woven rugs display. This was a smaller space, although there was still room for more rugs. Since Irene had been busy painting—and Sol was paying her more money than Abigail had—Abigail had been weaving her rugs alone again. She still hadn't used her special loom. She couldn't think of a project she was interested in. Now she had to focus her time on building up her stock of rugs again.

The rest of the store was still stocked with grocery and tool items, everything neat and facing outward. Things were also easy to find. Once business picked up, the store would do well.

The sound of the bell above the door tinkled and she spun around. Asa walked in, grinning. "Ready to *geh* to the bank?"

"It's open already?"

"Not until eight. But if we leave now we'll get there right at opening time."

She bit her lip. She couldn't get out of this, she knew. She picked up her shawl and said, "I'll get *mei* money."

He nodded as he walked over to the Amish section of the store. She thought he would pause to admire Sol's birdhouses or drool over Joanna's baked goods. Instead he went to the rugs and stared at them. "You do very *gut* work," he said, touching one of the blue-and-gray rugs.

"*Danki.*" She was pleased he noticed. "They're easy to make."

"They don't look that easy." He turned to her. "I know I still hadn't decided what to buy when I returned *yer* samples to Irene, but now I've figured out which one I want."

"Oh?"

"Want to guess?"

She smiled, studying him for a moment. What would Asa choose? She looked him up and down, and suddenly she wasn't thinking about rugs. He had his hands on his trim waist, causing his jacket to rise up a bit above his belt line. His shirt was tucked in. The man didn't have an ounce of fat on his body. She suddenly became self-conscious. She turned away. "Green," she said, saying the first color that came to mind.

"*Nee.* I don't like green at all."

She put her shawl around her shoulders, still not looking at him. *He is so beautiful . . .*

She halted her thoughts. She'd never thought Joel beautiful. Handsome, yes. But not enough to take her breath away, not like Asa was doing.

"Guess again," he said.

She didn't want to play this game, but she also didn't want him to suspect the line her thoughts were traveling. "Gray."

"Gray's pretty boring." He moved to stand in front of her. "Is that what you think I am? Boring?"

Nee. I don't think you're boring at all. The twinkle in his eyes as he looked at her, the sly grin he was giving her . . . what was wrong with her? "Brown," she said, this time sure that was the answer.

His smile widened and her heart thumped. "That's the one." He pointed to the brown rug on the display, which happened to be the largest. "I'll take this one." Then he dug into one of his pants pockets and pulled out his wallet.

"You don't have to pay, remember? That's why you're helping me with *mei* bookkeeping."

"I'm sure this rug costs more than a little financial advice and squaring up accounts." He checked the tag, then counted out the amount.

She looked at the cash as he held it out to her. "I feel like I should give you the *familye* discount."

He tilted his head. "I'm not *familye*."

Yet. She clapped her hand over her mouth as if she'd said the word out loud. Where had that thought come from?

Asa frowned. "Abigail?"

She removed her hand and snatched the money out of his. "I'll meet you at *yer* buggy." She didn't wait for him to respond. She just turned around and fled the store.

When she ran into the house, Aden and Sadie were in the kitchen. They had appeared later than usual this morning, which reminded her yet again that she was the third wheel here.

"Abigail, what's wrong?" Sadie asked as Abigail flew by her.

"*Nix*," she said. "Just going to the bank." She flew upstairs and went into her room. Out of breath, she shut the door and leaned against it. She couldn't keep Asa waiting out in the cold for long, but she had to gather her wits. Family. What had that been about?

Then another flutter appeared in her tummy. She was losing her mind. She had to be. It was nearly spring and she'd spent most of the winter stuck inside, either in her house or in the store. That had to explain why she had the words *Asa* and *family* in the same sentence in her mind. Cabin fever.

She looked at the money in her hand. Other brown rugs were on display, but he had chosen the biggest and most expensive one. The one that would make her the most profit. Did he do it on purpose? Or was that really the rug he wanted? And why was she overthinking a rug?

Her breath caught and she went to the bed and pulled out the shoe box she had underneath it. She rummaged through the receipts and found the envelope with her money. She grabbed her purse and ran downstairs.

"Abigail, when will you be back?" Sadie asked as she hurried back into the kitchen.

"Not sure—Aden, can you help with *mei* shift? Thanks!" She opened the back door and ran to the buggy. The faster they took care of this, the sooner she could get away from Asa and figure out what was going on with her feelings.

But Asa didn't seem in any hurry. In fact, his horse seemed to be sluggish once they were on their way. "Is there something wrong with *yer* horse?" Abigail asked.

Asa shook his head. "She's fine."

"We're going pretty slow. What if the bank closes?"

He looked at her and chuckled. "We're not going *that* slow. The bank is open until noon on Saturdays." He looked ahead, a puff of cold air coming out of his mouth as he spoke. "I just thought we'd take a slower drive today, since the weather is finally decent. But I can get her to move faster if you need to get back to work."

"That's probably a *gut* idea."

He nodded but looked disappointed. She glanced at his

profile. It wasn't helping that she couldn't keep her eyes off him. There wasn't anything different about him today than there had been the last time she'd seen him. She stared straight ahead again and kept her gaze that way until they got to the bank.

There was a hitching rail in front of the small bank, which Asa explained was a branch location of a major bank. He opened the door for Abigail. "Is this where you do *yer* banking?" she asked.

He nodded. "They're friendly here. They also have a *gut* interest rate and don't penalize you if *yer* balance drops under a certain amount."

She had no clue what he was talking about, and that bothered her. She once teased Sadie for reading a boring accounting book, but Sadie would know what Asa was talking about. Abigail let him take the lead as he went to the teller window. She stayed back as he explained that they wanted to open a checking account. The teller asked them to have a seat, adding that someone would be with them shortly.

Abigail sat down in one of the chairs and Asa sat down next to her. He leaned close and whispered, "You look nervous."

She glanced around the bank. "I am." She was about to give over her hard-earned money to people she didn't know. The fact that people did this all the time didn't quell her misgivings. "What if they lose *mei* money?"

"They won't. It's insured."

"What does that mean?"

"If something happens—the bank makes a bad investment, for example—then *yer* money is protected."

"Whose money are they investing?" she asked.

"Mine. Soon to be *yers*. Everyone's."

"Without our permission?" She gripped the strap of her purse tightly.

"Abigail." He put his hand over hers and gave it a gentle squeeze. "Do you want to leave? You don't have to open an account."

She looked down at his hand covering hers. He'd driven her all the way out here, and she didn't want him to have made a wasted trip. Besides, it was her fault for not knowing anything about banks. "*Nee*," she said. "You have *yer* money here. That's *gut* enough for me."

He removed his hand. "I can explain everything to you on the way home, if you want. How banks work, about interest, investing, savings, all of it."

She couldn't think of a more boring topic of conversation. But she needed to know these things. He also looked eager to teach her. "Okay," she said as a woman in a smart-looking business suit approached them.

Half an hour later, Abigail had a bank account. It was easy to get one, she discovered. And Asa was right—the banker was friendly. The only awkward moment was when she had asked if Abigail and Asa were getting a joint account.

"Oh, we're not married," Asa said.

"He's a friend," Abigail added quickly.

"Just helping her out," he said just as fast.

The banker had looked at them for a moment before continuing to fill out the paperwork.

As they walked out of the bank, the sun was high in the sky. "Do you want to grab something to eat before we head back to Birch Creek?" Asa asked. "There's a fast-food place next door."

Abigail didn't care much for fast food, but she was hungry.

By the time they would get back home it would be midafternoon. She nodded. "Sure."

They walked into the restaurant, the smell of fried food hitting her nose and causing her stomach to growl. She looked at the menu. She did like French fries, and the hamburgers didn't look too bad. Her eyes settled on a double hamburger and fry combo, which was what she'd get if she were by herself. She looked at Asa again as he studied the menu. Then he turned to her.

"Do you know what you want?"

She wanted a hamburger and fries. What she said was, "The side salad and a diet drink."

He frowned. "That's it? You're not hungry?"

"*Nee*, I'm not." Her stomach chose that time to growl. Loudly.

He arched a brow. "I don't think three pieces of lettuce and a sliver of tomato are going to fill you up."

"What's that supposed to mean?"

"It means you should get a burger if you're hungry." He frowned at her. "That's all."

She folded her arms across her chest, then realized that just made her coat look tighter around her body. "I don't want anything," she said, then turned around and headed for the door.

"Abigail—"

Tears bit her eyes as she opened the door and went outside.

Asa held up his hand to the woman behind the cash register. "We'll be right back." Then he dashed out the door after Abigail.

He found her walking toward the bank. Why was she upset? He thought things were going well between them. Really well. He had been surprised she'd been so nervous about getting a bank account, but when he saw the amount of money she deposited, he could see why she'd want to make sure it was safe. Her rug business must be doing really well for her to have already made that kind of profit.

Then she'd agreed to lunch, which had surprised him. He thought she'd refuse and want to go back home. He felt like he was making slow progress with her, and to be honest, he was enjoying the ride.

"Abigail, wait." He jogged toward her, leaping over a small pile of slush in the fast-food parking lot. She didn't turn around and he put his hand on her arm. "What happened back there?"

"*Nix.*" She didn't look at him. "I need to *geh* home."

"What about lunch?"

"I told you, I'm not hungry." As soon as she said the words, her stomach growled, again. Her face pinched in annoyance.

"*Yer* stomach says something different."

"*Mei* stomach needs to shut up," she muttered. "Asa," she said on a sigh, "just take me home."

He peered at her, hearing her voice crack. Then he saw her bottom lip tremble. She whirled around and hurried to the buggy. She didn't even wait for him as she climbed in. He untethered the horse, and as soon as he got in the buggy, he started to gather the reins—only to see her with her head in her hands.

"Abigail?"

She shook her head, still covering her face. They weren't going anywhere. The parking lot was empty and Asa had put the buggy shield on this morning to ward off the chilly weather. Since they had relative privacy, he moved close to her. "Tell me what's wrong, Abigail."

She lifted her head. She wasn't crying, but he could see she was trying hard not to. "What's wrong with me?" she asked.

"*Nix*," he said. "There's *nix* wrong with you."

"Then why wasn't I enough?" She looked at her lap, then spread her hands over her middle. "Maybe the problem is that I was too much."

He wasn't sure what that meant, but he could hear the disgust in her voice. "Abigail," he said tentatively. "Joel was a fool. I already told you that."

"You said he was an idiot."

"He's both. How he could let you get away . . ." Now it was his turn for emotion to catch in his throat. It was an unfamiliar feeling. Even when he'd left Shipshewana he hadn't felt this tightness closing around his neck. He'd felt anger that he'd lost his job and house in Shipshewana. Guilt when Susanna became ill. All that happened when he didn't obey God's clear call to leave everything he had and move back to Birch Creek, when God hadn't healed Susanna until Asa had given her up. Then he'd felt profound remorse that God had to do all that for him to listen. But he had never felt the pain now in his chest as he thought about how much Abigail was still hurting.

"I never got away." She looked at him, her eyes dry now. "He threw me away."

That was it. He couldn't sit there and not hold her. He put his arm around her shoulders and drew her close. He expected her to pull away, and he was prepared not to let her go. But she melted into him, turning her face into his coat. Then the tears fell.

She wanted her tears to end, but they didn't. She wanted to pull away from Asa, but she couldn't do that either. She was powerless over her body and emotions. Out of control. That's how she felt about everything. Her eating. Her business. Her future. She was sailing in the wind, like a kite with a broken string.

Until Asa put his arm around her. Until she felt not only his warmth but his compassion. And something else, something deeper that she had never experienced before. She turned her face away from him just long enough to wipe the back of her hand over her eyes, but she kept her ear on his chest, hearing the rapid thump of his heartbeat. For some reason, knowing his pulse was racing as fast as hers gave her some relief from her confusion. She lifted her head.

"It's all right to cry, Abigail. Especially after what you've been through." He drew his thumb across the top of her cheek.

The touch was featherlight, but she felt it to her toes. His gray eyes turned the color of slate, his black eyelashes moving to half-mast as he brushed her cheek again. His gaze dropped to her mouth and a tickle appeared in her chest.

"Are you feeling better?" he asked.

She had to be honest. "*Ya*. A bit."

"Sure you don't want anything to eat?"

The words hit her like a bucket of cold water. He hadn't been thinking about kissing her, like she thought he was. Like she had been thinking about kissing him. He was thinking about food. She pulled away from him. "Sure," she said with a shrug of her shoulders. Obviously he was hungry since he kept pushing lunch.

"Stay here," he said, then scrambled out of the buggy. She turned to watch him run to the fast-food place and disappear inside. That gave her time to collect her emotions. She couldn't act like that again around Asa. She couldn't be thinking about kissing him or paying attention to his pulse, which was probably racing because of lack of food. She didn't need to be melting down about Joel around him either.

A few minutes later Asa was back with a bag of food and two soft drinks. "We can eat on the road," he said, handing them to her. "Since you said you had to get home soon." He took the reins.

She placed the drinks on the floor so they wouldn't spill and opened the bag. Two hamburgers and two fries. Her stomach growled a third time. What a traitorous organ.

"*Geh* ahead and eat," he said as he maneuvered the buggy onto the street. "I'll wait until we get out of the traffic. Oh, and I didn't get you the salad. I got you some real food."

One more stomach growl and she couldn't take it anymore. She pulled out the fries, prayed a quick prayer, and started to eat. The fries were hot, salty, and, she had to admit, delicious. Without thinking, she handed one to Asa, who started chomping on it. "*Gut*. Better than leaves."

"I like salad."

"Me too. But as a complement to lunch, not as lunch." He glanced at her. "I'll take another fry."

She handed him one. "I should eat more salads," she said, speaking her thoughts out loud.

"Why? Because they're healthy?"

"Because I could stand to lose a few pounds. Okay, many pounds."

He gave her a side glance. "Who told you that?"

"The scale, *mei* expanding waistline, *mei* huge hips—"

"*Yer* hips are perfect." He was staring straight ahead, as if the comment had been a casual one. But it wasn't. He thought her hips were perfect? Asa, the epitome of physical perfection, liked her hips?

"I'll take *mei* hamburger now."

It took a second for his words to register. Then she dug into the bag and pulled out one of the burgers. She carefully unfolded the wrapping so he could hold on to the burger without making a mess. She expected him to take a bite when instead he said, "You shouldn't put *yourself* down."

"I'm not. I'm stating a fact. Those are two different things."

"You're stating an opinion. You think you need to lose weight because of a number."

"Not just that. *Mei* dresses got too tight. I had to make new ones."

"Well, that definitely calls for a salad."

She didn't appreciate his sarcasm. "You don't understand."

He took a bite of his burger. "Try me," he said, around the mouthful.

She couldn't speak. How could she admit to him something so personal? A flaw she was embarrassed about? How could she tell him when she was afraid to admit it to herself?

"I'm sorry," he said after the silence. "I shouldn't have pried." He paused. "It's just that you seem really bothered by it and I want to help."

"You can't help me with this," she whispered. "*Nee* one can." She looked at the wrapped hamburger in the bag, her appetite gone. She put her half-eaten fries in the bag and folded down the top.

Asa didn't say anything else, and they rode back to her house in silence. When he pulled into the driveway, he looked at her. "Abigail, I'm sorry. I feel like I hurt *yer* feelings."

She stared at him. He looked almost distraught. "I'm too sensitive. I know that." She smiled, trying to put him at ease. "It's fine. We're fine," she added.

He visibly relaxed. "*Gut.* Do you have time to show me *yer* receipts? Now that you have *yer* account set up, I can help you get *yer* ledgers in order."

She looked at the parking lot in front of the store. It wasn't too crowded, so perhaps Sadie and Aden were doing fine and didn't need her. "I'm sure you have something better to do with *yer* Saturday afternoon than *geh* through *mei* receipts."

"*Nee.* Remember, I like that kind of stuff."

"Let me check and see if Sadie needs *mei* help first."

He nodded. "I'll wait here."

After finding out Sadie and Aden didn't need her, Abigail came back to the buggy. Asa was sipping on his drink. "They don't need *mei* help right now. You can park *yer* buggy by the barn if you'd like. But I'm warning you, *mei* paperwork is a mess."

CHAPTER 15

Asa looked at the shoe box overflowing with small pieces of paper. He almost let out a low whistle, because Abigail wasn't kidding when she said her paperwork was unorganized. But after hurting her feelings earlier, he didn't want to upset her further. He wasn't even sure what he had done, but now he knew how sensitive she was about her weight.

He suspected there was more to it than that, though. Joel, the deaths of her parents—she had a right to be sensitive. If he wanted to earn her trust, he'd have to learn patience. *Is this* mei *lesson, Lord? Patience?* He'd never thought of himself as an impatient man. Then again, when had his patience been tested? When had the stakes been so high?

Abigail sat at the table, her fingers entwined. "That's *mei* filing system. And *mei* bookkeeping system. Sadie says I take after *Daed* when it comes to paperwork. She's still sorting out things she keeps finding in the office."

Asa nodded. "Everyone has their own system." He picked up a receipt that had fallen out of the box.

"This is not a system, Asa. It's chaos."

"Fixable chaos." He was eager to get started. This looked like a puzzle he would enjoy figuring out and putting back together. "Do you have a ledger book?"

Abigail shook her head. "I've got a notebook. Will that work?"

"*Ya.* But eventually you should get a ledger."

"Sadie uses spreadsheets."

"Those would work too." He started pulling out receipts and putting them in piles. "Help me sort these out. Here's a pile for purchases. One for sales. And one for miscellany."

"What is considered miscellany?"

"Purchases that don't have anything to do with *yer* business."

She held up a short receipt. "Like this one?"

He took it from her and examined it. It was a simple cash register receipt for $4.99. "What did you buy?"

Her cheeks pinked. "A dozen donuts."

"Miscellany." He set it on the pile. "Unless you need donuts for *yer* weaving."

"I don't need donuts, period."

Asa blew out a breath and left off the sorting. He'd had enough. "Abigail, I can't listen to you put *yerself* down anymore."

She shrank back. "Sorry."

"Quit apologizing." He looked her straight in the eye. "You need to stop cutting *yerself* down."

"I can't help it." She averted her gaze.

"I don't remember you being like this when we were *kinner,*" Asa said.

"I'm not the same as I was before."

True. He softened his tone. "I'm not going to judge you if you want donuts or a hamburger or a candy bar. It doesn't matter to me what you eat. It shouldn't matter to anyone else, either."

"You didn't hear . . ." She didn't look at him as she spoke.

"Hear what?"

She sighed. "When I first came back to church after I was in Middlefield with Joanna, I was looking for a seat. Someone made a comment as I passed by about how much weight I'd gained. It was a whispered comment and I know I wasn't meant to hear it. But I did. Joel broke up with me that afternoon. He didn't give me a reason, other than he wasn't in love with me."

"And you think that's because of *yer* weight?"

"*Ya.*" Then she shook her head. "*Nee.* Not entirely. He was seeing Rebecca while I was away. He told me."

Asa fisted his hands. Why was she so hung up on a guy who would cheat on her and discard her the way he did?

"But the thought is still in *mei* brain. That maybe he wouldn't be with Rebecca if I hadn't come back to Middlefield twenty pounds heavier."

"You would have wanted him back even though he cheated on you?"

She paused. "Maybe."

Did she really think so little of herself? "Abigail, listen to me. You deserve someone who will treat you well and put you first in his life. Someone who will love you the way you are, for the rest of his life." He couldn't prevent his gaze from scanning her body even if he wanted to. "Who thinks you're perfect the way you look right now."

He heard her breath catch and knew he'd revealed too much. So much for patience. He hadn't heard God's voice in several days, and the irony wasn't lost on him that the Lord had put him in this position and was now letting him sink or swim on his own.

"Do you think that, Asa?"

Her question made him freeze. He'd just promised himself

he'd hold back. That he'd be patient with her. But she was asking him with such genuine interest that he couldn't lie. He could never lie to this woman. "*Ya*," he said softly. "I do."

"Why?"

Of course she'd want to know why. How could he tell her? How could he show her?

He took her hand. "Come with me."

She resisted at first. "Where?"

"Just trust me, Abigail."

She glanced down at their hands joined together. Then she stood.

He took a deep breath and prayed he was doing the right thing.

∞

"The bathroom, Asa?" She looked at him as he shut the door in the small bathroom off the kitchen.

"Do you have a mirror somewhere else?"

She had a small one in her bedroom, but she wasn't about to let him take her upstairs. This was stupid and uncomfortable. She should have never told him about what she'd heard in church, or about her fear about Joel. He must think her an idiot for even considering taking Joel back. Which she wouldn't, even if he did break up with Rebecca. Although she had thought about it one time. Once. Then she had to go admitting it to Asa.

He turned on the battery-operated lamp and looked at her. Really looked at her, his gray eyes scrutinizing her from the top of her *kapp* down to her toes. But there was no criticism there. No judgment. Simply . . . appreciation.

Without a word he took her hand again. He faced her toward

the mirror, then stood behind her, his chin barely scraping the top of her *kapp*.

"Here's what I see," he said, then cleared his throat. "I see a pair of beautiful brown eyes that sparkle when you laugh—and when you beat me at Dutch Blitz."

That brought a small smile to her face. He pointed to it.

"I see a smile that takes *mei* breath away." He paused, then ran the back of his fingers over her cheek. "Soft, rosy skin." He pulled his hand away. "A cute round face."

She prickled at the word *round*. He must have noticed because he said, "I like round."

Abigail tried to move away from him, but he put his hands on her shoulders. She faced him. "You don't have to try to make me feel better."

"Is that what you think I'm doing?"

"I know it's what you're doing."

"I'm trying to tell you what I see when I look at you." Then he surprised her by closing his eyes. When he opened them again he said, "I guess I'll have to show you."

She couldn't breathe as he cupped her cheek with his hand. "If I didn't like what I see I wouldn't do this," he whispered. Then he leaned forward and kissed the top of her cheek.

One tiny wisp of a kiss. On the cheek, no less. And that had made her feel more than anything she'd ever experienced with Joel. "O-okay. You've m-made *yer* point." Oh no. She was reduced to stuttering.

"I don't think so. You're kind of stubborn, in case you didn't know." He kissed the top of her other cheek. "See? I like them both."

"Asa—"

He put his finger on her lips. "I'm not finished. Abigail, you don't understand how much it hurts me to hear you put *yerself* down. You're rejecting something I like, something I find attractive. I'm sure I crossed the line by not only pulling you into this bathroom to be alone with me, but by kissing you. So I won't blame you for being mad at me." He moved his finger away. "But I'm not sorry. And I don't regret it."

Well, if that wasn't the most perfect thing to say. "I'm not mad." And she wasn't. She'd never felt so special in her life. Without thinking, she put her arms around his neck. His hands went to her hips, right below her waist. She stiffened a bit, self-conscious that he was touching her in the one place she'd put on the most weight.

"Don't," he said, not moving his hands away. "I like all of you. Inside and out."

She relaxed, and he drew her closer to him. "I'm going to kiss you, Abigail. And not on the cheek." Before she could protest—not that she was going to, not this time—he bent his head and touched his lips to hers. Again his touch was light and tentative, yet made her feel things she'd never felt before. It was her that deepened the kiss, and he definitely didn't back away.

A knock on the door. "Abigail?" Sadie's voice sounded from the other side.

Asa's eyes filled with panic as they jumped away from each other. Abigail put her finger on her lips and drew back the shower curtain. She pointed to the door, then got in the tub. She stood as still as a statue as the curtain closed. Then she heard the toilet flush before Asa opened the door. Ya, *he's smart.*

"Sorry," Asa said. "I'm not Abigail."

Abigail held her breath. She did *not* want to be here when Sadie came in. But what other choice did she have? She couldn't let her sister see her and Asa alone together in the bathroom. She could still feel the tingle of Asa's lips on hers, and the slight burn on her cheeks where his stubbly chin had rubbed while they were kissing. She closed her eyes. *Lord, forgive me.* She couldn't let this happen again. Why was she so weak when it came to men?

"Oh," Sadie said. "I was looking for her. Someone wanted to purchase a rug and there wasn't a price on it."

"She must have run upstairs while I was in here," Asa said.

"Okay, I'll *geh* find her."

When Sadie disappeared, Abigail jumped out of the shower. "What did you tell her that for?"

He held up his hands. "Would you rather I tell her you're hiding in the shower?"

"Of course not." She moved past him. "But you could have thought of something else."

"*Mei* mind's not exactly working very well right now."

The low, husky way he said the words sent a shiver down her spine. She didn't dare look at him. Instead she went into the living room, took a deep breath, and yelled at Sadie upstairs. "I'm down here," she said, irritated that she still sounded breathless. Who wouldn't after a kiss like that?

"Oh," Sadie said, appearing at the top of the stairs. "Asa said you were up here."

"*Nee.* Been down here the whole time." She bit her bottom lip. At least it wasn't a lie. "What did you need?"

Sadie told her about the customer as she descended the stairs. "Can you talk to her? I didn't want to set a price for the rug and charge too much or too little."

Abigail nodded. She'd do anything to get away from Asa right now. It was bad enough that she had to see him as she walked into the kitchen. This time she couldn't look away. The dark smokiness was still in his eyes as he met her gaze. "I, uh, have to *geh* to the, uh, store." Wow. She sounded like a fool.

"Sadie told me." He leaned against the doorjamb of the bathroom.

How could he be so casual? The first thought that came to her was that he hadn't felt the same depth of emotion that she had. But that wasn't true. She knew it in her heart. He was just better at keeping his emotions together.

She and Sadie left for the store. It didn't take long to talk to the customer, who had eagerly agreed to pay what Abigail asked for the rug. Abigail rang her up, then took the receipt. She looked at it, took a pencil from the can by the cash register, and wrote down which rug was sold. She set the receipt aside and looked for something to do in the near-empty store, anything to keep from facing Asa again. She started straightening shelves and was able to do it for a while before Sadie came up to her.

"Isn't Asa in the *haus* waiting for you?" Sadie asked.

"*Ya.* I saw that these cans needed straightening, so I thought I'd do that before I went back inside."

"Abigail, Aden straightened those cans this morning."

Abigail could tell. When Aden straightened stock, he straightened it perfectly. She wondered if he even pulled a ruler out to make sure each can was a certain space away from the edge. Abigail forced a smile and said, "Oh. I hadn't noticed."

Sadie frowned. "Is something wrong?"

"Wrong? Why would anything be wrong?"

"*Yer* forehead is wrinkled, *yer* cheeks are red, and you keep touching *yer* mouth."

Abigail relaxed her forehead. She couldn't do anything about red cheeks and she had no idea she was touching her mouth. She had been thinking about the kiss, though. It was impossible not to. "I'm a little warm, I guess." The understatement of the year.

"Hmm. I thought it was chilly in here." Sadie pulled her sweater around her body. "You can *geh* back to the *haus*. As you can see, it's a slow *daag*."

"Where's Aden?"

"In the office. He's looking over paperwork from a gas company."

Abigail nodded. Although Sadie was good with money, she was trusting Aden to decide which offer for the gas rights on their property was the best one. Aden had taken his time, which Abigail had appreciated. "Are you sure you don't need any help?"

"*Nee*, I don't. Besides, you're being rude to Asa."

That was true. A stab of guilt went through her. *Don't be such a coward.* She could walk into the kitchen and pretend what had happened between them never happened. She'd tell Asa she didn't need his help with her books anymore. Sadie could help her, which was true, and she would when she caught up with the store's paperwork, which seemed endless. Abigail would put an end to spending time with Asa. She had to. She didn't trust herself to be alone with him, not after that kiss.

She mentally went over what she would say to him as she went back to the house. "Asa," she said, walking into the kitchen, putting her hand on her abdomen to steady her nerves.

But he wasn't there. She looked at the table. Her box of receipts was empty and put in neat stacks. The notebook was open on the table, and as she neared, she could see that he had organized the top page into columns. Debits. Credits. Expenditures. He'd also written down each receipt. He'd done all this in twenty minutes? She glanced at the clock. She'd been gone almost an hour.

She peered at the notebook. There was a folded sheet of
paper sticking out from under it. She pulled it out and opened it.

Receipts organized and recorded. It's a start. In more ways than one.

Abigail's eyes widened as she caught his meaning. She sat
down at the table. What was she going to do now?

CHAPTER 16

During the next week, Abigail didn't see Asa. Not that she expected to. He was busy working at Barton Plastics, and she was busy with her job at the store and weaving and knitting when she wasn't working there. Sadie was happy to see that Abigail was taking the bookkeeping seriously. "I'm glad you decided to write down the items on the spreadsheet," she said after Abigail had rung up a customer who bought one of Sol's birdhouses.

"I know. I should have been doing it more consistently before now." Which was true. But she had forgotten to do it before. Or more accurately, she couldn't be bothered. But after seeing what Asa had done with her own receipts, she realized it would be a lot easier to keep up with everything if she focused on keeping good records.

It's a start . . .

Her face reddened as she remembered his note, then remembered the kiss. It was nearly a week since he'd kissed her, and she was in her room working on a rag rug, this one a little more colorful than she'd made before. She'd ordered the fabric last week, and the light pinks, blues, greens, and yellows would be perfect for a baby or child's room. As she wove she tried to focus on the rug and not on Asa, or his kiss, or the way she felt as he had showed her in the mirror what he liked about her.

She had a hard time believing he was serious, mostly because it didn't make sense. It's not like they were friends growing up. Or that they had spent enough time together for there to be a connection between them. But their kiss had proven there was.

After working on the rug for an hour, she glanced out the window. The sun was shining. It had been such a snowy, cold, and dreary winter, including this whole month of March, that she couldn't resist standing by the window and basking in the sunlight. There was plenty of snow on the ground, but it was melting, and the icicles that hung from the roof were steadily dripping. She glanced at the small clock on her bedside table. Lunchtime.

She went to the kitchen and started preparing lunch for her, Sadie, and Aden. She wasn't a good cook like Joanna. She was barely a passable one. But Sadie and Aden had been very busy this week and she had taken over the meal preparation. Today they were having leftover vegetable soup and cheese sandwiches.

She'd set the soup pot on the stove when she heard a knock on the back door. It was Sol. She opened the door and let him in. "Hi," she said, then went back to the stove in the kitchen. She adjusted the heat underneath the pot.

"Hi." He didn't come far into the kitchen, as was Sol's usual way. She glanced at him again. Was he waiting for an invitation? "Do you need something?"

"Sadie mentioned that Asa Bontrager was helping you with *yer* bookkeeping."

Abigail paused, then nodded. "*Ya.*"

"How's that working out for you?"

The kiss flashed in her mind and she almost let out a sigh. Checking herself, she said, "He knows what he's doing." *He sure does . . .*

Sol's brow furrowed. "Think he'd mind giving me some advice? I haven't had time to keep track of *mei* books—been too busy making the birdhouses."

"Sure. I know for a fact he'd want to."

"If you see him before me, could you let him know?"

Abigail didn't plan to see him at all, but she nodded. "*Ya*. Do you want some lunch?"

He shook his head. "I just dropped off a few more bird-houses. I usually eat lunch with *Mamm* anyway."

Abigail smiled. She appreciated Sol's devotion to his mother. "If you ever change *yer* mind, you're welcome anytime. Rhoda too."

"*Danki*." His mouth quirked in a small smile and there was a little life in his green eyes. He was nice-looking. But nothing compared to Asa.

She had to throw up a mental stop sign. And she had to figure out how to get Asa out of her mind.

Sol left, and Abigail continued preparing lunch. She was setting out bowls when she heard another knock on the back door and gripped the edge of a bowl midair. She set down the bowl, walked through the mudroom, and saw Asa. What was he doing here? He waved at her through the door's window, but she couldn't move. She also couldn't let him stand outside. When she opened the door, a gust of cold wind blew in. It might be sunny outside and spring on the calendar, but winter wasn't ready to let go. "Why aren't you at work?"

"Hello to you too." But he grinned as he said the words and

shut the door behind him. "I took half a day off." He peered around her shoulder. "Something smells delicious."

"I'm making lunch—"

"*Gut*. I'm starving."

"I don't remember inviting you to stay."

His grin widened. "You haven't asked me to leave either." Then his smile dimmed. "You're not, are you?"

He looked so earnest and worried she forgot her nervousness. "*Nee*. You don't have to leave."

He walked inside and slipped off his coat. When she took it from him, he moved toward her and she instinctively backed up to the counter. Surely he wasn't going to kiss her right here in the kitchen when Sadie could walk in on them at any time? And if she was so worried about that, then why was she licking her lips, preparing herself for his kiss?

But he didn't. He kept a respectable distance between them, despite the fact that she could see he wanted the same thing she did.

"Maybe this isn't such a *gut* idea," she said.

"So you *are* avoiding me."

She held on to his coat. "*Nee*. We've both been working. That's not avoiding."

"You haven't been over to see Joanna this week."

Usually she tried to visit Joanna at least once during the week. The bad weather this winter had kept her off that schedule, but that wasn't the case this week. She'd kept her distance from her sister for a good reason. "How do you know I haven't seen her?"

"Because I went by each evening to see if you were there."

Her breath caught.

"Don't worry. They didn't know I was there for you. I have a standing invitation to supper over there. It's nice not to have to eat alone." He took one step forward. "But every night I hoped you would be there."

Any other time she would appreciate such straightforwardness. But this was too overwhelming. "Asa," she said, her voice sounding raspy and dry. She swallowed and tried again. "I think we should forget what happened the other day."

"Did you want *yer* receipts organized another way?"

"I'm not talking about that and you know it."

He nodded and took off his hat, then ran his fingers through his dark hair, which fluffed up the locks and made him look irresistible. Was he doing that on purpose? She turned away. "Sadie should be here any minute."

"Is that *yer* way of warning me not to kiss you?"

She jerked her head toward him. "*N-nee*—"

"Don't worry. I'm not going to. I did want to talk to you about it, though."

She folded his coat over her arm, hugging it tightly against her. "Why do we need to talk about it?"

"Why not?"

Because I want you to kiss me again. "Because it's weird . . . talking about kissing. People don't talk about stuff like that. It's too . . . personal."

He took another step toward her, and out of the corner of her eye she could see him lay his hat down on the counter. "I don't want you to think I *geh* around kissing just anybody."

That thought had crossed her mind. She was sure he'd had plenty of girlfriends in the past. Someone as kind and fun to be around as he was probably had every woman in Shipshewana after him.

"Actually," he continued. "You're the first *maedel* I've ever kissed."

She rolled her eyes. Did he really expect her to believe that? When she and Joel first kissed, it had been awkward, mostly for her because she had no idea what she was doing. Kissing Asa had been different. There was more tenderness, more . . . everything. Which made her think he had a *lot* of experience. But when she looked at him, doubt crept in. Gone was the easy confidence he'd had when he first arrived. He seemed bashful. Even a little lost. She realized he was telling the truth. "I'm *yer* first kiss?"

"*Ya.*"

"But I thought . . ." She couldn't admit she was thinking he was some kind of Amish ladies' man. "I'm surprised, that's all."

"I'm glad it was with you. And I know you're still getting over Joel and I don't want to push you, but I can't be anything but honest with you. I care about you. I want to spend time with you. I want to date you. I want to be *yer* boyfriend. I want . . ." He paused. "I want . . ."

The kitchen door opened and Sadie came inside. "Something smells *gut.*" She looked at Asa. "Hi," she said, looking a little surprised. "I didn't know you were here."

Asa took a step back and smiled as if he hadn't said some of the most amazing words she'd ever heard. "I wanted to ask Abigail if she needed any more help with her record keeping." He looked at Abigail. "Right?"

Abigail slowly nodded. Apparently he didn't mind telling a little white lie to Sadie. Which was good since Abigail's mouth couldn't form a single word.

"What a great idea," Sadie replied. "Whatever you said to her last week is working. She's recording all the sales now so we can keep better track of inventory, and she's like a new person behind the cash register."

Asa glanced at Abigail, a twinkle in his eye. "Is that so?"

"*Ya.*" Sadie sat at the table. "You're staying for lunch, then?"

"If it's all right with Abigail."

"*Ya.*" At least she could say that. She left the kitchen to hang up Asa's coat, still reeling from what he'd told her.

When she returned, Sadie and Asa sat at the table and started talking about accounting. It wasn't long before the conversation went over her head and she focused on serving lunch, which was better than thinking about her confused emotions. She put Asa's bowl in front of him, but he barely noticed.

"So you're looking at outside investments?" he asked Sadie, who at least touched her spoon when she glanced at her bowl.

"Not necessarily. More like expansion, and allowing more cottage industries to be featured in the store. It's not all about the money."

"What system are you using to keep track of the different accounts?"

Abigail put the plate of sandwiches on the table and then sat down as Sadie explained some kind of accounting system that sounded complex and detailed. But Asa was listening with rapt attention. He was interested in what Sadie was saying, and she seemed eager to talk about it.

Abigail cleared her throat. "Lunch is ready. Soup's probably getting cold."

They both looked at her as if her words had brought them out of some accounting dreamland where everything was numbers and lists and balance sheets and dollar signs. She bowed her head in silent prayer. Then they began to eat.

Sadie and Asa continued their conversation during the meal until Abigail's eyes glazed over. While Asa was talking about things she didn't understand and, honestly, thought were as exciting as watching a mopped floor dry, she noted his enthusiasm.

He really did have a passion for bookkeeping, and it didn't matter that it didn't make sense to her. She liked seeing him fully engaged, confident and knowledgeable. There was so much to admire about him. His intelligence, his ability to be there when she needed him, and his honesty. She had been on the receiving end of betrayal. She wouldn't go through that again.

Perhaps with Asa, she wouldn't have to. But it wouldn't be wise to get involved with him. She had to follow her mind, not her emotions. She didn't understand why he was interested in her. She didn't have beauty or brains. Not that she was stupid, but she wasn't as bright as him. Why, out of all the women in Birch Creek and Shipshewana, had he chosen her to kiss? To date? It didn't make sense.

Sadie finished her soup and sandwich and stood. "I better get back to the store." She looked at Abigail. "Do you mind if I take Aden's lunch to him? He wants to redo the tool display again, and he's been spending the morning taking measurements. When he gets like this I can't get him to take a break to eat. I figure if I take the food to him there's a fifty-fifty chance he'll eat it."

"Sure." Abigail found a thick plastic bowl with a lid and poured soup into it, then set a cheese sandwich on top.

"*Danki*," Sadie said. As she headed for the mudroom, she added, "I appreciate the ideas, Asa. I think it will really help make the accounting more streamlined."

Asa beamed as Sadie left. He seemed genuinely flattered and more than a little surprised.

Then he turned to see her looking at him and got up from the chair. "We need to finish our conversation."

"*Ya*, we do." She crossed her arms over her chest. "Asa, we shouldn't see each other anymore."

〜

Every good emotion he'd felt at Sadie's compliments disappeared with Abigail's words. "What? That's not what I meant at all."

"I know. You said you wanted to be *mei* boyfriend. I don't want a boyfriend." She shrugged, as if what she said carried little weight.

But she wasn't looking at him and he knew she wasn't as casual as she was trying to be. "Why are you pushing me away?" Impatience entered his tone, but he was getting irritated. Before Sadie had interrupted him he was about to pour out his heart. He'd already given her half of it. He was about to tell her he loved her. That he wanted to marry her. It wasn't logical because they hadn't even had one date. But life wasn't always predictable and orderly. He was learning that lesson fast.

She faced him, her mouth drawn tight. "You must not be used to being rejected," she said, sounding snide and very much unlike herself.

"If you're trying to hurt me, you're doing a *gut* job." That honesty thing again. *This is getting old, Lord.*

Her features softened. "I'm sorry. I shouldn't have said that. I don't want to hurt you."

"Then don't act like *mei* feelings aren't important." He turned away from her and gripped the side of the counter. He'd been taught all his life not to be prideful. And he really thought he hadn't been. But chasing after Abigail Schrock was chipping away at his ego and he felt pain with each blow.

He felt her hand on his shoulder and he closed his eyes. He hadn't lost her after all. He turned and faced her, putting his hand over hers. When he came over today, he vowed not to get too close. She was like fire to him, both magnetic and dangerous.

The kiss they'd shared last week had been heady. Feeling her soft hand underneath his palm, he realized that no matter the blows to his ego, no matter how vulnerable he had to be, no matter how impulsive he was acting, he would do anything to spend the rest of his life with her.

"I don't understand you," she said, looking up at him with those chocolate-brown eyes he loved so much. "We don't know each other very well. We don't have anything in common." She let out a bitter chuckle. "I had *nee* idea what you and Sadie were talking about during lunch."

"I could teach you."

She shook her head. "I'm not interested in learning. Don't get me wrong. I respect *yer* knowledge. I know how smart you are." She bit her bottom lip. "A lot smarter than me."

His eyes widened. He'd never been called smart. Not by his parents, not by his teachers, not by his employers. He'd always done a good job and he'd been complimented on his work ethic. But *Asa Bontrager* and *smart* weren't used in the same sentence. "*Danki,*" he said, her compliment touching him almost as much as her kiss had.

"For what?"

He removed her hand from his shoulder but didn't release it. "*Nee* one has ever said I was smart before."

"I don't believe that."

"It's true." He sighed, barely aware that he was rubbing his thumb over part of her hand and that she wasn't pushing him away. "People always assume things come easy to me. They definitely don't." *Like loving you.* He gave her a rueful grin. "I've actually spent the past four years studying accounting. I read every book I could find on the subject. Back in Indiana I became friends with one of the bank officers and we would have lunch and talk about investments and . . . I know, you're not interested."

She squeezed his hand. "*Geh* on."

"When I was in Shipshe I mentioned to *mei* parents that I wanted to quit the factory and open *mei* own bookkeeping business. That was met with very little enthusiasm. *Mamm* was worried I wouldn't make enough money to support a family. *Daed* didn't understand why I was interested in 'all those numbers and stuff.' He said that was for smart people, and I was better off at the factory."

"That was insulting."

He was pleased she was indignant on his behalf, but he had to set her straight. "He wasn't insulting me. He was concerned about *mei* future. And to be honest, growing up it wasn't like I had *mei* nose in a book all the time."

"So school did come easy to you."

"Up to eighth grade, anyway. So I stayed at the factory. Security is very important to *mei* parents. It's why we went to Shipshe in the first place. *Daed* lost his job here. He had a *gut* job at the RV factory, and I had one too. He didn't want me losing that."

"Even though you don't want to do factory work."

"Sometimes what you want doesn't matter. Other times . . ." He couldn't finish the thought. He could only stare at her, lost in the beauty of her face, the way she made him feel as he told her something he'd never told anyone, not even Andrew. She made him feel safe. Respected. That she could look beyond his outer shell and see what was on the inside.

"Asa." She pulled her hand out of his. "There's *nix* keeping you from being an accountant. Sol was here earlier. He needs someone to keep his books. Maybe Andrew does too, and

Joanna. Her baked goods have been selling very well, better than *mei* rugs and the birdhouses." She smiled. "I'm sure you can find enough clients in Birch Creek to open *yer* own business."

"You think so?" Was this another reason God had wanted him to come to Birch Creek? So he could find the courage to pursue his true passion? He'd never put that together before, but here was Abigail, gently pushing him in that direction.

"Absolutely. You should do what you want to do. What you're called to do. Life is too short not to." Her voice softened to a sweet, melancholy lilt. "You never know when you might lose the chance. Or never have the chance at all."

He knew she was thinking about her parents. He reached out to touch her again, but when she tried to pull away, he held on to her hand and closed the space between them.

"What are you doing?" Her eyes grew round with surprise.

"Taking *mei* chances." He brushed her cheek with the back of his hand. He loved the softness of her face, her sweet roundness. "I was serious about what I said before. I want to be *yer*"—he almost messed up and said husband, but he caught himself in time—"boyfriend. And before you say we don't know each other or we don't have anything in common, I'm telling you we do. We can get to know each other better and we can start by me taking you home from church on Sunday."

"I don't want a boyfriend." But she sounded less sure now. And she wasn't moving away from him.

"You already told me that. Now tell me to *mei* face that you don't feel anything when we're together." He lowered his voice to almost a whisper. "That the kiss we shared meant *nix* to you. Tell me that, and I'll walk away right now."

∞

Asa was good. He was really good. Her heart was in her throat as he looked at her, still holding her hand, her cheek tingling from where he had touched her. His gray eyes were once again at half-mast, his smile confident without being cocky. She would have found all this endearing and amusing if she wasn't scared to death.

"I . . ." He was right. She couldn't lie and say there was nothing between them, that she hadn't felt the connection even though it didn't make any sense. "I can't tell you that."

His grin widened, but she didn't feel any better. Six months ago she'd been ready and eager to marry Joel. Now she was kissing someone else, completely forgetting that Joel even existed. That had to be wrong.

"We're meant to be together, Abigail," Asa said.

"How do you know?"

"Because . . ." Something passed over his expression, something she couldn't decipher. Then it cleared and he brought her hand to his chest, flattening her palm against his heart. "I feel it. Here."

She felt it too. The thrumming of his heartbeat, as if he'd run a race. A person couldn't fake that kind of reaction. She knew it because her heart was beating in the same frantic rhythm.

"We'll take everything slow." He moved her hand from his chest and stood back. "We can start with a ride home Sunday afternoon. Maybe a rematch of Dutch Blitz one evening next week."

His promise made her relax a bit. Slow. She liked that idea. She also liked the idea of spending time with him doing something fun, like playing cards. "You're ready to lose again?" she said, this time not bothering to mask her smile.

"*Nee*. I'm ready to win."

There was a double meaning to his words. But before she

could agree to anything, she had to be clear. "I can't let *mei* heart get broken again."

"Your heart is safe with me," he said with absolute seriousness. "I promise."

Joel had promised her too. But Asa wasn't Joel. Asa made her feel more than Joel ever had, and she wanted to hold on to this feeling forever. Which was why she couldn't bear it if he rejected her.

You never know when you might lose the chance.

She needed to take her own advice. "All right," she said. "One ride home from church, and one rematch of Dutch Blitz. That's all I'm agreeing to."

He grinned and grabbed his hat. "That's enough. I'll see you Sunday."

After he left she sat down at the table, hoping she had made the right decision.

CHAPTER 17

W hat's wrong, Irene?" *Mamm* said. "You don't seem *yerself*
tonight."

Irene sat at the kitchen table finishing off the last of Abigail's
rugs. Abigail did most of the weaving, and then Irene bound the
ends so they wouldn't unravel. But her thoughts weren't on the
rugs. She was thinking about Sol. Since that day they'd smeared
each other with paint, he had been withdrawn and almost mute
whenever she showed up for work, as if nothing had happened
between them. But she remembered the way he'd looked at
her, his eyes filled with attraction and yearning. She had seen
a glimpse of the real Solomon Troyer. A guy who liked to have
fun, who liked to tease . . . and who was so broken and lonely he
made her heart hurt.

But she had felt something else when she allowed herself to
touch his cheek, feeling the scratch of his short, russet-colored
whiskers, seeing the small scar below his left eye that she hadn't
noticed before. Sol needed her. She was sure of that, just as she
was sure he wouldn't hurt her, at least not on purpose. And in

that moment she realized that she needed him too. His kindness, his steady loyalty to his mother and brother, his desire to be a better man. She needed someone like him in her life.

And then he left, basically dismissing her and running away like a wounded animal, leaving her confused about what to do next. She'd been pondering over it for the past two weeks, and things between them were at an impasse. "I'm fine," she said, focusing on stitching the last of the rug together, not wanting to talk about this with her mother—or anyone else.

Mamm sat down next to her. "You'll excuse me if I don't believe you."

Irene set down the sewing and sighed. "I'm not a *gut* liar."

"Which is a wonderful thing." *Mamm* smiled. "Do you want some tea?"

"*Nee.*" She wasn't hungry or thirsty. "I need to get this rug done. I don't want to get behind on *mei* work for Abigail."

"So you can focus on working for Sol."

Irene kept her head down and picked up the sewing again. But when she started stitching, she pricked her finger. "Ouch!" She dropped the needle and put her finger to her mouth.

Mamm leaned back in her chair and looked at Irene, her eyes serious behind her silver-framed glasses. "Are you sure you're going to be okay working with him?"

Irene pulled her finger away. "Why wouldn't I be?"

"I don't know. You seem . . . unsettled. Especially when I mentioned him." The corners of *Mamm*'s mouth turned down slightly. "Is there something going on between you two?"

Irene knew she couldn't lie to her mother. "I don't know."

Mamm's brow shot up. "Irene, if I had known you and Sol had problems I never would have suggested—"

"It's not what you think," Irene said, raising her hand. "I'll admit, there was a time I liked him. Before he was put into the bann."

"You did?"

"*Ya*. I was attracted to him." *I'm still attracted to him.* She shrugged, trying to be casual. "He is very *schee*."

"But Irene, he was so troubled."

"I didn't realize that at the time. Or maybe I did and had blinders on."

Mamm nodded. "If anyone can understand what that's like, it's me."

"I didn't know everything about him, though. And what he confessed in church . . . I was shocked. And I promised myself I would stay away from him."

"Then I *geh* pushing you two together."

"I'm glad you did." She leaned forward, her sore finger forgotten. "You were right. Sol does need someone to reach out to him. He has changed. And he's trying to do better."

"But?" *Mamm* asked.

Irene sat back in the chair. Dare she admit out loud what she had barely acknowledged in her mind? "The past is still there," she said quietly. "What he did . . . who he was. That's a part of him."

"And you're afraid of that."

"I'm not afraid of him."

"You're not afraid of the man he is now."

"*Nee*. I'm not. But he keeps pushing me away."

"Probably because he thinks that's the right thing to do."

"What if it isn't? What if *Daed* had pushed you away? What would you have done?"

She paused. "I would have stood by him," she said quietly.

Irene nodded. "Just like you are now." She paused. "How did you handle what *Daed* did?"

"You mean dealing drugs?" *Mamm* picked up a stray piece of thread off the table. "Not very well. I was angry. Really angry. We had just gotten married and he had joined the church. I had already joined the previous year."

"So you didn't know what he was doing?"

She looked at Irene for a long moment. "*Ya,*" she said softly. "I knew. Not exactly what was going on, but he was secretive. And he seemed to have more money than he should have from working for his family's bicycle repair business. Yet I never questioned him about it. I was young and in love. When you care about someone, you can be blind to the truth."

"When did you find out what he was really doing?"

"When I was pregnant with you. He confessed everything. He said that now that we were going to have a *familye,* he had to put that part of his life behind him. He quit the gang he'd been involved in, and said he was never going to sell drugs again. And I believed him. But then there was the day Andrew was eleven and you were thirteen . . ." She got up from the table and went to the counter. "I don't feel right telling you these things, Irene. Your father isn't here to defend himself. He's also not that man anymore."

"How do you know? How do you know he's been faithful to you while he's been away?" She shouldn't press, but she needed answers. For a good part of her life she had thought her father was one man, only to discover he was different. "How are you sure he hasn't decided to forget about us and move on with his life?"

"Because of his letters. If he had . . . if *yer vatter* had moved on from us, he wouldn't still be writing them. He takes a risk with every letter he sends." She folded a dish towel and placed it next to the sink before turning to face Irene. "But even if he didn't write, even if I never heard from him again, I have faith in him."

"Why?"

"Because I have to." She sat back down. "When you love somebody, you take the *gut* with the bad. Even though Bartholomew made mistakes, that didn't mean he was a bad man. When he was arrested he had confessed his sin to the bishop. Not to the entire church, because he didn't want them to be involved. If they knew what he'd done, then the gang of drug dealers might go after them. But he made his confession. He's paying the consequences for his mistakes."

"So are we."

Mamm's gaze misted. "*Ya.* And I'm sorry about that. I know *yer vatter* is too. It might be hard to believe, but I know this has strengthened us. The hardship on the family, it's made all of us stronger and more connected." She wiped her finger underneath her nose. "I can't tell you what to do about Sol. I just knew in *mei* heart that while *yer daed* was troubled, he was *gut* deep inside. And when we were together he proved that to me. You do have some *gut* memories of him, *ya*?"

Irene felt tears well up in her eyes. "*Ya.*" She remembered how her father used to walk with her on the beach and they'd look for seashells. Or they'd watch the gulls as they soared and dove into the ocean. Irene had been mesmerized by their graceful flight and could have watched them all day. *Daed* had never rushed her, never said, "Okay, that's enough." He let her watch them until she was ready to go. Then he would pick her up in his arms and carry her on his shoulders. She'd felt invincible when he did that, like she could touch the birds, or even the clouds if she wanted to.

"I love you, Irene," he would say, at least once a day, if not more. Which was why it had hurt so much when he left, when she thought he had chosen another woman over her mother. The pain was still there now that she knew the truth, but it was a different pain. A longing to see him again. "I do have *gut* memories."

"Then hang on to them, like I do."

Irene's eyes stung with tears. "If you had it to do all over again, would you marry *Daed*? Knowing what you know now?"

Her mother looked down at her lap for a long moment, so long that Irene was suddenly afraid of the answer. When *Mamm* finally looked up, she said, "*Ya*. I'd do it all over again. Not only because *yer vatter* gave me you and Andrew, but because I love him."

Breathing out a relieved sigh, Irene nodded. "I understand."

"I'm glad you do. Irene, pray about Sol, and *yer* feelings for him. Ask God what he wants from you, and what you should do. After knowing the truth about him and his past, you wouldn't have these feelings for him if there wasn't a reason. You have a kind heart. You need to let God lead it." *Mamm* rose from the chair and left the kitchen.

Irene tried to resume her sewing, but pricked her fingers several more times as her thoughts about her father and Sol melded together. When she finally finished the last stitch, she folded the rug and put it in the living room.

She went upstairs and readied for bed. Before she got under the covers she sank to her knees, and she prayed—for Sol and for her father.

Bartholomew walked out of work that evening, his back sore from working the twelve-hour shift. He would pick up another twelve hours tomorrow working for one of his coworkers who had a wedding to attend. "That's Jack," the man said to another one of their coworkers as he pointed to Bartholomew. "Always ready to help a guy out."

He reached his car and bent backward, hearing the crack in his lower torso. He inserted the key in the lock.

"Jack."

Bartholomew jumped at the sound of Mike's voice. He turned to see the federal marshal looking at him, his lantern-jawed face the sternest Bartholomew had ever seen it. "What are you doing here?" he asked, a knot forming in the pit of his stomach.

"We need to talk."

The knot turned into a cold, dead lump. His keys hit the ground. "Did something happen to Naomi? To my kids?"

"No," Mike said. "Not yet." He scrubbed his hand over his face. "How could you be so stupid?"

"What are you talking about?"

"We know you've been in contact with your wife."

Bartholomew stilled. How did they know? He and Naomi had been so careful—

"It has to stop." Mike looked at him, the anger sliding from his face. He blew out a long breath. "Hey, man, I'm sorry. I get it. I'm married too, you know. If I had to cut off contact with Marley . . . I don't know what I'd do. But you know what you signed up for. You agreed to stay in witness protection to keep your family safe. You've been putting them in jeopardy."

"I don't see how a few letters could do that."

"Because you underestimate your enemy. Their network is wide and they will never forget your betrayal. Until we have all the major players in custody, you're a marked man. Do you want that target on your wife and kids?"

Bartholomew slumped against the car. "You know I don't."

"Then we're clear. No more letters."

Bartholomew swallowed. "But—"

"Glad we cleared that up." Then he paused. "We want this to be over as much as you do."

I doubt that. Mike turned around and left.

His feet refusing to move, Bartholomew stared at Mike as he walked away. The parking lot was beginning to clear as workers left for home. They were going home to their spouses. Their children.

I need my freedom. He'd never wanted it more than he did now. But he would only get it in God's time. He knew that. He had to accept it. But he was losing patience. And now he'd lost the only thing that had kept his patience from evaporating altogether. How could he go on without any contact with Naomi? *How am I going to tell her?*

When he was finally able to move, he picked up his keys and drove home. A short while later he was in his bedroom, staring at a pad of paper, a pen in his hand. Anger over his circumstances had diminished long ago, mostly due to his continued connection with Naomi. How long could he keep the fury at bay now that he couldn't contact her anymore?

He stared at the paper. This would be the hardest letter he would ever write. But Mike was right. He couldn't put his family at risk anymore, even if it meant cutting them off completely. Wiping the tears from his eyes, his heart broke as he put pen to paper. *You are the love of my life . . .*

CHAPTER 18

Asa kept his distance before church service Sunday morning, and Abigail couldn't decide if that was a good or bad thing. Despite telling herself that Asa taking her home from church wasn't a big deal, she had taken a little extra time getting ready that morning, enough that she had kept Sadie and Aden waiting. She still found herself wanting to wish ten pounds away before she got to church, despite Asa telling her he liked her the way she was. That didn't seem possible, since she didn't like herself the way she was.

She tried to be detached from him during the service, but her gaze kept straying to the men's side of the Yutzys' barn. Right before the hymns started she saw him, sitting next to Andrew. And for the next three hours she kept her mind and gaze on him instead of on God and worship.

When Bishop Yoder started the prayer, Abigail closed her eyes and tried to focus on being in God's presence. But she failed. She hadn't focused on God in the past few months, not since her parents' accident. There had been too many distractions, and right now Asa was a big one.

"Abigail," Joanna said, as everyone else rose from the benches at the conclusion of the service. "Andrew and I would like for you to come for supper tomorrow night. I haven't seen you in so long. I've missed you."

Pushing her guilt out of her mind about not visiting Joanna, Abigail replied. "I've missed you too."

Joanna paused. "Do you mind if Asa's there?"

"Why would I mind?" Abigail said, a bit too quickly.

"I didn't want you to think we're setting you up with him. I know you're still trying to get over Joel."

Abigail pinched her lips together. She needed to tell Joanna what was going on with her and Asa. Maybe talking to her sister would help her make sense of it. If she was doing the wrong thing, Joanna would let her know. She was about to say something when Asa came up next to them. "You ready?" he said after telling Joanna hello.

"Uh, *ya*." She met Joanna's surprised look. "Asa's taking me home."

"I see." Joanna's brow lifted, along with the corner of her mouth. "We'll talk tomorrow night, *ya*?"

Abigail nodded. "Definitely."

After Joanna walked away, Asa asked, "What was that about?"

"*Nix*. We should get going."

Asa led her to the buggy and she climbed in, aware that a few people were looking at them with curious eyes. *Let them wonder*, she thought. She was tired of worrying about other people's opinions. She glanced at Asa. He didn't seem concerned at all that people were seeing him take her home. In doing so they were basically announcing that they were seeing each other.

He turned to her and grinned. "Mind if I take the long way home? Unless it's too cold for you today."

"It's fine." Now that it was the end of March, the weather had turned mild. This didn't mean bad weather was over. They would probably have a few more spring snows before warm weather set in for good. But this morning was perfect for a drive.

He pulled out of the Yutzys' driveway. "If you get too cold, you can always move a little closer to me. I don't bite, at least not usually."

That made her chuckle. "I'll keep that in mind."

Asa kept his horse at a steady but slow trot as they made their way to her house. He started the conversation off by asking her what her favorite color was, and from there they continued to talk for the next twenty minutes. She learned Asa's favorite color was blue, which didn't surprise her. His favorite food did—chili spaghetti.

"I never thought about putting chili on spaghetti," she said.

"You've never had chili with macaroni?"

"*Ya*, but not spaghetti."

"It's pasta. Same thing."

"*Nee*. Spaghetti is a lot different."

"True. And chili spaghetti is only good when it's topped off with cheddar cheese and diced onion."

"Remind me not to kiss you after you eat that."

He gave her a sly look. "In that case, forget the onions." He tapped the reins on the back of his horse, and the mare quickened her step. There wasn't much traffic on the road this morning. "So what's *yer* favorite food?"

"I don't know if I have a favorite. I just have foods I don't like."

"Such as?"

"Believe it or not, I don't like pickles."

His brow lifted as if she'd just told him she'd gone skydiving last summer. "That can't be possible. How can you be Amish and not like pickles?"

"I guess I'm the only Amish woman who doesn't. I don't like pickled anything."

"Pickled eggs?"

"Nope."

"Pickled beets?"

She wrinkled her nose. "Yuck."

"Pickled pigs' feet?"

"Definitely not." She looked at him. "Please tell me you don't like them either."

"Never had them. They could replace chili spaghetti as the best food in the world."

She folded her hands in her lap. "I highly doubt it."

They talked about more mundane topics, but Asa's charm and humor made them interesting. By the time he turned down her street, she was surprised how fast the ride had gone.

"So are *yer* parents coming to visit you soon?" Abigail asked.

Asa didn't say anything right away. That made her look at him, and she noticed he'd stiffened. "*Nee*," he said. "I don't think so."

"Do you keep in touch with them?" She realized that other than telling her about them wanting him to work in the factory, he hadn't said anything about his life in Shipshewana.

"Not really."

She wanted to ask him more. Like how his sisters were doing. Her curiosity was piqued, but they had turned into her driveway. What had made him return to Birch Creek? She turned, but he wasn't looking at her. When she looked at him, the ease in his expression disappeared. Had she said something wrong?

"Still on for Dutch Blitz?" he said, suddenly snapping out of whatever trance he was in.

"Of course. I'll be at Joanna's tomorrow night for supper."

"What a coincidence." He flashed her a smile. "So will I."

Did he have any idea how his smile changed his face from handsome to almost unbearably good-looking? But she knew there was more to Asa than his good looks, and she was finding the man underneath the handsomeness to be even more appealing.

"I'll see you tomorrow night, then," he said.

She nodded. "*Danki* for the ride."

"Anytime, Abigail. I mean that."

She looked at him for a long moment. "I know."

Asa waited until Abigail went inside her house. When the door shut behind her, he leaned back in the seat and blew out a long breath. That was close. When she asked him about his family, that had made him think about Susanna. He had to tell Abigail about her, and soon.

This was also the first time she'd asked him questions about Shipshewana. He should have prepared for it. But he'd spent so long blocking out his life there, trying to come to terms with what he had to leave behind. Shipshe represented pain and loss. Abigail represented comfort. And love.

As he had driven her home, he realized God was right in bringing Abigail to Asa's attention. He loved her wit, the way she didn't hesitate to give him a hard time, the ease with which they talked. There had been times during his relationship with Susanna that conversation had ground to a halt, and Asa had searched for something to say. It wasn't comfortable silence, like he'd had with Abigail during part of the ride home. Now he knew without a doubt that he and Susanna would have never worked out. She would have been a decent wife, mostly because she was eager to please. And while there was no spark between them, they were friends. Some friendships did make good marriages, but he wasn't satisfied with only "good." Abigail would be the best wife for him. *God, you know what you're doing.*

He smiled as he drove home. After he took care of his horse he went inside to spend the rest of the day resting. Or taking a nap. He was tired. He hadn't slept well the last two nights, thinking about Abigail. She'd given him a chance and he didn't want to mess it up.

He collapsed on the couch, one he'd bought secondhand last week so if anyone came over—like Abigail—she would have a place to sit down other than the rocking chair. He still hadn't touched the upstairs of his house, but he was ready to start working on it again. He was also seriously considering the idea of starting a bookkeeping business. Her confidence in him gave him confidence in himself. There were lingering doubts, though. Could he get enough clients to quit his job at the plastics factory? Could he successfully pursue a dream his family had dismissed? Did he have the courage to do it?

Asa turned on his side, his back to the back of the couch, and started to close his eyes. His gaze landed on the stack of letters on the floor a few feet away. There were five of them now, two from Susanna and three from his mother. He should have opened them. While he had felt a yearning for Shipshe shortly after he left, that had disappeared. He was focused on life here, not in Indiana, and he didn't want his old life to interrupt that. But he had put it off long enough. "Tomorrow," he said as he closed his eyes. He'd deal with the letters tomorrow night—after he beat Abigail at Dutch Blitz.

∾

When Irene arrived at Sol's Monday morning, his workshop was locked. She frowned. Well, she wasn't going to give up so easily. After praying not only on Friday night, but Saturday night and Sunday too, she was more sure than before that she and Sol were meant to be together. The hard part would be convincing him. Of course, she couldn't do that if he kept shutting her out.

She went to the house and knocked on the door, hugging her arms around her body. The day was cloudless but still cold, even though it was almost April. Winter seemed to stretch on endlessly this year. She shifted from one foot to the other, and then the door finally opened.

"Hello, Irene," Sol's mother, Rhoda, said.

"Hi. Is Sol here?"

"He's not in the shop?"

"*Nee*. It's locked."

"He might have stepped out to run an errand or something." But she didn't sound too convinced.

Irene wasn't convinced either. With the meticulous way Sol had cared for his mother since his father left, she doubted he would have run an errand without telling her first.

His mother's smile slipped a bit. "He probably went to the sawmill. He usually goes there once a week. Would you like to come inside and wait for him?"

Irene was a bit surprised at the invitation. She met Rhoda's eyes and saw something familiar in them. Loneliness. She was as lonely as her son. Irene's heart went out to her, but she had a feeling Sol wasn't at the sawmill. "I appreciate the invitation, and I'd like to take you up on it some other time."

"Sure," Rhoda said. "You're welcome to drop by anytime you like."

"I will." She bit her bottom lip. "Do you know if there's someplace else Sol might be? Somewhere he might go if he wants to, uh, think? Or be alone?"

Rhoda held on to the side of the door but didn't answer her right away. Irene wondered if she had crossed an imaginary line with the question until Rhoda said, "He might be in the barn."

Irene nodded and Rhoda closed the door. Her palms grew damp as she headed for the barn, nerves swirling in her stomach. She had no idea what she would say to him. *We belong together* didn't seem like an appropriate conversation starter.

She stilled her steps a few feet from the barn. Was she doing the right thing? Last night during her prayers she had believed she was. Now doubt was creeping in. Sol was complicated. There was no guarantee that if they were together he wouldn't fall into old habits and leave her. Perhaps he couldn't even promise that. But she had to have faith that he wouldn't. She had to have faith in him, the way her mother had faith in her father. *Lord, guide me.* Then she entered the barn.

Sol was in the corner of the barn on his knees, his forearms resting on a square hay bale, his head down. Was he praying? She watched him for a moment and realized that he was. Not wanting to intrude, she backed away, only to run into the barn doorframe. The harnesses that hung on the wall rattled and Sol looked up.

"I-I'm sorry." Irene held up her hands. "I didn't mean to bother you."

He turned to her, then slowly got to his feet. Pieces of hay clung to his knees. "It's okay."

"*Yer* workshop wasn't open, so . . . ." There was something about the way he was looking at her that halted her speech. His green eyes were stormy, almost tortured looking, and his brow was flattened above them, the wrinkles in his forehead deep and evident. "Sol? Are you okay?"

He shook his head. "*Nee*, Irene. I'm not."

She went to him. "What's wrong? How can I help?"

But he stepped away from her. "You can't help me. *Nee* one can."

"Sol, talk to me."

He started to pace, his hands fisting at his sides as if he were fighting some inner battle. All she could do was wait until he settled down. After a few minutes he stood in front of her. "I'm an alcoholic," he said.

"You used to be."

Shaking his head he said, "It doesn't work that way. I'll always be an alcoholic. It's part of who I am. And I struggle every day not to drink."

"Then you're keeping sober. That takes a lot of strength."

"I wonder if I'm strong enough," he muttered.

She couldn't resist moving toward him, even though he was making it clear he didn't want her near him. "You're strong, Sol. And with God's help, you'll be stronger."

He looked down at her. "You're so steady, Irene. So sweet."

"Not always," she said with a small smile. "Just ask Andrew."

But he remained serious. "I can see myself falling for you. Falling hard." He placed his fist over his heart. "There's something missing here, and when you're with me . . . it doesn't hurt so much."

Irene reached for him but he sidestepped her. "Don't," he said.

"Don't what? Care for you? Because it's too late for that, Solomon Troyer. You said you could fall for me, but I've already fallen for you."

"You'll change *yer* mind when I tell you the truth." He licked his lips.

"I'll be the judge of that." She stood in front of him, determined not to let him avoid her. "You're not the only one with secrets." Her heart squeezed in her chest. "You're not the only one in pain."

Sol couldn't move, even if he wanted to. Tears shimmered in Irene's beautiful eyes. How selfish could he be? He'd been so involved in his own problems, his own hurt feelings, that he hadn't thought that she might be going through a difficult time. She was always so positive, so upbeat. But she was right. She had a painful past with her father too. She had been abandoned. And even though it had been years ago, that kind of betrayal didn't disappear, not completely. "Irene, I'm sorry. I'm—"

"Shhh." She put her finger to his lips. His horse started munching on grain, the grinding sound filling the barn. "*Nee* one is beyond forgiveness, not even you. And what I'm about to tell you . . . you can't say a word to anyone. Promise me you won't."

He nodded. "I promise."

"*Mei* father used to be a drug dealer," she said, moving away from him and going to the hay bale. She sat down and looked up at him. "He never left *mei mamm* for another woman. That was a story *mei* parents created to keep us safe. Instead he was arrested and had to be put in witness protection."

Sol's eyes widened. "Why?"

"Because he had been in so deep with a drug gang in Florida that he could be killed. Or they would come after his *familye*." She sighed. "I haven't seen or heard from him since I was thirteen. That's why we moved to Birch Creek. To stay safe. I didn't know any of this until a few months ago. The entire time I thought he'd left *Mamm* for someone else. And I always wondered why she never said one ill word about him." She shrugged, looking down at her lap and threading her fingers together. "He turned our lives upside down. He broke *mei* heart. I haven't admitted this to anyone, not even to *Mamm*. I was ashamed of him, angry with him. But I also thought it was *mei* fault."

He sat down next to her. "Why would you think that?"

"I thought he left because of me. That I had done something wrong. That if I'd been a better daughter he would have stayed."

"Now you know that wasn't true."

"*Ya*, I know that now. But it's hard to get that out of *mei* head because I believed it for so long." She finally looked at him. "Even when I found out the truth I was still mad—I still am mad sometimes. He did something stupid and he broke the law. Because of his choices, we all suffered, especially *Mamm*."

"I had *nee* idea."

"*Nee* one does. And now you know why it has to remain a secret. *Daed* is somewhere, though I don't know where. *Mamm* doesn't even know. And until it's safe we won't know. He can't come back to us until then. But *Mamm* is sure in her heart that he will come back someday."

Like mei mamm. Sol doubted his mother would ever give up on his father. She, like Naomi Beiler, would be faithful to him until the end.

"Meanwhile, *Mamm*'s had to make peace with him being gone. To be at peace with raising two kids by herself, and dealing with everyone thinking her husband left her for someone else. I miss him," she whispered. "I know now that what he did had *nix* to do with me. But I also hurt. I hurt for *mei mamm*, for *mei bruder*." She sniffed. "*Mamm* forgave him. She loves him and she continues to forgive. I've forgiven him too. One day I hope I can tell him in person, so he knows that even though I'm angry and hurt, I still love him. I always will."

Sol nodded. He understood her contradictory emotions. He was furious with his father, not only for the past, but also for running away like a coward. But some part of him still loved his dad. It didn't make any sense, and he wasn't to the point where he could forgive *Daed* the way Irene had forgiven her father. He wondered if he ever would be.

"Sol, I'm telling you all this for a reason." She angled her body toward him. "*Nee* matter what you've done, there's always forgiveness. Especially when you've truly repented, and when you've taken responsibility for the past. *Mei vatter* is doing that right now. He's paying for his sins, but that doesn't mean they haven't been forgiven."

He couldn't keep himself from touching her. He thumbed away a stray tear and felt her stiffen. When he started to move his hand away, she held it to her cheek.

"I've liked you for a long time, Sol. Sometimes it was hard, when you were being cocky."

"When I was drinking," he said.

"*Ya*." She nodded, letting go of his hand. "But I've always known there was something deeper in you. A kind, genuine heart just waiting to be freed. I still believe that."

He leaned his forehead against hers. "Irene," he whispered, his voice husky and thick. "I wish I could believe that about myself."

"You can." She cupped his face in both her hands and looked

at him, their foreheads still touching. "You are forgiven, Sol. You asked for forgiveness in church that day. That wasn't just for our benefit. Or even for God's. It was for *yers* as well."

"But how can he forgive me for what I've done?" He pulled away from her, then turned his back to her. She could say this to him now, but she didn't know everything. She didn't know how black his heart had been.

"Sol, you can't box in God's grace. You can't assume that he's not going to forgive even the worst sin—"

"I beat *mei bruder.*" He blurted out his deepest secret, the one that would convince her he wasn't the man she thought he was. He faced her, his tone flat and emotionless. "I'm not only an alcoholic and a thief. I'm also an abuser. I used to beat him all the time when we were young . . . and not so young."

Her eyes widened. "What?"

"I'd probably still be that same man today. I wouldn't be hitting Aden, though. He wouldn't put up with that anymore. And he shouldn't. But I'd find another victim, another person to take *mei* anger out on. Only God put an end to it. He showed me who I really was. Broken. Dark." He swallowed. "Then he brought me back. Gave me a second chance." His lower lip trembled. He hated showing this weakness, especially to Irene. But he had to tell her everything, including his shame. "But what if I don't have the strength to fight that darkness?"

"You're not fighting it alone," she said, her voice shaking.

"I know." He gripped the edge of the hay bale, sharp strands of hay digging into his palms. "But what if God decides I'm not worth it? If he . . . abandons me?"

"Oh, Sol. He won't."

"I could mess up again. I could take the second chance he's given me and blow it."

"And then he will forgive you again. We're not perfect. You'll make mistakes, just like everyone else. But it won't be the kind you're thinking of. God has changed you, Sol. He's made you into the man you were meant to be."

His eyes burned. "You don't know how much I want that to be true."

"Believe it, Sol. All you have to do is believe."

CHAPTER 19

Monday evening Abigail fought a steady stream of nerves as she turned her horse and buggy into Joanna and Andrew's driveway. She'd dreamed about Asa last night. She could only remember snippets of the dream, but when she woke up she felt good. All day she had thought of him, enough that she had made several mistakes finishing up one of the rag rugs and she had to remake it. Despite the weather having cooled down today, her hands were slick as she held the horse's reins. Butterflies danced in her stomach. Or more like crashed into one another. As she pulled to a halt by the barn and hitched her horse to the rail, she couldn't deny that she was giddy with anticipation over seeing Asa tonight.

She took the corn casserole from the spot next to her on the seat. It was one of the few dishes she could make adequately. She didn't even bother coming up with a dessert, knowing Joanna would make something spectacular. A slight breeze swirled around her as she went to the front door and knocked. It was only four thirty. She was early. Asa probably wasn't even there yet. But she couldn't wait to get there.

Joanna opened the door and smiled as she let Abigail in. She took the casserole from her. "Smells *appeditlich*."

Abigail took off her coat and hung it nearby. As she suspected, Asa wasn't there yet. Neither was Andrew, Naomi, or Irene. "Andrew usually doesn't get home until after five. And Naomi and Irene went to the Yoders' for supper tonight."

Abigail nodded. "So it's just the four of us?"

Joanna pulled out a baking tray with fluffy yeast rolls. "*Ya*." She glanced at Abigail. "Is that all right?"

More than all right. But Abigail said nonchalantly, "It's fine." She caught Joanna's expression, and Abigail didn't bother to deny it. "I know what you're thinking."

"You do?" Joanna asked, the picture of innocence.

"That there's something going on with me and Asa."

"Is there?"

Abigail sat down at the table, smiling freely now. "I think so." She remembered the way Asa had looked at her before she got out of his buggy yesterday. "*Ya*. Definitely so."

Joanna went to Abigail and hugged her. "I'm so happy for you." Then she pulled back. "As long as this is what you want."

Abigail's smile dimmed. "I think it is." She looked at Joanna. "I'm scared, though."

"That you'll get hurt again?"

Abigail nodded.

"Asa's a *gut* guy. He always has been."

"I thought Joel was a *gut* guy too."

Joanna didn't respond right away. She was about to open her mouth to speak when Andrew walked in from the back of the house. He looked like he'd taken a shower. "Got home early," he said, going to Joanna. He put his hand on her shoulder. "Hi," he said softly, his mouth close to her ear.

"Hi *yerself.*" She smiled, a different smile, more radiant than the one she'd given Abigail.

Andrew looked at Abigail. "I hear we're doing a rematch of the Dutch Blitz game."

"*Ya.* Prepare to lose."

Andrew laughed. "I never knew you were so competitive."

Joanna set the rolls in a basket on the table. "She's always been that way. Don't you remember volleyball games at school?"

Abigail leaned back in the chair and folded her arms across her chest. "Nothing wrong with healthy competition."

"You spiked the ball in *mei* face, if I recall," Andrew said. "I knew you were tough at volleyball. I just didn't realize it extended to all games."

"I play to win," she said.

"So do I."

Abigail turned around as Asa walked into the kitchen. He came from the front of the house and she hadn't heard him knock. He flashed her a bone-melting smile. How had she resisted him this long? The bigger question was why. Nothing stood in the way of them dating but her own fear.

Abigail smirked at him as he sat down next to her at the table. Andrew and Joanna joined them, and they bowed their heads in silent prayer. Nearly an hour later, after supper was finished and the dishes washed, Joanna brought out the cards and tossed them on the table. But she and Andrew didn't sit down.

"You're not joining us?" Asa asked, his brow furrowed.

Shaking his head, Andrew said, "*Nee.* I'm not up for a blood bath. I didn't get much sleep last night."

"Me either," Joanna said.

But Abigail realized her sister wasn't looking at either of them, and Andrew looked anything but tired. When she glanced at Asa, he winked. They both knew Joanna and Andrew had planned to leave them alone. Abigail realized she didn't mind that at all.

"Not very subtle," Asa said, after they left.

"Not one bit." Abigail grabbed the cards, took them out of the box, and started to sort them. Then she paused, a stab of uncertainty flowing through her. "Do you mind that they left?"

He shook his head. "Do you?"

She hesitated, then shook her head. That made his eyes darken to near charcoal. The cards flipped out of her hand.

"Here. Let me help." He reached for a card at the same time she did, and instead of taking the card, he took her hand. He lifted their hands until both their elbows were on the table, then he locked his fingers with hers. "Maybe it wasn't a *gut* idea to be left alone," he said, his voice low and almost a whisper.

She couldn't respond. She glanced at their hands together. His long, lean fingers sandwiched between her shorter, chubbier ones. He leaned forward and pressed a kiss on one of her fingers, then released her hand.

"We should start the game," he said, not taking his eyes off her.

"Um, *ya*. We should." She didn't make a move to pick up the cards, though. Her finger still tingled from the tiny kiss, her heart thumping again.

Then he stood up and went around to the table. "Come here," he said, taking her hand.

She rose, and he led her to the living room, then to the small alcove underneath the stairs. He had to bend down a bit so he wouldn't hit his head, and the space was tight for the both of them.

Now her heart was thumping for a different reason. Although Joanna and Andrew clearly knew and approved of Abigail and Asa as a couple, Abigail didn't want her sister finding them in this compromising position.

Asa didn't say anything. He touched the side of her *kapp* with his palm, then traced his thumb over the top of her cheek. "I'm sorry," he said, although he didn't sound the least bit sorry. "I promised myself I wasn't going to do this."

"Do what?"

He put his hands on her hips and looked into her eyes. She refused to think about how wide her hips were, or have any other negative thoughts about her body. *He likes me the way I am.*

"This," he said, then kissed her. It was a quick kiss, but filled with meaning and promise. "I can't help myself."

She knew the feeling. More than anything she wanted him to kiss her again, longer this time, never letting go. She put her arms around his neck, feeling his thick hair brush the back of her hands. "We've got a game to play," she said.

"We'll get back to it." He grinned. "But how about one more quick kiss? For luck."

"You'll need it."

"I meant for you."

A sharp knock on the front door forced them apart. Her hand flew to her chest in surprise. She and Asa stared at each other. When neither Joanna nor Andrew showed up, he said, "I guess I'll answer it," his voice sandpaper rough. He went to the door, straightened, then opened it. "*Mamm?*" he said.

Abigail moved from the alcove as she saw a short woman with the same gray eyes as Asa's throw her arms around him. "I knew when I didn't find you home you would be here."

Asa stepped back, withdrawing from her embrace. He didn't

look happy to see her. If anything, he looked alarmed. "What are you doing here?"

"Didn't you get *mei* letter?" She shook her head. "Of course you didn't. Because if you did you would have opened it, and you would have read that we were coming tonight."

"We?" he asked, his full dark brow furrowing.

"*Ya.*" The softness from his mother's eyes dimmed. "We." She called over her shoulder. "Susanna. Come on in. Asa's here."

Abigail watched as the most beautiful girl she'd ever seen walked through the front door.

Asa couldn't move as his mother and ex-fiancée walked into Andrew's house. His lips tingled from kissing Abigail, and his brain and heart reeled from the feelings she instilled in him. The haze was still clearing as *Mamm* started taking off her black bonnet.

"Our suitcases are on the front porch, Asa," *Mamm* said. "Bring them inside, would you, please? Is Naomi here?"

Still stunned, Asa couldn't respond. What were they doing here? Now he wished he would have read the letters. Then he would have been prepared for this visit. Better yet, he would have told them not to come.

"She's not here."

Asa turned at the sound of Abigail's voice. She looked bewildered as her gaze went from *Mamm* to Susanna.

"Oh." *Mamm* held her bonnet in her hands. "I was hoping we'd get to see her tonight. Tomorrow is another day. Asa, our suitcases, please?"

Asa gave Abigail another glance, then retrieved the suitcases. How long were they planning to stay? More important, why were they here? His mind whirred with what to say as he set the cases down in the Beilers' living room and shut the door.

Mamm was already moving to Abigail. "So nice to see you," she said, embracing Abigail with a less enthusiastic hug than he'd received. Then again, his mother had always hugged him as if she were about to squeeze the life out of him. "I'm so sorry about *yer* parents."

Abigail nodded. "*Danki.*" She kept looking at Susanna, who was standing near the door.

"Like I told you, Susanna, Asa and Andrew have always been inseparable. I knew he would be here if he wasn't home." She turned to Asa. "Where is Andrew?"

"In his part of the *haus.* With Joanna."

"Right. Naomi told me he was married." *Mamm* looked at Abigail. "I'm assuming that's why you're here. To visit *yer* sister."

Asa rubbed his forehead. He had a lot of explaining to do, especially to Abigail. "*Mamm*, why don't we *geh* back to *mei haus*?"

"But you haven't introduced Abigail to *yer* fiancée yet."

Asa's worst nightmare just occurred. He saw the color drain from Abigail's face.

"We're not engaged anymore," Susanna said quietly.

"Of course you are." *Mamm* brushed her off with her hand. "You've just had a little misunderstanding, that's all. Susanna, say hello to Abigail."

"Hi." She held out her hand, her voice as high and musical as ever. "I'm Susanna."

Abigail shook Susanna's hand, gaping at her blankly. "I'll be going now," she said in a monotone voice that made Asa's panic rise higher. This was a mess. A huge mess.

"Give Sadie our best, and our condolences," *Mamm* said. "I'm sure we'll be by the store sometime this week."

Abigail turned around and nodded, then took her coat and left through the front door.

Asa started to follow her. He had to explain . . . everything. He opened the door.

"Asa, where are you going?"

He turned and looked at his mother. He also had things to explain to her. And to Susanna, although he thought he'd already set everything straight with her before he left Shipshe.

"*Frau* Bontrager?" Andrew said as he came into the room.

"Andrew." His mother enveloped Andrew in a hug almost as tight as the one she'd given him. "It's *gut* to see you. Congratulations on the wedding. I'm sorry we couldn't be here for it."

Asa closed the door and gave Andrew a look. He'd invited his family? Asa hadn't known that.

"*Mei* mother understood," Andrew said, looking at Asa as he spoke.

Asa realized that Andrew hadn't known either. Naomi must have invited her. Which would have made sense, because the two women had been friends when they lived next door to each other. Not that Asa was thinking clearly about any of this. All he could think about was the devastation on Abigail's face. What he would say to her. How he would explain—

"Asa," Susanna said. "We need to—"

Joanna walked into the room that moment, gave Asa and Andrew one questioning look, then turned into the perfect hostess. While she made sure *Mamm* and Susanna were welcome and comfortable, Asa and Andrew went into the kitchen.

"What's going on?" Andrew said.

"I don't know." He shoved his hand through his hair. "I had *nee* idea they were coming." Which was his fault for not reading the letters. He could kick himself for that. "I don't have a place for them to stay, either." He explained the house situation.

Andrew nodded. "That's not a problem. We have room upstairs, so they can stay here." He smirked. "This place is turning into a regular hotel."

But Asa didn't find any of this funny. "I have to talk to Abigail. *Mamm* introduced Susanna as *mei* fiancée."

"I thought she wasn't anymore."

"She isn't. But I don't know if Abigail heard Susanna say that."

"You can take one of *mei* buggies. Joanna and I will get *yer mamm* and Susanna settled. Where should I tell them you went?"

Asa paused. A lie wouldn't be right. It wouldn't do any good either. "Tell them the truth. Tell them I went after Abigail."

CHAPTER 20

Abigail was numb as she drove home after leaving Asa, his mother, and his . . . fiancée. She couldn't believe it. He was engaged? This whole time he had a fiancée in Shipshe and he never said a word. Chased after her like he was unattached. No wonder he'd been cagey about his answers when she asked him about Indiana.

Her heart hurt, this time worse than any pain she'd felt other than the day she found out about her parents' deaths. It was as if blades were slicing her inside. How could he do this to her? How could he look at her with such passion, touch and kiss her with such . . . love?

But it wasn't love, any more than what Joel had felt for her was love. Lord, she was stupid. And desperate. Her head had known to stay away from Asa. Not to trust him. That he'd been too good to be true. He was probably even lying to her about never kissing anyone before her.

Her heart was just as stupid as it had always been.

In the dark of the road, all she could see was Susanna. She was stunning. Crystal blue eyes, large and round with endless eyelashes that were even longer than Asa's. Her complexion was flawless, almost translucent. And of course she was tiny. Everything about her was petite, graceful, and perfect.

Everything Abigail wasn't.

She wanted to cry. She needed to cry, but she couldn't. She was too angry. Too mad at herself for being a fool, for falling for Asa's charm and looks and smooth talking.

When she reached the house, she took hold of the reins and guided the horse back to the barn. She lit the lantern, put the horse up, then shut the door to his stall. She leaned her head on the rough wood, wishing she could crawl into a hole and stay there for the next ten years.

She turned at the sound of a buggy pulling into the driveway. She recognized it right away. Asa must have pushed his horse to a fast trot to get here so quickly. She put her back to his buggy, flinching as she heard him run up behind her.

"Abigail?"

She closed her eyes at the sound of his voice. It shouldn't, but Asa saying her name still elicited an excited shiver through her body. Then again, he probably knew that too. He had her desperation pegged from the beginning. In so many ways he was worse than Joel, when all along she'd thought he was so much better.

Taking a deep breath, she straightened. She wouldn't let him know he got to her. She could at least keep her dignity. She pretended he wasn't there and walked past him. But he took her by the upper arm, retaining her.

"Abigail, please. I need to explain."

She turned to him, making sure her voice was as steady as a placid lake. "I hope you enjoyed *yerself.*" Her voice cracked on the last word. So much for dignity. "I hope you had *yer* fun."

Pain flashed in his eyes, an ache so deep that she could almost feel it. "Do you really believe that's what I was doing? Enjoying myself at *yer* expense?"

"I don't know. Why don't you talk about it with *yer* fiancée?"

"She's not *mei* fiancée."

"That's not what *yer mutter* said." She yanked her arm out of his grasp.

"It's a long story."

"Not interested." She started to turn away again.

"I love you, Abigail."

Those three words held her in place. She bit her bottom lip until she tasted blood. Then she turned to him. "How dare you say that to me?"

"It's the truth." He closed the short distance between them. "I've loved you ever since I came back to Birch Creek."

"You expect me to believe you?"

"I'm praying that you do." He took her hands in his, his gaze desperate. "It's hard to explain, but God sent me here. He told me to leave Shipshewana and everyone behind and come back to Birch Creek. That included leaving Susanna."

"You were going to marry her."

He swallowed, his grip tightening on her hands. "*Ya.* I was. But I know now it would never have worked between us. God must have known it, too, because otherwise he wouldn't have sent me here . . . to fall in love with you."

She pulled away from him and stormed into the barn. When he followed her, she whirled around. "Do you really think I'm that pathetic? That I'll fall into any man's arms who pays me five minutes of attention?"

He looked confused. "Of course not."

Anger consumed her. He was toying with her. Lying to her. He didn't love her. He wanted one thing—the one thing all men wanted. Joel had wanted it, and she had seen that same look in Asa's eyes when he kissed her before Susanna had shown up. Hot tears coursed down her cheeks. "Fine. You know what. I'll give it to you."

"Abigail, I don't know what you're talking about—"

She took off her coat and threw it on the ground. The voices in her head screamed that this was all she was worth. They pounded the message into her heart. She'd never have the love of a man like Rebecca had with Joel. Like Susanna had with Asa. Self-loathing overwhelmed her. She pulled the top pin out of her dress, the cool air from the barn hitting her collarbone, reminding her of the fleshy rolls of fat she carried. The tears came faster as she moved the fabric aside.

"Abigail, what are you doing?" Asa rushed to her. She yanked on her dress, but before she could reveal herself Asa's hands closed the fabric shut. "That's not what I want."

Her breathing turned ragged, pain lashing at her from all sides. She tried pushing his hands away but he wouldn't move them. He wasn't hurting her. And in the far recesses of her mind she realized he was saving her from doing something monumentally stupid.

"I would never take advantage of you," he said.

"So now you're saying you don't want me?"

He closed his eyes tight. "You know I do."

But his words fell onto the desert in her heart. All she felt was pain and rejection and shame. "*Geh* away, Asa."

"Abigail, please."

She finally looked up at him. His beautiful eyes swam with tears. She could almost believe he was genuine. Almost. But to believe that, she had to accept that she was worthy of his love, and she couldn't do that. Not after Joel. Not after Asa had kept the fact that he was engaged from her. Not when she felt ugly and worthless. She pushed his hands away and clutched at her dress.

He picked up her coat and handed it to her. She shrugged into it and pulled the front closed.

"I'm not leaving until I explain about Susanna." He didn't move away from her, his gaze locked with hers. And as much as she wanted to, she couldn't look away from him, either.

"She and I were engaged to be married. That is true. But *was* is the operative word, because we broke up before I came to Birch Creek."

"Then why does *yer mutter* think differently? Why is Susanna here?"

He sighed. "I don't know. *Mamm* really likes Susanna. She's the one who fixed us up."

"I can see why," she said bitterly. "Two perfectly beautiful people."

"Fine, Abigail. If you're going to make this about looks, then I'll admit Susanna is pretty. But you? You're beautiful, both inside and out."

Abigail folded her arms over her chest and huffed. Did he really expect her to believe him, even though she desperately wanted to?

He shut his eyes, as if he were praying. She'd seen him do this before. Or was he trying to find a way to lie to her again? "Asa—"

"I'm not leaving before I'm finished," he said, more firmly than she'd ever heard him before. His eyes were open now, dark gray and filled with seriousness. She had no choice but to hear him out.

"Other than not liking *mei* job that much, everything was *gut* in Shipshe. Even the job wasn't that bad, and I would have stayed there for the rest of *mei* life. It paid *gut* money, it was stable. The perfect job for a *mann* who was about to get married and, God willing, have a *familye*."

With every word her heart shrank. "Then why are you here if life was so perfect in Indiana?"

"Because like I said, God told me to leave. He told me to give up everything and come to Birch Creek."

She listened as he explained about losing his job, his new house catching fire, and Susanna getting sick. "I couldn't ignore God any longer," he said. "So I told Susanna it was over and came back here."

"You broke up with her when she was in the hospital?"

"I didn't have any choice!" He heaved in a breath, then let it out slowly. "The minute I left, she started to heal."

"So you left her to save her." Abigail's heart softened a tiny bit. Then again, she wouldn't expect anything less from Asa. He was that type of man—good-hearted and kind. At least she'd thought he was. "You ended the relationship because you love her."

"I love you," he said, his voice tight. "I don't love Susanna."

"But you did."

He feathered a hand through his hair. "I'm not going to lie to you. I *can't* lie to you. I *thought* I loved her. But I didn't realize what love was until I met you. That's the truth."

The sincerity in his eyes almost made her give in. She lifted her chin, meeting his gaze. "Why?"

He frowned. "What do you mean, why?"

"Why do you love me? How can you when we've only been on one date? When we're only starting to get to know each other?"

"We grew up together."

"We knew each other as kids. That's not the same. And it's not an answer." She lowered her voice. "You said you could never lie to me. Tell me . . . why do you love me?"

A shadow passed across his face. "Because God told me to."

She stilled. She'd been prepared for any clichéd, ludicrous answer but that one. "God told you to love me?"

"*Ya.*" His tone sounded like someone had let the air out of a massive balloon. "He told me you would be *mei frau.*"

"Is this a joke?"

Asa shook his head. "I would never joke about something like this. You and I . . . we're God's will. He said it to me as plain as he told me to come to Birch Creek." He swallowed. "I think he wanted me here for you."

Abigail huffed. "So you and God are doing me a favor? Taking pity on the lonely fat girl *nee* one wants?"

Storm clouds formed behind Asa's eyes. "I told you not to do that."

"What? Be honest? Can you stand there and say to me that if God hadn't told you to come after me, you would have given me a second look? You would have asked me out on *yer* own?" She could see the answer in Asa's eyes before he said the words.

"*Nee.* I wouldn't have."

Pain pierced her heart like a dart. Of everything he had told her up until now, the only thing she was absolutely sure of was what he'd just admitted. She wouldn't have even been an afterthought in his mind. She could feel the tears form in her eyes again as she dropped her arms. Her coat front opened, and she knew her dress was still unpinned, but she didn't care.

He moved toward her. "Abigail, the circumstances don't matter. What matters is I love you."

She couldn't stand to look at him anymore. "Leave, Asa."

"*Nee*, not until—"

"*Geh* before I scream and Aden comes out here."

Asa paused, then backed away, holding up his hands. "All right. I'll *geh*. But this isn't over." His voice broke. "It can't be."

She turned her back to him, her shoulders slumped, her despair and humiliation cloaking her like a sopping, rotten rug. The pin from her dress lay at her feet, lantern light glinting off the thin sliver of silver. She'd offered herself to him out of anger and frustration, truly believing that he wanted her, at least physically. But she'd been wrong. He didn't want her. He only thought he loved her because of some crazy coincidences in Shipshe that he somehow had twisted into thinking God was speaking to him. It didn't make any sense. All she knew was that he'd done the one thing she had begged him not to do—tear her heart to pieces.

Then again, she'd allowed him to.

She waited until she heard his footsteps disappear. Then she fell to her knees and sobbed.

CHAPTER 21

Asa felt sick. He stood outside the barn and listened to Abigail crying. He wanted to go to her again, to try to reason with her. To tell her he loved her, and say it so many times she would finally believe him.

But he didn't move. She wouldn't see him. She wouldn't believe him. And he couldn't blame her. She had told him that she couldn't stand having her heart broken a second time—and he had shattered it all over again.

He'd do anything to take back what he'd said about how he knew he loved her. And how he wouldn't have given her a second look if things were different. But he couldn't do that either. It was the truth. He would have overlooked Abigail Schrock if God hadn't knocked sense into him. He would have missed the chance to fall in love with the one woman he knew would make him happy for the rest of his life. Now he had no idea how to repair the damage he'd done.

Pain lodged in his throat as he made his way to the Schrocks' home. Even though she wouldn't see him, he wouldn't let her be alone. Not after what happened. He knocked on the front door. His whole body shook as he tried to contain his emotions. When the door opened and Sadie stood there, he swallowed, unable to keep his voice from breaking. "Abigail needs you," he said.

Sadie's eyes widened. "What? Where is she?"

"In the barn." He jerked his thumb in the direction of the building. "Hurry, Sadie." Then he turned around and left.

By the time he arrived home, it was late. Both his mother and Susanna liked to go to bed early and get up early, so he didn't go to the Beilers'. Instead he went to his house and tried to get some sleep. But sleep was elusive as he tried to figure out what to say to them. He didn't want to hurt either of them. But he couldn't give in to them, either.

The next morning he headed to Andrew's, exhausted. He paused in front of his friend's house, still uneasy. Then he shoved his hat low on his head as he went up the front porch steps. He couldn't put this off any longer. He knocked and let himself in, expecting everyone to be in the kitchen eating whatever delicious breakfast Joanna had whipped up that morning. As soon as he stepped inside, he could smell waffles cooking and bacon sizzling. But the living room wasn't empty. His gaze landed on Susanna.

She stood, smiling. "Andrew said you'd probably be here this morning, so I waited for you."

He swallowed. "Susanna—"

"We need to talk."

Asa stilled as her smile disappeared and determination entered her eyes. He steeled himself and said a silent prayer as he took off his hat. "Okay."

She gestured for him to sit on the couch. When he did, she sat next to him. She licked her lips, not looking at him. He couldn't say anything. It was as if they were both frozen. Finally he had to push through his fear.

"Susanna—"

"Asa—"

They both smiled. They'd always been comfortable around each other. But he wasn't interested in staying comfortable.

"I'll *geh* first," Susanna said. They were sitting close, but not touching. That wasn't unusual either. Other than holding hands, they hadn't done anything else. When she wanted to wait for her wedding for her first kiss, he agreed. He always agreed. He had been fine with everything, letting everyone make decisions for him. *Not anymore.*

"I didn't want to come here with *yer mamm,*" she said.

Asa arched a brow. "You didn't?"

"*Nee.* But you know how she is. She can be persuasive when she wants to be. And I didn't want to hurt her feelings. Asa, she can't accept that we're not together anymore."

"What about you? I know I broke up with you at the worst time."

"That's just it, Asa. You didn't." She sighed. "I guess you didn't read *mei* letters."

He shook his head and glanced away. "*Nee.* I couldn't. I felt horrible for leaving you when you needed me the most."

"If you had read *mei* letters you wouldn't have felt guilty anymore. You would have known how grateful I am that you ended our engagement."

He looked back at her. "Grateful?"

"*Ya.* I'd known things weren't right with us for a long time. But I couldn't bring myself to end it. Our *mamms* were so happy that we were getting married, and you seemed happy. But none of it felt right to me. There wasn't any . . ."

"Spark?"

Her cheeks turned red. "*Ya.*" She brushed her hands over the skirt of her dress. "I needed to feel more, Asa. Not just from you, but *for* you. And I tried. But every time I thought about us together . . ." She finally looked up at him. "I'm sorry. I have to be honest."

"I'm glad you are." He was surprised. He was also relieved. They were on the same page after all. "I care about you, Susanna. But as a friend."

"Same here. Which is why I understood why you left. You've always tried to do the right thing. And when it came down to listening to God, you made the right choice. For both of us." She smiled a little bit. "It looks like you may have found the right *maedel* too."

"I have." He settled back against the couch, his shoulders slumping with relief. "She's not too happy with me right now."

"But she loves you."

He looked at Susanna. "How do you know?"

"I saw the way she looked at you. I also saw that she was hurt to find out about me."

"I should have told her."

"*Ya*, you should have. But I'm sure you'll make everything right with her soon enough."

"If I can get her to talk to me."

His *mamm* entered the living room. "There you are, Susanna. And Asa." She clasped her hands together, beaming. "It's so *gut* to see you two together again."

"*Mamm.*" Asa stood, Susanna quickly joining him. "We have something to tell you."

"I knew it! You've worked things out and the wedding is back on!" She went to Susanna and gave her a hug. "I'm so happy for you both."

Asa glanced at Susanna as he embraced his mother. She'd always been a demonstrative woman, never shy with her feelings or her words. He had known it would be harder to talk to her than Susanna. When they parted he said, "*Mamm*, I need to talk to you."

"After breakfast. You won't believe how fluffy Joanna's waffles are. I must get her recipe. Come," she said, looking at Susanna. "Let's *geh* eat."

"*Mamm*," Asa said, stern enough to get her attention. Then he nodded to Susanna. She gave him a small nod back and left the room.

"Asa," *Mamm* said, looking at him, all joy in her eyes gone. "What's going on?"

"Susanna and I are not getting back together."

She waved her hand. "I'm sure she has a hard time forgiving you for what you've done. But she'll come around. You have to give her a little time." She leaned closer to him. "You'll need to woo her back."

Asa ran his hands over his face. "*Mamm*, I'm not wooing anybody." Well, he'd probably woo Abigail, but his mother didn't need to know that. Not yet, anyway. "Can we sit down and discuss this? Please?"

His mother lifted her chin the way she did when she was being prickly. "Fine," she said, sitting down on the couch primly. He moved the rocking chair in front of her and sat down so he could face her square on. He leaned forward and clasped his hands between his knees. "*Mamm*, Susanna doesn't want to marry me. I don't want to marry her. We don't love each other.

We care about each other as friends, but that's as far as things are going to *geh*."

"Because you made a mistake." *Mamm*'s eyes narrowed. "I don't understand you, Asa. *Yer* life was perfect. Everything was falling into place for you."

"*Nee*, it wasn't. At least not the things I wanted."

"What else did you need? You had a *gut* job—"

"That bored me to death."

Mamm paused before continuing. "Not all jobs have to be exciting. The important thing is that it was steady."

"You sound like *Daed*."

"That's because *yer vatter* was right. He knows what it's like not to have work. I don't want you to *geh* through that worry with *yer familye*."

"I know." He reached for his mother's hand. "And I know it's because you love me. But I have to follow *mei* own path. The one God has lined out for me. I'm going to be an accountant."

His mother frowned. "That's more exciting than factory work?"

"It's more satisfying." He wasn't going to bother explaining why he liked accounting and numbers and finances. He had to stick to the point. "I'm also going to get married, at least I hope."

"Finally you're making sense. And you can be an accountant in Shipshe."

"I will be an accountant here. Birch Creek is thriving financially. This is a *gut* opportunity for me to do something I love, and I know I can find clients."

Mamm let out a breath and let go of his hand. "All right, you're going to live in Birch Creek. I'm sure you can convince Susanna to move here. It's not that far from her *familye*, and she can visit anytime."

"*Mamm*, listen to me. You have to accept that Susanna and I aren't together anymore. I'm . . . I'm in love with someone else. With Abigail."

"Abigail? You're cheating on *yer* fiancée?" *Mamm* gasped.

He rubbed the back of his neck. *Patience, remember?* "*Nee*. I'm not cheating on Susanna because we're not together. I wouldn't do that to her—or anyone else." He frowned. "I can't believe you'd think I would."

She pressed her lips together. "I'm sorry," she said softly. Then she sighed. "I'm also disappointed."

"I'd appreciate it if you wouldn't insult Abigail," he said, barely able to keep his tone even.

"*Nee*. I'm not disappointed with her. She's a lovely *maedel*. I was just hoping . . ." Her eyes shone with tears. "I miss you, Asa. I was shocked when you left home. Then I was worried when you didn't answer *mei* letters. You're *mei* only *sohn*. I had dreams for you."

"But they're not *mei* dreams. I can't keep living *mei* life to please other people. God brought me here for a purpose—multiple ones, I'm finding out. He hasn't told me to leave. In fact, I feel more certain than ever that Birch Creek is home." He took his mother's hand again. "But I can come visit," he said, smiling.

"*Ya*. And we can visit too." Her smile faded. "Is Susanna upset with me?"

"*Nee*. She understands. But she has to live her own life too. I'm not a part of that. I was never meant to be."

Mamm nodded. "I see that now. I'm sorry I caused trouble for you and Abigail. The way she left so quickly . . ."

"I should have read *yer* letters. I should have told her about Susanna. I've made a lot of mistakes lately."

Mamm patted his hand. "*Mei sohn,* I have confidence that you will make everything right. You always do."

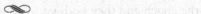

When Abigail opened the door, she had expected to see Asa. She'd experienced his persistence firsthand. It was a quality that at first irritated her, but now she loved that about him. Love. She did love Asa. But she also had to stand her ground. She had to go back to her first love—God. She also had to work on loving and accepting herself. She couldn't depend on anyone else.

However, instead of Asa, Susanna stood there. Pretty, petite Susanna. Abigail could see how Susanna and Asa made a striking couple.

"Can I come in? I'd like to talk to you, if that's all right."

Abigail's first response was to say no. She didn't want to deal with her or Asa today. But it wasn't Susanna's fault that Asa had kept her a secret from Abigail. "Come in," Abigail said, opening the door wider.

Susanna stepped inside. She looked around the living room. "You have a lovely place."

"*Danki.* How did you find out where I lived?"

"I asked Naomi."

The two women stood there for a moment, Susanna not meeting Abigail's gaze, Abigail wondering why she had let the woman in her house. Then remembering herself she said, "Do you want something to drink? I can make some tea, and we have some brownies in the kitchen." She marveled at how she could talk normally to Asa's fiancée—ex-fiancée—like she was there for a normal visit.

"*Nee.* I'm not hungry."

Neither was Abigail, but that didn't mean she wasn't craving those brownies right now. "We can sit down." She gestured to the couch and they both sat.

Susanna folded her hands on her lap. Everything about her was compact and graceful. She looked at Abigail. "I'm sorry I surprised you by coming to Birch Creek."

Abigail frowned. She was apologizing?

"Asa's mother can be very persuasive, and I'm not *gut* about telling people *nee.* I should have refused to come with her."

"You didn't want to see Asa?"

Susanna shook her head. "*Nee.* Not because of what you might think. Asa and I were engaged, but we shouldn't have been. We were never right for each other."

Abigail was confused. "Then why were you engaged?"

"We lived next door to each other and our mothers were really close friends. It was *mei mamm* who suggested Asa come over one evening for supper, and then we ended up talking afterward." She smiled. "He's very *schee* and nice, but you already know that. It was easy for us to start dating. Then both our mothers got involved. They started planning the wedding almost after our second date. And actually for a while we really thought we were in love. We got along very well. We were comfortable around each other." She folded her lips in. "But there wasn't a spark. I know Asa didn't feel much either, but he never said anything. He's easygoing and likes to see people happy, sometimes at his own expense. So I knew I'd have to be the one to break it off."

"But I thought he broke up with you?"

"He did. And I was too sick to tell him I was relieved. I wrote to him and explained that I was fine with our breakup.

That he did us both a favor. Turns out he never read *mei* letters."
She looked at Abigail. "He carried a lot of guilt about how our
relationship ended, even though he was following God's will.
So I am glad that I got to talk to him and straighten things out.
We're in a *gut* place now."

For some reason, Abigail was glad to hear that. Now that
she knew Susanna's side of the story, her resentment disappeared.
Asa had been telling Abigail the truth. He hadn't betrayed her
like Joel had.

But that didn't mean everything would be fine between them.

"He loves you, Abigail," Susanna suddenly said.

Abigail froze. "How do you know that?"

"He told me. And I can see it in his eyes when he talks about
you. I know you're confused about what his *mamm* said, and I
don't blame you. She really wanted the two of us to get married.
But I think part of the reason Asa was sent to Birch Creek was
to be with you."

Her words made Abigail skeptical. God wouldn't turn a
man's entire life upside down for Abigail's sake. She wasn't Asa's
reward for his obedience. Whatever brought Asa to Birch Creek,
she doubted she was a part of it.

"Give him another chance, Abigail. I've never seen him like
this. Not being with you is breaking his heart."

Abigail froze at the words, his pain causing her pain. "I don't
know if I can."

"Why not? All of this has been a misunderstanding. It hasn't
changed how he feels about you." She peered at her. "Or how
you feel about him."

Glancing down, Abigail said, "I care about him. A lot."

Susanna stood. "I should be getting back. Naomi is the only
one who knows I'm here, and Asa's mother will start asking

227

where I went. Please think about what I said. I want Asa to be happy, and I believe he will be with you."

Abigail thanked Susanna and showed her out. Even though it was still daylight out, all she wanted to do was hide under the covers. Instead she sat on the sofa and thought about what Susanna said. Asa loved her. And somewhere deep inside Abigail knew it was the truth, just like she knew her feelings for him ran deeper than just caring. She loved him too.

It's not enough . . . for either of us.

All this time Asa believed he was following God's will. He had obeyed the Lord, even though it had cost him everything. His mind and heart had been open to God. When was the last time Abigail had been that vulnerable with the Lord?

She had been filled with hurt, grief, and insecurity. But instead of turning to God, she had put her faith in Joel, then immediately turned to Asa with little resistance. It had been easy to do. It would also be easy to get back together with him.

But she couldn't depend on Asa to heal her pain and solve her problems, and it wasn't fair to expect him to. She was tired of being hurt and confused. She closed her eyes, her heart crying out to God. *Lord . . . help me.*

She felt a nudge deep inside her soul. She went upstairs and stared at her loom. At the box of materials on the floor next to it that remained untouched. She'd been afraid to use this loom because while her mother had faith in her abilities, she didn't. Making rugs had been easy. Comfortable. Using an intricate loom would be difficult. She would make many mistakes until she created something worthwhile.

Abigail took the loom to the center of the room. Chose yarn from the box, then took the shuttle and the shed stick—and started to weave.

CHAPTER 22

Asa stood next to his mother as the taxi pulled into Andrew's driveway. He had taken the day off to spend with her and Susanna before they left for Shipshe. But even as he tried to focus on visiting with *Mamm*, he couldn't keep his mind off Abigail.

The driver turned off the engine and got out of the car. "Can I help you with your bags?" the tall, thin man said, adjusting the bill of his Cleveland Indians baseball cap.

Asa was about to tell him no when Susanna spoke. "Yes, please." She turned to Asa. "Good-bye," she said, giving him a smile. "I'll pray for you and Abigail."

"*Danki.*" Despite everything, he would miss her. "I'll pray for you too."

She gave him a short wave as the driver picked up her small suitcase. Asa turned to *Mamm*, who dabbed at her eyes with a handkerchief. "I really thought you would be coming back with me."

"*Mamm*," he said, then gave her a hug, not caring if anyone saw him. He pulled away. "I'll come to visit you and *Daed* and *mei schwesters*. I promise. But I have to stay here."

"I know." She sniffed and put her handkerchief in her purse.

"That doesn't mean I won't miss you. Or write to you. But this time promise me you'll read *mei* letters."

"I promise." He picked up her suitcase and took it to the car. "Take care of *yerself*," he said.

"You too, *sohn*." She patted his cheek, then got into the backseat with Susanna.

He waved as the car pulled out of the driveway. He would miss his mother, but he was glad she was heading back home. It was still morning and he had time to seek out Abigail. He couldn't leave things the way they were. He had prayed all last night, and to his irritation God was silent. Why had he withdrawn now, when Asa needed his guidance the most? The only conclusion he'd drawn was that God wanted him to go after Abigail. Asa wanted to go after Abigail. He was ready to do anything to get her back.

Naomi sighed as the taxi driver pulled into the post office. She'd spent the time during the drive here to pray for Asa and Abigail. She and Asa's mother had talked last night, and while Asa's mother had said she accepted that her son wasn't going to marry the woman she thought was perfect for him, Naomi could tell she was still wrestling with her disappointment. Ordinarily Naomi would have wanted her friend to stay longer, but it was good that she and Susanna had gone back to Shipshewana. Asa needed to work things out with Abigail without anyone else's interference. She had come to love Abigail as if she were a daughter, and Asa had always been an unofficial member of the family.

Then there were Irene and Sol. That situation had ended up being more complicated than she ever thought. Irene clearly had feelings for him. But Sol was troubled. Then again, Bartholomew had been too. She knew firsthand the miracles God could work in someone's life. Bartholomew had turned himself around. Naomi had to believe Sol could, too, and she had to let Irene trust her own judgment.

The driver pulled the car into a parking space. "I'll only be a minute," Naomi said to him. He nodded and pulled out his phone.

As she walked into the post office, a familiar anticipation came over her. She had to put her adult children into God's hands. Meanwhile, at least she had Bartholomew's letters to look forward to. The last time she'd heard from him was back in January, after Andrew's wedding. It wasn't unusual for him to go for a few months without writing. If he sent too many letters, he might cast suspicion. But surely there would be a letter waiting for her in the post office box today. She inserted the key, opened the small door, and smiled.

But a few moments later, her world crashed. The letter shook in her hands. She couldn't believe what she was reading. How could this be happening?

"Are you all right, ma'am?" said the woman standing next to her.

Naomi glanced and saw the woman had her key inserted in the lock of her own post office box but hadn't opened it. Realizing she needed to gain her composure so she wouldn't draw any more attention to herself, she started to say she was fine. But she couldn't form the words. All she wanted to do was tell the woman to mind her own business. Instead Naomi pressed her teeth against her bottom lip and shook her head.

The woman turned to her, concern present on her face. "Is there anything I can do for you?"

Knowing she was perilously close to breaking down, Naomi

shook her head. "No," she said, her voice quavering. "There's nothing anyone can do." She rushed outside, her lungs straining for air. She glanced at the driver of the taxi that brought her here. He was waiting in the car, looking at his phone. She took the opportunity to walk around to the side of the post office where she couldn't be seen by anyone. The cold, brutal wind sliced through her, but she didn't care. She looked at the letter in her hands and read the words over again.

Naomi, my love. This will be my last letter. I wish I could explain why, but I can't. You know how this works. I'm sorry that I've failed you again. Please pray that we will be together soon. Always remember that I love you.

Bartholomew

How could this be his last letter? And out of the blue like this, with no warning? She had always known that keeping up their correspondence was risky and against the rules they had agreed to when Bartholomew was put into witness protection. Something must have happened to keep him from writing. And of course he couldn't give her an explanation. She was supposed to accept the circumstances, the way she had accepted everything else in their lives, especially their separation.

But she couldn't accept this. She couldn't accept not having any contact with the man she loved. God had promised her years ago that she and Bartholomew would be reunited. And she had held on to that promise, believing that because they were still able to communicate that God was with both of them. And now . . . now the doubts started setting in. The weariness. The empty hole in her heart deepened as she covered her face with her hands and started to cry. "Why, God?" she whispered through her tears. "Haven't I been faithful enough? Have you forsaken me and *mei* husband?"

There was no answer in the brisk wind that whipped around her body. She started to shake, her nose and fingers stiff with cold. She couldn't stay out here much longer. Forcing herself to gain control of her emotions, she took a tissue out of her purse, wiped her cheeks and blew her nose, then went back to the taxi.

"Get what you needed?" the man said, setting his phone on the passenger seat.

Naomi gave him a curt nod, then stared out the window as he drove her home. She didn't say anything else, her mind still trying to grasp that she didn't know when or if she would ever hear from Bartholomew again.

When she arrived home, she paid the driver and went to the front door. She took in a deep breath. The cold burned her lungs. She couldn't let her children see her like this. Yes, they were adults, but she still had a responsibility not to show them her weakness or lack of faith. She vowed to be strong the day they took Bartholomew away, and so far she had. Irene and Andrew had lost their father. They weren't going to lose their mother too. She straightened her shoulders and walked to the kitchen. Irene and Joanna were there, surrounded by baking supplies on the table—flour, a rolling pin, a bowl, oil, and a rotary beater.

"How do you get the dough so thin?" Irene asked as she skimmed the roller across the floured ball of dough.

"You need to apply a little more pressure. But not too much." Joanna took the pin from Irene and expertly rolled out the crust. Before it was completely flat she handed it to Irene. "Now you try."

Naomi didn't move, watching her daughter and daughter-in-law as they worked on the pie crust together. Normally this would make her smile, the two of them doing a simple task and being at such ease with each other. Joanna had suffered several blows in the past year, but she was coming into her own as Andrew's wife. Yet instead of being happy, she choked back tears. She must have made a noise, because both Irene and Joanna looked up.

Irene smiled. "Hi, *Mamm*. We didn't hear you come in." As soon as she spoke, she frowned and put down the rolling pin. As she hurried toward Naomi she said, "*Mamm*? What's wrong?"

"*Nix*." But Naomi could barely get the word out.

"You're shaking."

"Because I'm cold." She tried to muster a smile, but she couldn't. All her strength seemed to leave her body.

Irene put her arm around Naomi's shoulders and guided her to the table. Naomi didn't protest and sat down while Joanna brought her a glass of water. Both women sat next to her and Naomi saw them exchange a glance. Then Joanna stood up. "I should *geh* and let you two talk," she said.

Naomi shook her head. "You're a member of this *familye*. You know what happened to *mei* husband. There are *nee* secrets here." She turned to Irene. She hadn't expected to reveal why she was upset, but she couldn't stay silent. And Irene had a right to know what was going on, now that she was aware of Bartholomew's circumstances. "I got a letter from *yer vatter*. It's . . . his last one to me."

"What?" Irene asked, her brow lifting. "Why?"

"I don't know." *Always remember that I love you.* She tried to keep those words in her heart, where she always kept his written declarations of love. But maybe it was a lie. Maybe he couldn't write to her because he found someone else. Maybe the years apart and the years of him living in the *Englisch* world had finally broken him—and in turn broke them. She started to shake again.

"*Mamm*," Irene said, "You're pale and trembling. You need to lie down."

"*Nee.*"

"There's something seriously wrong. Please, do as I say."

She didn't have the strength or desire to argue. Naomi rose from the table, feeling like she was going through the motions. She went up to her room, Irene close behind her. She sat on the edge of the bed, wringing her hands over and over. "I just want to be alone," she whispered.

"I don't think that's a good idea right now."

She snapped her head up and glared at Irene. "I said leave me alone!"

Irene looked shocked. But she simply nodded and backed out of the room, then shut the door.

I should apologize . . . I shouldn't take mei *anger out on her.* But Naomi couldn't hold it in anymore. She started to cry again . . . and wondered if she'd ever stop.

CHAPTER 23

Sol rubbed a sheet of fine-grade sandpaper against the side of a log cabin birdhouse. These were becoming his most popular and requested types of houses, with the painted ones coming in second. He glanced at the front door and frowned. Irene should have been here by now. He tried not to worry. She wasn't his responsibility. *But I want her to be.* He couldn't deny how he felt about her anymore. He cared for her, more than he thought possible. After their talk on Monday they had fallen into an easy working relationship, even though he couldn't help but sneak glances at her when she wasn't looking.

Or maybe she had noticed. Maybe he'd made her uncomfortable without knowing it. Maybe she'd changed her mind about working for him. Maybe she knew she was better off without him in her life . . .

Nee! He put his hands over his ears, as if he could hear his negative thoughts out loud. His mind was going down that path of negativity, of self-pity, of doubting that he was a changed man.

236

How could he be a part of Irene's life if he couldn't get out of the mental hole he kept digging? He picked up the sandpaper and started scouring the wood. Moments later he slowed, realizing he was ruining the birdhouse. He tossed down the sandpaper at the same time he heard the door to the workshop open. When he turned, he saw Irene standing there. Relief flowed through him, quickly replaced by concern.

It only took a second to notice the tears in her eyes and her red nose. "Irene," he said, opening the door wider. "What's wrong?"

"I don't know what to do," she said, her voice thick. She paused, looking around as if she were lost. "I didn't know who to turn to. Andrew has Joanna and I . . . I had to see you."

He had no idea what she was talking about. He gestured for her to come inside. He shut the door and faced her, genuinely worried.

"I'm sorry. I know I'm late for work." She was wearing a coat, but her arms were hugging her body as if she were freezing inside.

"Forget about work." Sol searched for a chair, found one, and pulled it over. He pointed to it. "Sit down and tell me what's going on."

Irene sat, but she didn't speak, which was unlike her. He knelt in front of her. "Irene, please. Talk to me."

"It's *Mamm*. Something happened yesterday, and I don't know what to do."

"Whatever it is I'll help you through it."

"I've never seen her like this." She lifted her head and looked at Sol, her eyes liquid with tears. "*Mamm* has always been *mei* rock. She's always been there, being both mother and father to me and Andrew. She had to be."

Sol nodded, remembering what she had told him about her father. "Is Naomi sick? Is she hurt?"

Irene shook her head. "She's not sick, not like you think." Irene started to cry. *"Mei daed . . ."*

"What happened to *yer daed*?"

"I don't know. I don't know anything about *mei* father, nothing since he left. I didn't even know he and *Mamm* were writing to each other all these years until I learned the truth about why he left. But now he's cut off communication, and she's devastated. She hasn't left her room since she came home yesterday. She won't talk to me or Andrew. I don't know what to do to help her."

Sol wasn't sure what to do either. His mother was still stoic, still sure that his father would come back. And despite his conversation with Aden the day they'd hosted the church service, he was starting to hope she was right, at least for her sake. Because he couldn't imagine his own mother's reaction if his father never returned.

"I feel so helpless," she said, crying freely now.

He felt helpless too. She'd been a light in his life since she started working for him. She never asked for anything in return except a fair wage for her work. But she had done so much more for him. She had listened to him. She hadn't judged him. She gave him a chance. She believed in him. And now she was in need and he was at a loss.

He looked down at his hand holding hers, then he took her other hand. "Irene, let me pray for you. Let's pray for you and *yer mamm*."

Irene nodded and he bowed his head and started to pray. He faltered at first, unsure what to say, not used to praying out loud and especially at a crucial moment like this. But after a minute the words started to flow. He didn't know where they came from. He prayed for Irene and her father, for Naomi, his mother, his brother, the Schrock sisters, and finally for his own father. It was only after he had brought his father before God in prayer that he realized he had strayed from his original purpose. He quickly ended the prayer and looked up. "I'm sorry."

"Sorry for what?" she whispered.

"For going on and on. For praying for *mei familye* when I should have focused *mei* prayer on *yers*."

"Sol," she said. "Every word was from *yer* heart. I could tell. You had a connection with God during that prayer. I know he heard you. Don't be sorry." She touched his cheek, then she was holding his face in her hands. *"Danki,"* she said, then kissed him on the cheek. Her eyes widened, as if she was surprised by the move. Then she released his face. She wiped her tears on the back of her hand. "I feel better. Is it okay if I call off work today? I should probably get home and check on *Mamm*."

"Of course. The birdhouses aren't going anywhere."

She gave him a watery smile. *"Danki."*

"Are you sure you're okay?"

"Ya. I am. I needed that." She looked up at him. "I needed you." She paused, catching his gaze for a moment. Then she turned around and left.

You need me . . . but not as much as I need you. Although he was still concerned about her and Naomi, he couldn't help but smile. He had been able to help and comfort her after all.

Naomi heard a soft knock at her bedroom door. She didn't get up to answer it, instead turning over in her bed and bringing her quilt up to her chin. She didn't want to see Irene or Joanna or Andrew, all of whom had tried talking to her over the past two days. Why couldn't they leave her alone? Deep inside she knew they were trying to help, to encourage her, but her heart was too broken to receive it. All she could think about was Bartholomew. As long as they had letters, they had a connection. But now that thin thread had been snapped, and she had no idea when or if she'd ever hear from him again. And while she tried to have faith, tried to believe in him and in God not allowing them to be apart forever, she couldn't grasp it. Not right now.

She thought about the last time she'd seen him, six years ago. A good memory, one she thought of often over the years. The last time they'd embraced. Kissed. Were able to reaffirm their love during those few stolen moments. Now even that was tainted. Would that be the last time she'd ever see him?

The knock sounded again, a little more insistent this time. "*Geh* away," she said, clutching the edge of the quilt. Her wedding quilt, a gift from her best friend, who was still in Florida. They had lost contact over the years, which had been necessary for Naomi and the children to remain safe. She had made new friends in Birch Creek. The sacrifice had been worth it. All of it had, because she had always believed that eventually she and Bartholomew would be together. But what if it all had been in vain? What if all her belief had been for nothing?

What if she would always be alone?

"Naomi?"

She turned slightly at the tentative female voice. Rhoda? What was she doing here? Naomi cleared the tears from her throat. "I'm not feeling well, Rhoda. I'm not in the mood for company."

A pause. "Naomi, I'm not leaving until you and I talk."

Naomi frowned. Rhoda sounded more forceful than she'd ever heard her. Naomi stood, smoothed back her hair, and opened the bedroom door a crack. "I'm not presentable," she said.

"That doesn't matter. Not between friends." Rhoda smiled, and Naomi saw genuine concern and softness there. "Please, Naomi. Let me in."

Resigned, tears still spilling over her cheeks, she opened the door. She walked to her bed and sat down. Rhoda sat in the rocker in the corner of the bedroom. It was the same one Naomi had rocked Irene and Andrew in when they were babies. Rhoda didn't say anything for a long time, just rocked back and forth as Naomi wiped the tears from her cheeks and tried not to cry anymore. But it was as if her heart and eyes were leaking, that the dam she'd kept patched together for so long had burst into pieces.

Finally Rhoda said, "How can I pray for you?"

Naomi looked into Rhoda's eyes. She didn't see any prying or judgment. Just compassion and the simple offer to pray. Naomi was grateful for it all. But she was also at a loss. "I . . . don't know."

Rhoda went to her and sat beside her on the bed. She took Naomi's hand. "Then I'll just sit here with you."

Naomi looked at her. "How did you know to come over here?"

"I saw Irene this morning when she came to work with Sol." Before Naomi could say anything, Rhoda added, "She looked upset."

Guilt nagged at Naomi, but it didn't penetrate her sorrow. Right now she didn't have the strength to comfort her daughter. "Is she still with Sol?"

"She came home. She's the one who let me in."

"So she told you what happened."

"*Nee.* I'm here because when I saw Irene leave work early, I felt a nudge . . . here." She put her hand over her heart. "I wasn't sure what was wrong, but God was telling me to come see you."

Naomi squeezed Rhoda's hand. Here was the only other person in the community who understood Naomi's pain, even if their circumstances were different. They both had lost their husbands. Neither of them knew when they would return. Both of them had to hold on to faith—and also, Naomi now knew, they had to hold on to each other. "I can't explain," she said, her voice cracking. "But I need strength. Mine has run out."

"Because you've had to be strong for so long." Rhoda's eyes softened. "Because you've spent years holding in the pain."

Naomi nodded, and for some reason she was sure Rhoda wasn't talking only about Naomi's situation. "*Ya.* That's exactly right."

"Then we'll pray for strength. But not our own. Strength only God can give."

Both women closed their eyes and prayed. Naomi didn't feel her strength come back. But she did feel a small sense of peace. *My promises are true. My promises are real.* God's promises could overcome her doubt. She realized that's what she needed more than strength. She needed to be reminded that God was here, that he hadn't left her or Bartholomew. That they would get through this like they had gotten through everything else. Now wasn't the time to cave in or bend to doubt. It was time to lean on God.

Rhoda released her hand and Naomi opened her eyes. Rhoda smiled a tiny bit. "You look better already."

Naomi chuckled. "I feel better . . . a bit."

Rhoda paused, glancing down at her lap. "How do you do it?"

"What do you mean?"

Rhoda looked up. "How do you get through each day . . . hour . . ." She looked down again. "I think about Emmanuel almost every minute. Wondering where he is, when he's coming back." She gripped Naomi's hand. "But what if he doesn't? What if I never see him again? How can I *geh* on?"

"You hang on to hope. It's all you have." She straightened, realization dawning. She hadn't lost hope. She'd faltered for a short while, let doubt and insecurity creep in and take over. But now she had regained her footing. And even though it may be twelve more years—or twenty, or thirty—before she saw her husband again, she would cling to that hope as tight as she could. "Hope and faith, Rhoda. That's what has sustained me . . . and it will sustain you."

"Then you believe Bartholomew will return? Even after he . . ." She glanced away. "After he left you for someone else?"

How Naomi wished she could tell Rhoda the truth. But she couldn't. It was bad enough that Irene, Andrew, and Joanna knew. She couldn't risk anyone else in Birch Creek knowing the real reason she and Bartholomew were apart. "There's always a chance," she said. "I will never give up on him."

Rhoda's gaze moved back to Naomi. Her lips lifted in a small smile. "Then I will never give up on Emmanuel, either." She released Naomi's hand. "Are you feeling up to eating a bit of lunch? It will be a late lunch, but that's all right."

Naomi nodded. "Lunch and company would be nice. Let me get dressed and I'll prepare something."

Rhoda rose. "You don't have to prepare anything. I saw Joanna in the kitchen when I arrived and she was making a sandwich for you to have later. I'll finish getting *yer* meal ready while you get dressed."

Relief coursed through Naomi, but not because she didn't have to make a meal. For the first time since she moved to Birch Creek she felt she had a true ally. Not just a friend, but someone who could walk this new, unknown journey with her. An ally born out of pain. They were very different women, but they were now bonded by the fact that their husbands weren't there. How could a blessing come out of that tragedy? Yet it had. "Thank you," she said, drawing Rhoda into a hug.

Rhoda quickly returned it and stepped away, her expression showing her surprise at the spontaneous show of affection. Color brightened her cheeks. "I'll see you in a few minutes."

When Rhoda left, Naomi looked up at the ceiling, her mind moving past the drywall and the roof and to the heavens. "*Danki* for pulling me back." No, her circumstances hadn't changed. Both Bartholomew and Emmanuel were gone. But Naomi had her hope back. With that she could get through anything. She paused and prayed that Rhoda could do the same.

CHAPTER 24

Bartholomew walked into the seedy-looking bar. He knew he would find Mike here. He scanned the small joint looking for the burly guy. Since it was a Friday night, it was hard to spot him in the crowd, but after a few minutes he found him, sitting in a back booth alone, nursing an amber-colored drink. Bartholomew slid into the seat across from him.

Mike looked up, surprised. "What are you doing here?" His gaze darted around. "You shouldn't be in a place like this."

Bartholomew leaned back in the seat. He hoped his body language was calm because inside he was seething. "Afraid someone will find out about your on-duty activities?"

"I'm off duty. Have been for the past hour. And if you know so much about me, you would know that I don't drink on duty."

He nodded. He was aware Mike was off duty, but he couldn't resist making the verbal jab. After he'd written his last letter to Naomi, something inside him snapped. Since then he'd been a mess. He couldn't take it anymore, and he'd done something he'd never done before—followed Mike instead of Mike following him. "I know," he said, not flinching. "Just like I know that back at my apartment complex is an unmarked car with one of your agents sitting in the front seat keeping an eye on me."

"I guess you gave him the slip?"

Bartholomew smirked in reply. Being part of a drug ring had given him some skills he never forgot, and had never planned to use again. But tonight he'd been desperate.

"How did you find me?" Mike asked.

"I followed you from your office. I bet you come here every Friday night after work to unwind."

"If you had my job, you'd be drinking too. Even my wife understands I sometimes need this buffer before I go home at the end of a hard week." Mike took a sip of the liquor. "I'm impressed. If you hadn't taken a wrong turn years ago, you could have had a career in law enforcement."

"If I hadn't taken a wrong turn, I would be home with my wife and my kids. Where I belong."

"Back with the Amish, then. I thought after twelve years you'd be used to modern comforts."

"Comforts don't matter if you're not with the people you love." Bartholomew was turning maudlin but he couldn't help it. Computers, air conditioning, cars—they were convenient but they didn't stem his desire to go back to his family and his roots. If anything, living in the *Englisch* world had made him appreciate the simplicity of his former Amish life. He'd been too young, stupid, and greedy to appreciate it before. He set his jaw, refocusing his attention on the reason he was in this dive of a bar. "I'm giving you a heads up that I'm done."

Mike's brow lifted. "Done with what?"

"With witness protection. With being away from my family." Leaning forward, his emotion got the best of him, and he had to force the next words around the lump in his throat. "I can't even contact my wife anymore, Mike. Do you know how hard that is? I have followed all of your rules—"

"No." Mike held up his hand. "You haven't. You were specifically told not to contact your family. You've been writing to your wife for years."

"Can you blame me?"

Mike's chest heaved. "No. I can't."

"Those letters kept me sane." He wasn't going to say this out loud, but they fed his heart and soul. He fisted his hands under the table. "I've lost everything now. I can't live like this."

"You may not live at all if you leave our protection. You do remember why you're here, right? You turned state's evidence. Because of that there are people out there who want to shut you up permanently."

"That was twelve years ago. The drug gang wasn't that big."

"It was an international ring, Jack. You were a small fish, but a fish with information."

"Which must be outdated by now." He narrowed his gaze. "Either you're part of the worst law enforcement agency in history or there's something you're not telling me. I don't believe you just found out I was writing Naomi. I think you knew how important it was for me to be in contact with her. But then something changed. Something you're not telling me."

Mike's gaze didn't leave Bartholomew's. After a long pause he pushed his drink away. "I'm not authorized to tell you anything."

"But?"

"There are no buts. You're released from protection when we tell you. When the job is finished. End of story."

Bartholomew leaned back in the seat, taking in what he thought Mike was hiding. "You mean when you've caught everyone. And

I have a feeling you might have a break on that front, maybe you even have only one person left." When Mike's gaze flicked to the left, Bartholomew had his answer. "Use me as bait."

Mike picked up his drink and drained it dry. He slammed the glass on the table. "This conversation is over."

"Fine." Bartholomew stood. "I'll draw whoever it is out myself, then. I'm sure I can't do a worse job than your agency has."

"You can't do that."

"Want to bet on it?"

Mike tossed a five-dollar bill on the table and got up. He took Bartholomew by the arm. "We're taking this outside."

He'd never seen this look on Mike's face before and it set off alarm bells in his mind. During the past two years he'd been assigned to Bartholomew, he had been slightly friendly and pretty easygoing. Now he was agitated, his thick brow stern over icy blue eyes. Which confirmed to Bartholomew that he had been on the right track. He yanked his arm out of Mike's grasp as they left the bar and walked out to the parking lot.

They went to the far end of the lot where there weren't very many cars around. Bartholomew spun around. "Are you going to tell me what's going on? And I want the whole truth or I promise you I will take care of this myself."

Mike nodded his head in the direction of the dark blue sedan, a car Bartholomew recognized as his. They walked over to it. "Get in," Mike said. "Then we can talk. We'll pick up your car later."

They drove away from the bar, which was on a back road on the west side of town. As Mike turned onto a gravel road with no streetlamps, Bartholomew was losing patience. "Who is it?" he demanded.

"Wes Trickey."

Bartholomew shook his head. Despite Wes's last name, the guy was anything but tricky. Or clever. Wes had been only sixteen when he started dealing drugs and joined the gang. He'd just turned twenty when Bartholomew had been arrested, and from what Bartholomew remembered, Wes wasn't street savvy. "How has he eluded you for this long?"

"His family is well connected in Sarasota. Father is a state congressman, and his mother comes from old money." Mike shook his head and gripped the steering wheel. "Talk about wasted potential. So far his parents have kept him out of our reach. But he must have finally drawn the last straw because word is out that he's been disinherited. And with all the major players behind bars now, he's on his own. He's running out of friends."

"Then he should be easy to apprehend."

"He's gone underground. Like I said, he's desperate." Mike sighed. "We can't find him. And until we do, we have to keep you on the move. I was going to tell you tomorrow, but we're sending you to a new location."

Bartholomew shook his head. "No. I'm not moving again. I told you, this ends now."

Mike stepped on the brakes. The car screeched as it slowed. He pulled over and put the car in park. "We didn't spend twelve years protecting you just to have you get killed. Give us some more time—"

"No." He slammed his fist on the dashboard. "This is not life, Mike. Not one worth living." He turned to him. "I'm tired of hiding. Of not doing anything. Let me help you bring Wes in."

Mike shook his head. "I can't authorize that."

"Then go to the person who can and get the authorization."

Mike squeezed the steering wheel. "You're serious about this."

"Dead serious."

"You're throwing that word around too lightly," Mike said. He sighed. "I'll see what I can do."

"And when Wes is in custody, I'll get to go home, right?"

Mike turned to him. "Yes. You can see your family again." His cell phone rang and he pulled it out of the pocket of his suit jacket. "Yeah, I got him. He can be stubborn when he wants to be. I'll bring him back. No, rookie, I won't report you . . . this time." He shut off the phone. "You've got the newbie scared witless he's going to lose his job."

"Wes isn't the only one who's desperate."

"Even if I do get the okay to let you help us, you don't know what you're getting into."

"Doesn't matter. Whatever I have to do . . . it will be worth it."

When Abigail woke Monday morning, she went to her window. The sun was peeking over the horizon. It was the second week of April and the weather had finally turned warm enough to open the windows during the day. She crossed her arms and leaned against the window sash.

She thought about her fight with Asa. It hadn't been far from her mind all week as she found refuge in her bedroom and with her loom, coming out only for meals and to help with household chores. Sadie told her to take off as much time as she needed from working at the store. But Abigail knew both of her sisters were worried about her. For a while she was worried about herself.

Asa had stopped by once during the week, but Abigail had refused to see him. She wasn't angry with him anymore. Time and distance had made her realize that. While he should have told her about Susanna, he hadn't been overtly dishonest with her. It was her extreme reaction to what happened that scared her more than anything—that, and facing him again.

She'd thought about how she had basically offered herself to him, thinking he was just like Joel. How embarrassing. But there was more to it than humiliation. She didn't trust herself, didn't trust her own judgment. If she couldn't trust herself, how could she make a relationship work?

She turned and looked at her loom. All week she'd been weaving, and with each attempt she'd made mistakes. She'd redone so much work she'd lost track, and she had nothing to show for it. She couldn't move forward with her weaving, and she felt like she was at a standstill with her life. She couldn't hide in her bedroom forever. She couldn't avoid Asa forever. But how could she face her family, her friends, the community . . . when everyone knew by now what happened with her and Asa?

Her stomach rumbled. She'd been eating less lately, but that didn't seem to have much effect on her waistline. Not that she cared anymore. Her weight was the least of her problems, and she felt foolish for making such a big deal out of it in the first place. She dressed and went downstairs. She'd make breakfast for Sadie and Aden this morning, instead of the other way around.

But when she walked into the kitchen, she was surprised to see Joanna putting a pan of cinnamon rolls in the oven. "When did you get here?" Abigail asked, going over to her sister.

"Andrew brought me over about an hour ago." She turned to Abigail. "I wanted to surprise you with *yer* favorite breakfast."

"I have a lot of favorite breakfasts," Abigail said with a half-smile.

Joanna grinned back. "I also thought we could talk."

"Where are Sadie and Aden?"

"They decided to take a walk this morning. Aden's ready to set up his beehives, now that the weather has turned warmer." Joanna went to the table and sat down. The limp she had from the accident was barely noticeable. "The rolls need to bake for a little while."

Abigail joined her sister at the table. Joanna poured them both a cup of coffee. "How are you doing?" she asked.

Abigail sighed. "Confused." She looked away. "Feeling like a failure."

"Because of Asa?"

"Asa, Joel." She thought about the loom upstairs. "Everything."

"Abigail." Joanna touched her sister's shoulder. "You're not a failure. Remember, I left *mei* husband standing at the proverbial altar."

"*Ya*, but you two worked it out."

"And you and Asa will work things out too."

"But what if we're not supposed to?" She looked at Joanna. "I thought I loved Joel. I think I love Asa. But I haven't given myself any time to . . ."

"To what?"

Tears fell from her eyes. "To breathe. To grieve for *Mamm* and *Daed*. To figure out what God wants me to do."

"Then take that time," Joanna said. "*Nee* one's pushing you." She frowned. "Except Asa."

Abigail shook her head. "He's not pushing me. He only dropped by once this week."

"Then he knows you need some space."

"*Ya.* Space." She stared at her coffee cup. Where would she find space in a small community like Birch Creek? She straightened. "I'm going to Middlefield."

Joanna's brow lifted. "What?"

"I'm sure cousin Mary won't mind if I stay with her for a little while. She's always said we have an open invitation."

"Abigail, you don't have to leave—"

"*Ya,* I do. For a little while." She took Joanna's hand. "Just until I figure things out."

"Figure what out?" Sadie asked as she walked into the kitchen.

"Abigail's going to Middlefield," Joanna said. "Help me talk her out of it."

But Sadie didn't say anything as she sat down. Abigail wiped her eyes as she looked at her older sister. Finally Sadie asked, "Is this what you really need to do?"

"*Ya.*" And it was. She stayed with her cousin while Joanna was in the rehabilitation center. All she had to do was make a phone call and Mary would welcome her with open arms. For the first time in weeks she felt a spark of confidence. This was the right decision, at least for the time being.

"Then we'll miss you." Sadie got up and hugged Abigail's shoulders. "And we'll be waiting for you when you come back."

CHAPTER 25

When Asa came home from work Monday night, he was exhausted. Not just physically, but drained to the core. He hadn't wanted to be at Barton Plastics. He was starting to detest the job that bored him. Before, he would have dealt with it, talked himself into being content with what he had, shoving down his real interests and dreams in order not to make waves. But that was before God had gotten his attention and shaken him loose. Before he fell in love with Abigail and sparked to life.

He was about to open the front door when he heard a buggy pull into his driveway. He recognized the driver and stilled. Abigail. His heart leapt in his chest. He'd tried to see her this week, only to have Sadie turn him away. He wasn't surprised, but he'd been disappointed. Okay, more than disappointed. But he wouldn't force Abigail to see him. And although it had been hard to stay away, he thought he'd made the right decision. Now that was confirmed. She was here. His patience had yielded reward.

He walked toward her, trying not to rush his steps or act like a little kid on Christmas. As he reached her, she pulled on the reins and halted her horse. "Abigail," he said, smiling.

"Hi." She looked down at the reins in her hand. "I . . . I hope it's okay that I came over."

Everything was okay now, he wanted to say. Instead he nodded and reached for the reins. "I can take *yer* horse back to the barn for you."

She shook her head. "I won't be here that long."

His smile faded, and dread churned in his stomach as she climbed out of the buggy. She stood in front of him, and he sensed something different about her. Yes, she was still beautiful, and her sweet spirit called to his heart. Yet there was something else, something he couldn't define but his soul sensed. And then he knew . . . she wasn't here for him.

"I'm sorry," she said, as if he'd said his thoughts out loud. "I'm leaving for Middlefield in the morning."

Middlefield? She was leaving Birch Creek? "Abigail, don't. We can work things out. Start over. I'll do anything—"

"But that's just it," she said. "It doesn't matter what you do. You might be able to fix us . . . but you can't fix me."

"You don't need fixing."

She nodded. "*Ya*, I do. I need to get back to who I am, Asa. To put God at the center of *mei* life so I can be true to him, to me, and to the people I love." She looked up at him. "That includes you."

"You love me?"

Her smile was bitter. "*Ya*, Asa. I do love you. And I'm sorry—"

"*Nee* more apologizing!" He hadn't meant to raise his voice, but sudden anger overtook him. "Susanna said she talked to you.

She even told you to give me another chance. And you're still saying *nee*?"

She nodded, and he exploded.

"I don't believe this!" He glared at her, the pain in his heart stoking his anger. "You mean everything to me, Abigail. You're the reason I came back to Birch Creek."

"I thought God was the reason."

He stilled. "He was—is." Now confusion overtook him. "But God sent me here for you."

"I believe part of that is true. I also think he sent you here to help me see the truth. Not about us, but about myself." Her eyes filled with tears. "I'd ignored God for so long, Asa. I didn't have him first in *mei* life. I put *mei* faith in Joel, and then in you. I can't do that anymore."

Asa dropped his hands from his waist. How could he argue with this? Yet he wanted to. She could have him and God.

No, she can't. Not yet.

A knot formed in Asa's throat. Now God decided to speak? He looked at Abigail, tears streaming down her cheeks. *I thought I was supposed to fight for her. Wasn't that the lesson here, Lord? That life isn't easy, that I have to work for what's important?*

Wait.

He heard that one word clearer than he'd heard any of God's other instructions. And it cut him to the core. To wait, he'd have to say good-bye. And there was no deadline, no time given for how long he'd have to wait, or even what he was waiting for.

She took his hands in hers. "*Danki*, Asa. *Danki* for showing me the truth, and for loving me."

"What do we do now?"

Turning from him, she said, "We move on." She released his hands and climbed back in the buggy.

Asa turned away, unable to watch her go. He didn't want her to see how upset he was, how hard he was fighting his tears. *Wait.* What did that mean? Would he and Abigail find their way back to each other? If they didn't, he didn't know how he could survive it.

You have me. That is enough.

He took in a deep breath, feeling God's presence as dusk surrounded him. God was enough. He had been when Asa left Shipshewana and arrived in Birch Creek with nothing. And although he had rebuilt his life and fallen in love, that fact hadn't changed. God was enough, whether he had plenty or nothing. That was the lesson he had to learn. Perhaps Abigail had to learn it too.

The next morning Abigail waited outside for the taxi to pick her up to take her to Middlefield. She had already told Sadie and Aden good-bye, and they were working in the store. They had assured her that between the two of them they could handle running the store and getting Aden's beekeeping business going. Abigail believed it. They were two determined people, and as a team, they were unbeatable.

She smiled as she saw two blue jays chase after each other in the warm sunshine. This time her smile was genuine, coming from her soul. There were still small aches in her heart for her parents and for Asa, but she knew she was making the right decision. God was leading her away from Birch Creek for a time. He would lead her back when he wanted her to return.

A buggy pulled into the driveway, and for a moment her peace evaporated. Surely Asa wasn't here to talk her out of leaving? She didn't think she had the strength for another confrontation with him. Her heart dipped as she remembered the sadness in his beautiful gray eyes. But she'd also seen grudging acceptance. They both knew the time wasn't right for them to be together—if they were supposed to be together at all. Then she saw who was in the driver's seat and froze. Joel.

She stared at him as he got out of the buggy, long and lean and blond and as handsome as ever. Nothing compared to Asa, though. Her heart didn't skip a single beat as he approached her.

"Abigail, can I talk to you for a moment?" His brow flattened, his eyes taking on a serious expression. Whatever was on his mind was weighing heavily on him. She nodded. There was no reason to be uncomfortable around him anymore. "Sure."

He looked around the yard. "In private?"

"*Nee* one's here."

Joel looked at Abigail's suitcase, which was on the ground next to her. "I heard you were going back to Middlefield."

"How—"

"You know the grapevine works fast around here." His frown deepened. "You're not leaving because . . . because of me?"

She almost laughed. Of course he would think that. He was selfish enough to date someone else while she had been helping her sister heal, so why wouldn't he think the world revolved around him? "*Nee.* I'm not leaving because of you."

Relief crossed his face. "*Gut.*"

"Does Rebecca know you're here?" she asked.

He shook his head. "*Nee.* She doesn't."

"Then maybe it's not a *gut* idea for us to talk."

"But we need to. At least I do." He rubbed his cheek with the flat of his hand. "I need to apologize to you, Abigail. I should

have done this a long time ago. But I was selfish. I wasn't thinking about you, only about myself."

"And Rebecca," Abigail couldn't help but add.

"*Ya*. And Rebecca."

Abigail could see his beard was already growing in. He and
Rebecca had been married less than a month. She waited for
jealousy to rear its head. She was basically in the same place she'd
been when he'd broken up with her—alone. But no, she wasn't
alone. She had her family. She also had God, and a new path
stretched in front of her.

"Forgive me?" he asked, looking earnest, and more than a
little worried. "Forgive me for how I treated you when we were
together. For breaking up with you the way I did. For cheating
on you." He looked at the ground. "I treated you poorly. You
deserved so much better."

She'd been waiting to hear those words from him, although
she'd never expected to. "I forgive you."

He let out a relieved breath. "*Danki*. I really am sorry."

"I know." She smirked. "I can tell."

"And I know you won't believe this, but I did care about
you. I still wish you well, Abigail."

"And I wish you well, Joel." Nothing had worked out the
way she had expected with him. But she knew in her heart it
wouldn't have. She hadn't been ready to marry Joel, just like she
wasn't ready to have a relationship with Asa. "Just make sure you
treat Rebecca the way she deserves."

"I plan to." He looked down at her. "You really are special,
Abigail. I hope you know that."

"I do," she said with a lift of her chin. As he walked away, she
whispered again, "I really do."

He left, and she hugged her arms around her body. Special. He'd never said that when they were together. She let out a short laugh. How ironic.

She lifted her face to the warming sunshine. Spring was finally here, and with it, a new beginning—and she was looking forward to it.

CHAPTER 26

You don't know what you're getting into . . .

Y The words reverberated in Bartholomew's mind as he
sat in the warehouse parking lot in his beat-up junker of a car.
Two weeks after he and Mike had talked, he was now waiting
for Wes Trickey to show up. Mike had been right about Wes's
desperation and Bartholomew had been right about the kid's lack
of street smarts. It hadn't taken long for word to get to Wes that
Bartholomew Beiler was looking to get back in the drug trade.
Now he was waiting for Wes's phone call to direct him where
they were going to meet. He tapped the top of his cell phone, a
burner the feds had given to him, along with the wire he wore
on his chest.

He knew he should be scared to death. Over the past week
he had been given access to Wes's information, what he'd been
up to the past twelve years, and the depths he had sunk to since
his family had cut him off. Armed and dangerous was what Mike
had said. Bartholomew was taking his life in his hands by doing
this. He knew it.

But instead of panic he felt calm. He'd been truthful when he told Mike that his life meant nothing now that he was completely cut off from Naomi and his children. And he had spent hours in prayer, asking for courage. That and thinking of Naomi and his family kept his heartbeat at a steady rate. He rolled down the window slightly and the scent of the ocean wafted to him. He hadn't been in Sarasota for over a decade. The ocean breeze brought back memories, but some of them good ones, like meeting and marrying Naomi. He remembered how much Irene liked to watch the seagulls.

The phone rang and he answered it. "Beiler," he said.

"You alone?" the scratchy voice on the other end said.

"Yeah." They sounded like a bad cop television show. "Enough with the cloak-and-dagger, Wes. Are we gonna meet up or not? I can find someone else to work with me on this. Plenty of dealers out there. Don't waste my time."

Wes's breathing was heavy over the speaker. "I got questions."

"Let's meet face-to-face so I can answer them."

"Is this close enough?"

Bartholomew heard a tap on the driver's side window. He jumped and turned to see Wes standing outside his car, a gun pointed at Bartholomew's head. He gulped. Although there were several marshals in strategic hiding places in the area, they were little comfort now. All Wes had to do was pull the trigger . . .

"Get out," Wes snapped.

Bartholomew opened the door as Wes stepped away, the gun still pointed at him. Gathering his calm, Bartholomew said, "The gun's not necessary."

"Oh, I think it's necessary." Wes sniffed, and in the yellow light of the warehouse lot Bartholomew could see shadowed pock marks on Wes's face. He smelled like urine, and Bartholomew knew he'd been making meth, if not using it.

But a stronger emotion than fear slammed into him. He was face-to-face with what could have been his future if he hadn't been arrested and put into protection. God had saved him from this, he realized. The past twelve years had been hard, but he was alive. He had been in contact with Naomi. He was healthy. He wasn't a skin-and-bones mess desperate for money and another fix. God had made sure Bartholomew paid for his mistakes, but he had also shown him mercy. The deep truth of that fact hadn't hit him until now.

"What are you staring at?" Wes wiped his nose with his sleeve.

"You're holding a gun on me. Of course I'm going to stare." Bartholomew held up his hands. "I'm not armed."

"How do I know that?" Wes's arm grew unsteady as his speech sped up. His gaze darted around. "How do I know you're alone?"

"Do you see anyone else here?"

"Those cops, they're sneaky, you know." Wes started to shift on his feet. "I guess we can talk here. Tell me the plan."

"Plan?"

"Yeah. You've got a plan, right? How we're getting back in the game?" Wes gripped the gun tighter. "And it better be more than homemade meth labs and selling to country-club kids." He aimed the gun at Bartholomew's chest. "You better tell me you have a plan, Beiler. One to make a big score. One that will make the Mexicans sorry they left me alone in the wind."

Bartholomew's mind scrambled. Were the feds hearing this? Wasn't it enough for them to arrest Wes? Bartholomew didn't have a plan, at least not one Wes would buy. He'd spent years regretting ever going near drugs. Now he had to think about how he and the thin, pathetic man in front of him were going to take over the drug world.

"You got three seconds to start talking or I put a bullet in your heart." Wes raised the gun. "Or your brain. I don't care what I hit."

"Wes, don't do anything stupid. Don't add murder to your crimes."

Wes grinned, and Bartholomew could see he was missing teeth. "Too late. Been there, done that."

Bartholomew's blood ran cold. Where was Mike?

"I'm waiting, Beiler. You got three seconds."

"Wait," Bartholomew said, backing up against the car. Cold sweat dripped down his face. "Don't—"

"Three . . . two . . ."

"One."

Bartholomew sagged with relief as he saw Mike coming toward Wes, gun drawn. "Put down the weapon, Trickey, or you'll be the one with a hole in the head." When Wes hesitated, Mike yelled, "Drop it!"

Wes put down the gun, his grin shifting to a glare as several officers came out from behind barrels and stacks of cargo. Mike slid his gun into his holster, then grabbed Wes's arms and shoved them behind his back.

"Doesn't matter, I'll be out on bail in a few hours," Wes sneered, his gaze remaining on Bartholomew.

"You threatened to kill someone," Mike said. "The only place you're going to be is in prison for a very long time. And before you squawk about lack of proof, we have you on tape." He shoved Wes toward another officer, who took Wes away.

Bartholomew leaned against the car, willing his speeding

pulse to return to normal. Mike came up and put his hand on Bartholomew's shoulder. "You okay?"

"I will be . . . eventually." He looked to see the officer and Wes disappear behind a stack of oil drums.

"Good." Mike released his grip. He leaned against the car next to Bartholomew and put his hands in his pockets. "We would have got to him someday," he said. "Trickey's not that smart."

"He never was." Bartholomew straightened as he blew out a long breath. "Yeah. I see why you drink now."

"Not often," Mike said. "But sometimes . . ." He shrugged. "Anyway, thanks for your help. You did good, Beiler. And you've more than made up for what you did all those years ago." He moved to stand in front of Bartholomew. "Go home. Go see your family."

As Mike walked away, tears welled in Bartholomew's eyes. Home. Family. In a day or two he would see Naomi, Irene, and Andrew again. He couldn't help but sink to his knees, thanking God that he would finally be whole again.

Irene turned her face toward the sunshine as she rode next to Sol in the buggy. It was mid-April, the warmest day yet that month. Spring was in the air, and she could see signs of it— daffodils and jonquil leaves pushing through the earth, the sound of birds twittering, and most of all the sun. It felt good to enjoy the warmth after a long winter.

It felt even better sitting next to Sol.

Since that afternoon more than two weeks ago when he had prayed for her and her family, they had fallen into an easy friendship. He was more relaxed around her now, quicker to smile and crack a joke. But he kept a physical distance between them and she wondered if it had something to do with her kissing him on the cheek. It had been forward of her, but she had been so filled with peace after his prayer that she couldn't contain herself. Since then *Mamm* had been quiet and hadn't mentioned *Daed*'s letter, but she wasn't as upset as she'd been when she'd come home from the post office. Irene still didn't know what was going on between her parents, and she couldn't ask. It was frustrating, but working and being with Sol helped divert her thoughts. She enjoyed painting the birdhouses, but looked forward to seeing Sol even more.

Life was good, with one exception. She missed Abigail. She'd received one letter from her friend since she left for Middlefield, and while it was friendly, it was also vague. She'd been a little hurt that Abigail hadn't told her good-bye, but she also understood. After everything that happened with her parents, Joel, and then Asa, Irene wouldn't begrudge Abigail her space or question her decisions. She just hoped she would return to Birch Creek soon.

She glanced at Sol, who was staring straight ahead as he drove the buggy. When he offered to take her home after they finished working Saturday afternoon, she'd eagerly accepted. Since the day had been mild she had walked to his house, and she wouldn't have minded walking home . . . but it was much better riding with Sol. "*Danki* for the ride," she said, turning to him. "That's kind of you."

"I don't mind." He didn't look at her, just stared straight ahead. "It's the least I can do after you've painted so many birdhouses."

"Which you paid me for."

"I should have paid you more. The painted ones are selling better than the plain ones."

She was pleased to hear that, but she kept it to herself, not wanting to appear boastful. A car moved past them, driving slowly and considerately as it passed the buggy. There wasn't much traffic on this road, but she imagined since it was a beautiful day people might be out going for a ride. She waited for him to say something else, but after a lengthy silence she looked out the buggy again, breathing in the fresh air.

"Irene," he said, pulling a bit on the reins and slowing down his horse. "I . . ." He shook his head. "This is going to sound stupid."

"Sol, I hope you know by now you can say anything to me."

"I do." He turned and looked at her for a brief moment. "And I'm glad for it. I don't have many friends, Irene. Jalon's still hung in there with me. But not everyone trusts me, and I know it will take time for me to earn that trust. I just wanted you to know that I appreciate our . . . friendship."

She couldn't help but feel a little disappointed by that word, and the memory of her kissing his cheek made her face heat. Sure, she was glad they were friends. But she wanted more. Her mother had told her to follow her heart, and it was leading her to Solomon Troyer. But that didn't mean he reciprocated the feeling. The thought of that disappointed her. But friendship was better than nothing. "I'm glad you feel comfortable with me."

"I do." He paused. "Very."

This husky tone made her glance at him. He wasn't looking at her anymore. He was staring ahead, his cheeks slightly colored. She looked at the reins he held in his hand. His knuckles were white. Something was going on with him, which had her a little worried.

She frowned when he turned the buggy down an unfamiliar road. "I thought you were taking me home."

He continued to drive, not answering her, his knuckles still gripping the reins with an almost deathly tightness. It wasn't until they went down another road, then to a dead end nearby, and he pulled the buggy to a standstill, that he looked at her.

She looked around and saw they were alone. "Why did you bring me here?"

His gaze was more intense than she'd ever seen it. "I care about you, Irene. I care about you a lot."

Her heart thumped in her chest. Finally, she could admit her feelings to him. "I care about you, too, Sol."

"Because I care, I need to be completely honest with you. And I haven't been." He put his hand on her shoulder, holding her still. "I haven't told you everything. And once I do . . . you might change *yer* mind about me."

CHAPTER 27

Irene wasn't sure what was going on. She'd never seen Sol like this. She also wasn't sure how she should react. His hand on her shoulder was unnerving, but not threatening. She didn't know where he'd brought her. From what she could tell, there was no one around for miles. The road dead-ended into a field with woods to the left. It was just her and Sol, and he was acting strangely.

Then he released her arm. "I haven't been here since . . ." He closed his eyes, breathed in deep, then opened them. "I promise once I explain everything I'll take you home." He took off his hat and shoved both hands through his hair. "You told me about *yer vatter*. Now I'm going to tell you about mine."

She listened as he talked about the beatings his father had given both him and Aden when they were young. About how his father made him beat Aden when he got a little older, to keep both of them in line.

"He said he was teaching me to be strong." Sol hung his head. "That me punishing Aden instead of him would make us both better men. He was so wrong about that."

Irene fought the urge to hug him. She sensed he would reject any offer of comfort. Then he started explaining that his father had hoarded money. Not just his own money, but the community's. "It was all greed," Sol said. "And I went along with it. I didn't care. I was drunk most of the time, Aden was afraid all the time, and *Mamm* ignored everything. But I don't blame her. She had her own way of coping with what was happening in our *familye*." Then he turned to Irene. "Everything came to a head when he wanted me to marry Sadie Schrock."

"*Yer bruder's wife?*"

Sol nodded. "He wanted access to the Schrocks' property. There are oil rights on that land *mei* father wanted to get a hand on. And I saw marrying Sadie as an opportunity to escape *mei* life." He let out a bitter chuckle. "But Aden stepped up. Offered to marry Sadie, and she accepted. *Daed* didn't care which one of us married her. The difference was that Aden loved her. And he protected her and her *schwesters* from *mei* father. That's when *Daed* started losing control."

Irene was trying to digest what he was saying. She didn't want to believe any of it . . . but deep inside she did. She'd known the bishop was a hard man, distant, very legalistic, and much different from the bishop she remembered in Florida. He'd visited *Mamm* on occasion, always saying he was doing his duty to look after a woman without a husband. But Irene always sensed censure in the man's eyes and voice, as if he blamed Naomi for her husband's abandonment. Of course, he had thought *Daed* left *Mamm* for another woman. But how was that her mother's fault? She'd never liked Sol's father, only respected him because she had to. Now her stomach lurched as she thought of what Sol had been through.

"I wouldn't blame you if you didn't believe me," Sol said. He turned from her and faced the front. The horse nickered before munching on the grass at the end of the gravel road.

She moved next to him. "I do believe you." She shook her head. "What you've been through . . ." she whispered.

Sol abruptly turned to her. "Don't feel sorry for me. I put so many people through so much pain. Aden, Sadie, *mei mamm* . . . *Daed* was right to put me in the bann, even though he was doing it for his own selfish reasons. If he hadn't, then I wouldn't have listened to God." He clenched his fists. "I'd still be drinking, still be hateful . . . and *Daed* would still be here."

"Do you want him to come back?"

Sol shook his head, his eyes turning into green chips of ice. "*Nee.* I don't care if I ever see him again."

Irene's blood chilled. "Surely you don't mean that."

"I do." The muscles in his jaw twitched. "He's caused me and *mei familye nix* but heartache."

"But you have to forgive him." Irene angled her body so she could face him. "Jesus said—"

"I know what Jesus said!"

She flinched at the anger in his voice.

"I'll take you home now."

"*Nee,* let's talk about this."

But he was already turning the buggy around, and he didn't say another word on the way to her house. By the time he pulled into her driveway the sky was a dusky gray and she could barely see his expression when she turned to him. "Sol . . ."

"I'm sorry, Irene. But like I said . . . you'd change *yer* mind about me once you knew the truth."

"You're wrong about that," she said. "I haven't changed *mei* mind at all. I just hope one day you'll be able to see *yerself* the way I see you . . ." Her voice caught in her throat. She paused, wishing there wasn't so much distance between them, distance he had put there. Not by admitting the hard truth about his upbringing, or even the brutal honesty of not being able to forgive his father. He was caving in on himself and she could see it . . . feel it. He was pushing her away, and she wasn't sure she was strong enough to push back.

When she went inside, she passed by the kitchen, barely nodding to her mother as she went upstairs. She closed the door to her room and sank to her knees. She didn't have the strength or ability to heal Sol. Only the Lord did . . . and the Lord's work was exactly what she prayed for.

Sol knew he'd made a mistake telling Irene about his father. He should have known she'd ask him about forgiveness. And he couldn't lie to her. He hadn't forgiven his father. He wasn't sure if he ever truly would.

Consumed with his thoughts, he let his horse take the lead on the way home. But Jasper hadn't taken him home, and when he'd paid attention to where he was, he realized his horse had taken him back to the dead-end road. "*Dummkopf*," he muttered, irritated more with himself than with the horse. He pulled on the horse's reins, but was met with resistance. He frowned and tugged a little harder. But the horse pulled straight ahead, ignoring Sol's attempt at directing it in any other direction than forward. "Halt!" he said, yanking even harder. The horse finally held up.

The fading rays of sunlight made it difficult for Sol to see. "Come, Jasper," he said. "Let's *geh* home."

But the horse wouldn't move. Jasper stood stock-still. Sol jumped out of the buggy to check on him. Maybe there was something wrong with the animal. But after giving him a thorough once-over, he couldn't find anything. "What's going on with you?" he said, stroking the horse's nose. "Why did you bring me here?"

Sol froze as a shiver ran between his shoulder blades. He turned and looked at the woods, barely making the outline of the trees in the dim light of dusk. A few yards away, deep in the woods, was the small wood shack that had belonged to his father. *Daed* had kept the cabin a secret until Sol stumbled upon it when he was drunk one night. Then after *Daed* left, Sol took Aden there, showing him where their father had hidden the community's money and put Sol in the bann.

His stomach churning, he headed into the woods. He had a flashlight in his buggy, but he didn't bother to get it. He knew these woods. He had spent more than one drunken night in the cabin, and after being in the bann, he had spent three days wandering in circles, detoxing from alcohol, his soul stripped bare by God. This was where his life had changed. Where he knew he couldn't dull his pain with alcohol anymore or take out his anger through physical abuse. He couldn't continue to keep his father's secret about hoarding money that not only belonged to the community but was needed by its members. Here he'd faced his sins, his brokenness, his ugliness.

But there was one more thing he had to do. As he continued in the dark woods, he found the cabin. Opened the door. Walked inside and saw a cracked, splintered plank of wood that had somehow torn loose from the wall. He ignored it and fell to his knees in the center of the cabin.

"Help me to forgive him," he said, his heart feeling like it was being ripped apart all over again. "Give me the strength to forgive *mei* father."

The next day Irene searched for Sol at church, but she didn't see him. His mother, Rhoda, was there, but there was no sign of Sol. After the service she approached Rhoda, asking where Sol was.

"He didn't come home last night." Rhoda's hands twisted together. "I'm sure he's all right, though. He's done this before. Just not since . . ." Her gaze flicked away, then back at Irene. "He usually comes back in a *daag* or two."

Irene nodded and thanked Rhoda for the information. But when she turned from Sol's mother, it passed through her mind that he had gone on a drinking binge. She pushed that thought away. She believed he had changed. She believed in him. Whatever happened, he hadn't spent the night out drinking. She was sure of that.

But where was he? She found her mother and told her she wanted to leave, but *Mamm* decided to stay a little longer and visit. "I'll catch a ride home with Andrew and Joanna."

Irene nodded as she turned and tried not to rush to her buggy. Within a few minutes she was on the road, trying to figure out where to search for Sol. Would he be at Aden and Sadie's? Or maybe he had gone home this morning and was at his own house, or in the workshop. She slowed down her horse and calmed her heart. She wasn't going to find him with her thoughts racing. *Lord, where is he?*

She didn't get a clear answer, and she realized she could spend the day wearing out her horse looking for Sol only to discover he might not want to be found. She blew out a breath. She needed to give him space. She turned around and headed back to her house. All she could offer him now were her prayers.

When she arrived home, she guided her horse to the barn,

unhitched it from the buggy, and started to lead her to her stall. When she entered the barn, she froze. Standing in the middle of the barn with his hands in the pockets of his broadfall pants was Sol. Without thinking, she dropped the horse's reins and ran to him, throwing her arms around his waist and hugging him tight. "Where have you been?"

His arms went around her shoulders, but he didn't fully return her embrace. She pulled away and looked up at him. There was a smeared patch of dirt on his forehead and his long reddish hair was sticking up, as if he'd been pulling on the ends. His eyes were bloodshot but he didn't smell like alcohol.

Her horse whinnied. Irene held up one finger. "Don't *geh* anywhere." She quickly took care of her horse while Sol waited, not moving from the spot where she'd found him. When she returned to stand in front of him, she asked again, "Where have you been? Where were you all night?"

"How did you know I was gone that long?"

"*Yer mamm* said you didn't *geh* home last night." She batted his arm on impulse. "Don't ever worry me like that again!"

"I didn't mean to worry you." His voice sounded scratchy, like a nail against a rusty can. "I need to *geh* home and let *Mamm* know I'm okay. But I had to come by here first." His chest heaved. "Irene, I'm sorry about yesterday. You were right, and Jesus is right. I have to forgive *mei* father. Not just for myself, although I know that's important. But I want him to see that God changed me. That I'm not the weak man he always said I was. That I became strong—that I am strong—only because God has made me so. I want him to come back and apologize to *Mamm*. To Aden. I want . . ." Tears shined in his eyes. "I want him to have what I have. I want him to be healed."

"Oh, Sol."

"I think . . ." He swallowed. "I think I've forgiven him."

Without qualm she put her arms around his neck and hugged him, not caring that he was still wearing yesterday's clothes and smelled like he'd spent the night in the woods. "You're an amazing man," she said in his ear. "To overcome what you've overcome." She hugged him more tightly.

But he pulled away. "Only through God, Irene. Don't give me the credit. God dealt with me again, but that doesn't mean I'm okay. Far from it. I still want to drink. I don't know if that urge will ever *geh* away. And while I don't feel the anger I had before . . . I'm afraid of what will happen if I do get angry. I don't want to hurt anyone ever again."

Meaning dawned on Irene. This is what he needed her for. He needed someone to believe in him, to stand beside him and support him. To remind him of the man he was now and keep him from believing he was still the man of his past. She wanted to be that for him. She wanted to walk this journey with him for the rest of their lives. But how could she convince him of that?

There was only one way. She brushed a russet lock of hair back from his forehead. She kissed the skin revealed there. "I love you," she said, knowing that it was highly possible that he didn't love her back. Yet that didn't hold her back from telling him the truth. He needed to know how she felt. That he was worth loving. "I love the man you've become and the man you will continue to be."

His hand moved to her waist even as he said her name. "Are you sure?"

"More than anything." She leaned forward and kissed him. He didn't respond at first, then he was kissing her until she could barely breathe. His hand tightened at her waist as he broke the kiss.

"I'll wait for you, Sol. I'll wait until you love me."

He smiled, and she'd never seen anything so beautiful. "You don't have to wait for me to love you, Irene. I already do." After kissing her again Sol said, "I need to *geh*." He paused, gazing into her eyes. "Even though I don't want to."

Her heart warmed. Gone was the trepidation that had been there earlier. Now she saw what she'd yearned for in his green eyes—peace. "I understand. Where is *yer* buggy?"

"Other side of the barn. I was worried *yer bruder* would come home before you and chase me away."

"Andrew wouldn't do that." Irene realized Sol still had a long way to go until he believed he wasn't a pariah. "You're *familye*, remember?"

"By marriage." A fact that he didn't need to say out loud. Yet his cheeks turned almost the shade of his hair as they walked out of the barn. "I'll see you tomorrow, *ya*?"

"Of course." She followed him to his buggy. His horse was contentedly munching on the grass behind the barn.

Sol climbed in and took the reins. "Maybe we can talk about a few things after work. Important things," he added. He smiled again and Irene caught his meaning.

"I can't wait."

She said good-bye and stepped away from the buggy. She was waving as he pulled out of the driveway. Before he was completely gone a car pulled up next to it and waited for Sol to leave before pulling into the driveway. Irene waited to see who was stopping by her house in a car. That was unusual.

The front passenger side door opened and a man who was a little taller than Andrew stepped out of the car. He was *Englisch*, with short, sandy-blond hair cut close to his scalp and was wearing a long-sleeved plaid shirt, jeans, and sneakers. He pulled a duffle bag out of the front seat and shut the door, giving the driver a little wave. The driver backed out and the man faced Irene, but he didn't come any closer.

A weird feeling overcame her and she couldn't move. There was something familiar about him . . . her stomach felt like it dropped to her feet. "*Daed?*" She put her hand over her mouth.

He nodded, but didn't make a move toward her. "Hello, Irene."

Suddenly it was as if she were thirteen years old again. She launched herself into his arms. He dropped the duffle bag and hugged her tight.

"You're home," Irene said, tears streaming down her face as she held on to her father's neck.

"*Ya*," he said, his voice thick. "I'm finally home."

CHAPTER 28

Asa stripped off his church vest, hung it on a hanger, and put it in his closet. He closed the door and turned to look at the bedroom. His old bedroom, the one where he grew up. When Abigail left, he'd thrown himself into fixing up the house. God was keeping him here, and he couldn't live in a dump. He'd also put in his two weeks' notice at the plastics plant on Friday. He was done working in factories. He'd taken on Sol, Andrew, and Freemont as clients, and was ready to hang out his shingle as an accountant. When he'd finally made the decision, he'd felt freer than he had ever felt in his life. He also felt like he had a purpose.

He went downstairs to the kitchen to fix a sandwich, then take a Sunday afternoon nap. As he passed by the front door, he heard a knock. His heart flipped. Abigail? Was she back? He hurried to the door, opened it, and saw Andrew. "Oh," Asa said, opening the door wider.

"Glad to see you too." Andrew snickered and walked into the living room.

"Sorry." Asa shut the door and gestured to the new couch

he'd bought last week to replace the old one he had before. It wasn't fancy, but it was nice. He'd chosen a dark blue color, briefly wondering if Abigail would like it, then realizing he couldn't make his purchases—or any other decisions—based on her opinion. Not when she wasn't in his life anymore.

Andrew sat down and crossed his ankle over his knee. He was still wearing his church clothes, including his black hat, which he took off and tossed beside him.

"I don't have much to offer you for lunch," Asa said.

"That's okay. Joanna's putting together something." He patted his belly. "She's going to have me fattened up soon enough."

Asa sat down in the rocker. "I can think of worse fates."

Andrew's expression sobered. "*Ya.*" He uncrossed his legs and leaned forward. "I came by to see how you're doing. I'm sorry I haven't been around much."

"You're married," Asa said with a shrug. "That keeps a man busy."

"It does." Andrew grinned, but it disappeared quickly. "Have you heard from Abigail?"

He shook his head. "I don't expect to."

"Maybe you should *geh* see her."

"*Nee.*" Asa leveled his gaze at Andrew. "Absolutely not."

"I didn't take you for a prideful man, Asa."

"It's not pride." He leaned forward. "Don't get me wrong. I still care for Abigail. I still . . ."

"Love her?"

He swallowed. "*Ya.* And that's why I'm not chasing her to Middlefield or wherever else she decides to *geh. Mei* place is here, in Birch Creek. That hasn't changed just because Abigail left." He pushed his hand through his hair. "I used to think that was why God brought me here. Because Abigail and I were meant to be together. But that's not why. I have purpose now, Andrew. I'm going to start *mei* own business soon." He looked around the living room. "The *haus* is shaping up."

"What about Abigail?"

He blew out a breath. "I don't know. I've had to put that in God's hands. And it's been the hardest thing I've ever done."

Andrew nodded. He picked up his hat and stood. "I better get home. I'm glad to see you're doing okay."

"Better than okay." He stood and faced Andrew. The words were true. He missed Abigail, but he had a life here. A new beginning. And if he and Abigail were meant to be together, God would make a way. He truly believed that.

∞

Irene sat in the living room with her father and mother while they waited for Andrew to come home. Her mother and Joanna had dropped him off at Asa's before coming home, and now Joanna was in the kitchen preparing a cold lunch. Irene and Naomi had offered to help but Joanna had insisted on letting them all have time alone. Homer was also there with her, waiting for any scrap that might accidentally—or on purpose—fall on the floor.

Irene looked at her parents and smiled. They were sitting together on the couch, close but not touching. Yet they couldn't stop looking at each other. Irene could feel the love between them, and it made her tear up again. Her mother had believed her father would come home one day—and now he was here.

"Are you sure they've captured everyone involved in the drug ring?" *Mamm* asked.

Daed nodded. "*Ya*, finally." His answer was curt, and he didn't elaborate. Irene wasn't going to ask. She would probably never know what her father had gone through the past twelve years, and that didn't matter. What was important was that he was here. He looked at Irene and then back at *Mamm*. "It's so *gut* to be home."

Irene noticed he'd slipped back into Pennsylvania *Dietsch*. Then he looked at Irene. "So who was the young man I saw leaving when I arrived?"

"Bartholomew," *Mamm* said, giving him a warning look.

Daed frowned. "Sorry. I was only teasing."

"It's okay." She grinned. "His name is Solomon Troyer."

"Irene works for him," *Mamm* explained. "Painting bird-houses."

"Oh." *Daed* looked chastened. "Sorry. I thought . . . never mind. I should mind *mei* own business."

"*Nee*, it's all right." She looked at both her parents. "I like him. And he likes me." No reason to admit that they were in love, not when it was so new. She wanted to keep that to herself.

The faint sound of the back door opening silenced them. "Andrew's home," *Mamm* said.

Daed stood up. "I'll *geh* see him, then."

When he left, *Mamm* watched him walk out of the living room. "I can't believe he's home."

"Me either." She went to sit next to her mother. "We all have so much catching up to do."

"I think you have some catching up to do with me," *Mamm* said. She leaned closer to her. "I didn't know Sol was here."

"It was an unexpected visit."

Mamm's face beamed, her smile wider than Irene had ever seen it. She hugged her mother. "You look happy," she said.

"I am," *Mamm* whispered, hugging Irene tight. "I'm so very, very happy."

Me too. Sol loved her, and now she had her father back. It was more than she'd ever hoped for.

∞

Later that evening, after supper, Naomi couldn't wait to be alone with her husband. Now they were upstairs in their room, and her heart was so filled with joy she thought it might burst.

"I can't believe you're here." Naomi lifted her hand to touch Bartholomew's face. He looked so different, yet the same. The warmth in his blue eyes, his square jaw, hair so soft she couldn't resist touching it. These were all familiar. But the grays that threaded through the short, sandy-blond strands, the stress lines on his forehead, the slight slump of his posture—these were the changes.

"You look the same," he said, his voice a low, husky whisper that sent a shiver down her spine. He ran this thumb over the top of her cheek, right below her glasses. "Still beautiful."

She almost melted at the tears in his eyes. She took his hand and led him to the edge of her bed. Their bed. She could hardly believe it. It would be their bed now, just like everything else here. They shared it now. *Not mine, but ours.* He sat down next to her, keeping his hand in hers.

She gazed at him again. "I don't know what to say."

"It's like being on our first date again." He smiled. "Getting to know each other."

"Yet already knowing."

He nodded. "Something like that." He lifted their clasped hands together. "I can't tell you how good it feels to be here with you. I've dreamt of this moment for years." He shifted his gaze to her. "Along with other moments."

She blushed. "Me too," she admitted, unable to look him in the eye. He made her feel like a young girl all over again, stripping away the years of worry and longing and sacrifice.

"Naomi." He touched her chin and he turned her to face him. "Don't be afraid."

"I'm not."

"*Yer* hand is shaking."

"I'm just . . ." She didn't know how to describe it. "Happy," she said, tightening her grip around his hand. "So very, very happy."

Bartholomew kissed her forehead. "Me too. I'm also sorry."

She put her fingers to his lips. "You don't have to say it."

"*Ya*, I do." He moved her hand. "I'll say it every day for as long as I live. I can't make up for what I've done to you . . . to our *familye*."

"There's nothing to make up. You're here. That's what matters." She ran her hand across the sides of his short hair. "I don't know how I feel about this, though," she said, desperate for some levity. She'd spent so long without him that she didn't want their first moment alone to be filled with sorrowful reminders.

He ran his hand through his short hair. "*Ya*. But it will grow." He glanced down. "I'll need new clothes too."

She extricated her hand from his and went to the closet. She pulled out a shirt, then a pair of pants. "Will these do?"

He joined her at the closet. "You saved these?"

"I knew you'd come back. I wanted them to be here when you did."

He took them from her. "You had that much faith."

"I did. In God, and in you."

"Even after I couldn't write to you anymore?"

She paused, knowing she had to tell him the truth. "I was

upset. *Nee*, more than upset." She gazed up at him. "I was devastated. The thought of never hearing from you again was more than I could bear. And I thought . . ." She turned away from him.

"You thought what?"

"That maybe I was wrong. That God hadn't promised me you would return, that it was just wishful thinking." She glanced at him over her shoulder. "That maybe you had found someone else."

He hung the clothes back in the closet, then came up behind her and put his hands on her shoulders. "You're the only one for me, Naomi. There never was, never could be, anyone else. I love you." He turned her to face him. "And I will never leave you again. I promise." He bent and kissed her.

She melted into his embrace, and poured her heart out to him . . . as she had been waiting to do for so long.

CHAPTER 29

I rene's hands trembled as she fastened the last bobby pin onto her *kapp* as she stood at the bottom of the stairs. She tried not to think about all the people waiting for her outside on this hot September day, but to focus on the fact that soon she would be Mrs. Solomon Troyer. Getting married so quickly wasn't typical, but she and Sol had waited long enough. Nerves mixed with anticipation. She wanted to be a good wife to Sol. He had come so far over the past few months, and she had too. She had learned how to have faith and trust in her husband to be, even when there were still a few people in the community who questioned whether Sol really was a changed man. But she couldn't do anything about their opinion of him. All she could do was follow her heart.

She slipped on her black bonnet and tied it under her chin, then breathed deeply. It was time. She started for the door that led to the backyard of her parents' house where the wedding ceremony would take place.

286

"Irene."

Pausing at the sound of her father's voice, she turned around. He stood there, a sheepish smile on his face. She was still getting used to having him here, but she was so grateful for his presence. He was wearing his Sunday clothes, the new ones *Mamm* made shortly after his return. He'd grown his hair out, and it covered the tops of his ears. She returned his smile.

"You ready for this?" he asked.

"*Ya*," she said, her nerves calming down a tiny bit. Then she smirked. "Are you?"

He walked toward her. "Honestly . . . *nee*."

She frowned. "*Nee*?"

His blue-eyed gaze searched her face. "I missed so much with you and Andrew," he said, his voice low and full of regret. "You're *mei dochder* . . . *mei* little girl. And now I'm handing you over to someone else." His eyes misted. "I have so many things to make up for—"

"*Daed*, don't." She touched the sleeve of his white shirt. "This is a new beginning, for all of us. We need to celebrate the present, and let God take care of the future."

Her father nodded. "How did you get so wise?"

"I'm not." She grinned. "I'm just repeating what Sol said to me last night."

"So he's the wise one." *Daed* leaned over and kissed her cheek. "I love you, Irene."

"I love you, too, *Daed*. I'm so glad you're here to share this *daag* with me and Sol."

He gave her a small nod, then went outside. A minute later Irene followed him, ready to marry the man she loved.

∞

Asa stuffed his hands in his pockets as he waited for Irene to appear. From his position in the congregation, he could see Sol, who was standing next to the bishop with a big grin on his face. The man had changed over the past five months. The love of a good woman would do that, Asa guessed, trying to stem his jealousy, trying not to think of Abigail. He thought that as time passed it would be easier, that now that she was out of sight she would be out of his mind and his heart. If anything, her presence was stronger. More than once he'd been tempted to defy his own vow not to go to Middlefield. He just wanted to see her, to take in her beautiful round face and soft brown eyes, to feel her in his arms one last time, to kiss her pretty mouth . . .

He looked away. That was why he couldn't go to Middlefield. If he did, he wouldn't be following God's timing, he'd be forcing his own. That never worked out for him. So he'd bide his time as long as he had to. If patience was a virtue, then he was the most virtuous man in Birch Creek.

A murmur went through the wedding attendees, and he turned to see what the commotion was about. His breath hitched as Abigail stepped into the yard. He glanced up at the sky, his heart hammering as he silently acknowledged God's perfect timing. He shouldn't be surprised that she would show up at the exact moment he was thinking about her.

She didn't move any farther into the crowd, but she did give her friends smiles. Then Irene came out, and the wedding was underway.

But Asa couldn't concentrate. He kept looking at Abigail, even though she never met his gaze. He tapped his foot, wishing the vows would move faster, then feeling guilty because Irene and Sol deserved their wedding moment. Once again he had to be patient . . . but at least he knew that in a short time he would get to talk to Abigail again.

∞

Abigail smiled as she watched Sol and Irene exchange vows. A genuine smile, and she was happy she'd made the decision to come to Irene's wedding after all. When she'd been invited two weeks ago, she wasn't sure she was ready to come back. She'd been settled in Middlefield, getting to know her cousin and the people who lived in Mary's district. She'd also been very productive with the loom she had there, creating beautiful wall hangings she knew would sell well in the grocery store. But while she'd been happy, she'd missed her family. Her friends.

She had especially missed Asa.

She knew he was here. She'd seen him when she arrived, but she had to pretend not to notice him. Which was hard. He was still devastatingly handsome, possibly more so than the last time they'd been together. Her pulse thrummed as she tried to focus on the ceremony. She could see how deeply in love Irene and Sol were. They complemented each other, and made each other better. Everyone could see that. Sadie said they had asked to have the wedding at the Schrocks' house because it was larger than the Beilers' and the Troyers'. Aden and Sadie had been happy to accommodate them. Sadie even mentioned to Abigail that the tension between her and Sol had eased over the summer.

Irene and Sol kissed, and Abigail glanced around the room. She was surrounded by people she loved—and people who had found their soul mates. Andrew and Irene's parents had been reunited. Irene had written to Abigail, explaining how her father had admitted he had left his family and asked for forgiveness and to be accepted back into the church. He was forgiven, and now worked with Andrew in his farrier business.

Then she saw Andrew and Joanna. Other than Andrew and Abigail, no one knew Joanna was expecting. She was only a couple of months along, but she glowed, and Andrew's eyes were filled with love when he looked at her. Then she saw Sadie and Aden, standing close to each other. Abigail would have never put the two of them together, but God did. Now she couldn't imagine them apart.

Then her gaze landed on Asa, and she couldn't pull it away this time. He was watching Irene and Sol, and Abigail looked to see who he was sitting next to, if he had found someone else while she was gone. If he had, she wouldn't blame him or resent him. As for her, no one in Middlefield could compare to Asa, not only in looks but more important in kindness and heart. The ache in her chest that had been there for months intensified. She missed him so much—his kindness, his charm, his love.

He looked up as if sensing her looking at him. The corner of his mouth lifted into a small smile . . . and she couldn't breathe.

She turned away and slipped behind the barn. She pulled in deep gulps as she tried to slow her pulse. She shouldn't have come back. She wasn't ready for the onslaught of emotion flowing over her. Plus, she wanted a brownie. But that's what she did when she was stressed—reached for food. She shook her head. She didn't need food. What she needed were her feelings to simmer down.

"Abigail."

Well, that didn't help. She couldn't turn around right away at the sound of his deep voice. They'd been here before, several times, him checking on her when she was distressed, comforting her when she needed him, being a good friend, and then, for a short time, something more. The pounding of her heart roared in her ears as she finally faced him. She cleared her throat. "Asa."

He put his hands in his pockets. "Nice day for a wedding, *ya*?"

She nodded, her heart hammering at his nearness. "*Ya*."

Their gazes locked, and she saw the yearning in his gray eyes. "I'm sure Irene will be glad to know you're here."

Was she the only one? Abigail couldn't voice the question. She couldn't pull her gaze from him, either. "*Ya*," she said, her tongue almost tripping over the word. "I'm glad she's so happy."

"She is." He looked at his feet for a moment, then back at her. "What about you, Abigail? Are you happy?"

She pressed her lips together. "*Ya*. I am."

"So you like Middlefield?"

"It's nice." The small talk was getting on her nerves. Then again, what did she expect? For him to gather her into his arms? *You left him, remember?* And she had been right in doing so. But at that moment all she could think about was how much she wanted him to hold her.

"Does that mean . . ." He paused, his eyes not leaving hers. "That you're going back?"

She thought about the suitcase in the kitchen. The taxi had a flat tire on the way here or she would have been at the wedding early. She would have already put her suitcase in her bedroom. Whether she would have unpacked it, she didn't know.

He took his hands out of his pockets. Stepped toward her. Cupped her cheek in his hand. "I missed you," he whispered, running his thumb across the top of her cheekbone. "I missed you so much."

Something inside her broke at his gentle touch. "I missed you too."

He pulled away from her. "I told myself I would be patient," he said. "That I would wait on God, and on you. But now that you're here . . . I don't know if I can be patient anymore."

His words sent a shiver from the top of her head to her heels.

"I still love you," he continued, his voice turning raspy. "Not because God told me to. Because I can't help but love you. I always will, even if you turn around and walk out of *mei* life forever."

She nearly melted at the tears pooling in his eyes. She couldn't say anything. She could barely catch a breath.

"I just wanted you to know that." He gazed at her for one long moment, then started to turn away.

"Asa?"

When he faced her, she launched into his arms. "I'm sorry," she said, letting the dam inside her burst into pieces. She leaned her cheek against his chest as his hands went to her waist. For once she wasn't self-conscious about him touching her there. Instead she closed her eyes, feeling cocooned in his embrace and his love. "I'm sorry," she repeated against his shirt.

"It's okay." His cheek rested on the top of her head, even though they were both in full view of anyone who was looking out the kitchen window. "I'm just glad to be holding you," he added with a whisper. "I thought I'd never get to hold you again."

"I needed time," she said.

"I know. We both did. I'm glad you realized it, because I wasn't listening."

She lifted her head and looked up at him, losing herself in his beautiful eyes. "It's because of you that I *started* listening. I can't thank you enough for that."

He looked at her, his hands moving from her waist to cup

her face. "Please tell me you're coming back to Birch Creek. That you're coming back to me."

She gazed up at him, her heart so full of love and peace that she knew God was speaking straight to her soul through the unabashed words of this man. "*Ya*," she said. "I'm here to stay."

He pressed his lips against hers, his kiss gentle and loving, a reflection of himself. When he pulled away she said, "I love you, Asa. That never changed, even while I was gone. And I'll love you forever, *nee* matter what comes between us."

"*Nix* will," he said. "Nothing will ever come between us again."

"You're right," she said, unable to resist giving him a teasing look. "Seeing that God brought us together, after all."

"Remind me to thank him," Asa said, grinning, his lips hovering over hers. "Later."

CHAPTER 30

Abigail sat at the table in the kitchen and looked at her family. Every one of them was here at Aden's request—Andrew and Joanna, Sadie, Asa and her. When Asa sat down next to her and held her hand under the table, Abigail smiled at her husband. She and Asa had married earlier in March, having decided to take their relationship slow when she returned to Middlefield.

Although she and her sisters were happy with their husbands and, in Joanna's case, also with her new son, Samuel, who was spending the afternoon with his *aenti* Irene and *onkel* Sol, there were still times of grief, times when Abigail couldn't bear to see her parents' empty seats at the table. She still felt the pain of their loss, but it was soothed by knowing that she had this family, this new family that she loved and who loved her.

Asa gave her hand a squeeze and released it. Then underneath the table he tapped his foot against her bare one. He wore socks, one of several pairs she had knitted on her fine loom. When she presented him with the first pair at Christmas, he'd acted like she'd given him something priceless. When she questioned him about his reaction, he said he didn't want to take her handiwork for granted because it was so special. Just like she was. Since then she had knitted socks, scarves, and even a few sweaters on the loom, and they sold quickly in the store along with her tapestries.

Asa leaned over to Abigail and whispered in her ear. "I wonder what this is all about."

Abigail shrugged. "I don't know. It's Aden's first *familye* meeting."

"Hey," Joanna said with a smile. "*Nee* whispering, you two."

Abigail folded her arms across her chest. "As if I haven't seen you and Andrew whispering before."

"So you were eavesdropping?"

"*Nee*. At least not much."

Everyone laughed as Aden came back into the kitchen. He sat down in their father's chair, which had now become his chair. He had slipped into the role of family patriarch with ease and confidence. He gave Sadie a smile and then put a letter on the table.

"I appreciate you all coming this afternoon." He looked at Joanna. "I really appreciate the brownies you brought, too, Joanna. They're *appeditlich*."

"As always," Andrew said, giving Joanna a smile. Joanna looked down shyly.

Abigail nodded. She'd had two, and didn't feel a bit guilty about it. She knew now that she had to enjoy life, to not let guilt and pain shadow everything—including brownies.

"As you all know, I've been looking at all the offers for the gas rights here on the property. I've been taking *mei* time, praying about it, and talking with Sadie about it." He cleared his throat.

"I appreciate you putting *yer* trust in me with this. I wanted to make sure that whatever the decision, it would be the best one for all of us." He pushed the paper over to Sadie, who handed it to Andrew. "That's the company I think we should sell the rights to. They didn't have the largest bid, but they had the most integrity. And as you can see, the money they offered is substantial."

Andrew's eyes widened as he scanned the letter. Without a word he handed it to Joanna, who put her hand to her mouth as she read. She gave the letter to Abigail. Asa leaned over as Abigail read the letter—and gasped at the amount. She jerked her head up and looked at Aden. "Is this for real?"

"*Ya.* It's very real."

She turned to Asa, who also looked shocked. This was more money than she'd ever imagined. If they took this bid, they could close up all their businesses and never have to work again. She handed the paper back to Aden, who folded it back into thirds.

"I can give you all the information about the company. I've done a lot of research—"

"We trust you," Abigail said, the word *research* making her eyes glaze over. The last thing she wanted to do was to read about a drilling business. But Asa's eyes sparked with interest. "At least I do. Asa?"

"I trust you, Aden. But I'd like to read up on the company anyway."

Aden nodded. "I'll get you the paperwork in a minute." He turned to Andrew and Joanna. "What do you think?"

Andrew looked at his wife. "Joanna? It's up to you. This is *yer* legacy."

She shook her head. "It's our legacy." She gestured to everyone. "All of ours. And if Aden says this is the right company, then I support his decision."

Aden's shoulders slumped a little, as if he'd been worried this process would have been more difficult. Sadie put her hand on his forearm and smiled. "I told you," she said in a quiet voice. "I told you they would all be fine with what you decided."

"Once we receive the money, it will be split into thirds," Aden said, lightly brushing his hand over Sadie's before she removed it from his forearm. "I think it's only fair that I tell you what Sadie and I have decided to do with our share." He glanced at Sadie, this time taking her hand and holding it on the table. "We have everything we need. Two thriving businesses. A beautiful *haus*. Our family." His green eyes grew glassy. "We don't need anything else. So we're giving our share to the community fund."

Abigail drew in a breath. Even though it was a third of the proceeds, it was still a significant amount. Then she looked at Asa. She could see her thoughts reflected in his eyes. "We'll do the same." He nodded and smiled.

"So will we," Joanna said.

Sadie held up her hand. "You don't have to do that," she said. "We don't want to pressure you or make you feel like you have to. Whatever you do with *yer* money is *yer* business. We won't judge."

"But you're right," Abigail said, taking Asa's hand. She placed both their hands on the table, just like Sadie and Aden's. "We have what we need."

"The money isn't ours," Joanna added, her and Andrew's hands joining everyone else's. "It's the Lord's. He's blessed us so much." Her voice sounded strangled. "We need *nix* more."

The room was silent as the sisters and their husbands looked at one another. Tears swam in Sadie's eyes, Joanna was already crying, and the lump in Abigail's throat nearly strangled her. "*Mamm* and *Daed* would approve," she whispered thickly.

"*Ya*," Joanna said.

"*Ya*," Sadie added.

Aden looked at Asa. When he spoke, his voice wasn't steady, either. "I'll get you that paperwork so you can look over it. Also, I mentioned to Freemont that we would be making a sizable contribution to the fund. He nearly passed out and said he was glad you were in charge of the community fund and not him."

Sadie rose. "Abigail, Joanna, would you help me with the dishes?"

Abigail nodded and stood, along with Joanna. Aden, Andrew, and Asa left the kitchen, mumbling something about going to the store office to look over the drilling paperwork and specifics.

Sadie filled the sink while Joanna cleared the table and Abigail took a hand towel out of the drawer. This wasn't her house anymore. She loved the cozy home she and Asa had made for themselves in his childhood home. But a part of her would always be here, among her sisters, whom she loved.

Joanna set a stack of dishes on the counter and Sadie turned off the water. They faced each other, then clasped hands. "God made beauty," Sadie said.

"—and love," Joanna said.

"—from ashes." Abigail put the towel on the counter and opened her arms wide. Then the three of them hugged. *Thank you, Lord.*

Acknowledgments

When it comes to support, I've got the A Team on my side: editor extraordinaire Becky Monds, Sue Brower, Kelly Long, Tera Moore, my husband, James, and my children, Matt, Sydney, and Zoie. They have supported me throughout this book and the entire Birch Creek series, and for that I'm very, very, *very* grateful. As always, a special thanks to you, dear reader, for taking another literary journey with me.

Discussion Questions

1. Even though they had been separated for weeks and hadn't talked to each other since Abigail's return to Birch Creek, she assumed that Joel was going to propose. Instead, she discovered he'd been unfaithful. Have you ever experienced betrayal? How did God help you move past it to forgiveness?

2. Do you agree with how Asa initially responded to God's call for him to return to Birch Creek? Why or why not?

3. Abigail's body issues stemmed from her own self-doubt. How did Asa's persistent love for her mirror God's love for us?

4. Sol didn't believe he was worthy of love. When was a time you felt unworthy of something? What helped you believe that you are worthy?

5. Which character in *A Love Made New* did you feel embodied the definition of being faithful?

6. Do you think Emmanuel will ever return to Rhoda and Birch Creek? Why or why not?

7. Abigail thought about how God took a terrible situation (her parents' death) and turned it into something beautiful, easing

all three of the sisters' grief. Think of a time when God took a tragedy in your life and transformed it into something you never expected. What lessons, if any, did you learn from the experience?

Get lost in a new series by Kathleen Fuller!

THE AMISH BRIDES *of* BIRCH CREEK

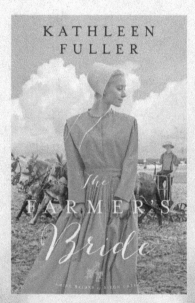

(coming June 2019)

Available in print and e-book

About the Author

With over a million copies sold, Kathleen Fuller is the author of several bestselling novels, including the Hearts of Middlefield novels, the Middlefield Family novels, the Amish of Birch Creek series, and the Amish Letters series as well as a middle-grade Amish series, the Mysteries of Middlefield.

Visit her online at KathleenFuller.com
Twitter: @TheKatJam
Facebook: WriterKathleenFuller

Printed in the USA
CPSIA information can be obtained
at www.ICGtesting.com
JSHW031145150724
66428JS00011B/95

9 780310 353676